Break

the

Heart

of

Me

By Elizabeth Dewberry Vaughn

MANY THINGS HAVE HAPPENED SINCE HE DIED

BREAK THE HEART OF ME

Nan A. Talese

Doubleday

New York

London

Toronto

Sydney

Auckland

Break the Heart of Me

Elizabeth Dewberry Vaughn

PUBLISHED BY NAN A. TALESE
an imprint of Doubleday
a division of Bantam Doubleday Dell Publishing Group, Inc.
1540 Broadway, New York, New York 10036

DOUBLEDAY is a trademark of Doubleday,
a division of Bantam Doubleday Dell Publishing Group, Inc.

"Song for a Dark Girl" by Langston Hughes. From *Selected Poems* by
Langston Hughes. Copyright 1927 by Alfred A. Knopf, Inc. Reprinted
by permission of the publisher.

The author also gratefully acknowledges Harold Ober Associates, Inc.,
for permission to use the line "Break the Heart of Me," from "Song for
a Dark Girl" by Langston Hughes, as the title of this novel.

Library of Congress Cataloging-in-Publication Data

Vaughn, Elizabeth Dewberry.
    Break the heart of me / Elizabeth Dewberry Vaughn. — 1st ed.
        p.   cm.
    I. Title.
    PS3572.A936B7   1994
    813'.54—dc20   93-8162
                                                              CIP

    ISBN 0-385-41425-0

Book Design by Gretchen Achilles

Printed in the United States of America
All Rights Reserved
February 1994

10   9   8   7   6   5   4   3   2

This book was written
with the support of
grants from the Georgia
Council for the Arts, the
Alabama Arts Council,
and Ohio State
University, for which I'm
deeply grateful.

To Elaine Markson, Nan
A. Talese, and especially
Robert Vaughn, for your
faith in this book, I am
more grateful than I
know how to express.

E. D. V.

Way down South in Dixie
    (Break the heart of me)
Love is a naked shadow
    On a gnarled and naked tree.

—Langston Hughes

I HAVE NOW SEEN THREE DEAD BODIES IN MY LIFE—MEMAW, Paw Paw, and Bo Schifflett, Junior. Well, four if you count my mama. Which I don't.

The first one besides Mama was my grandmother. I went in the den where she'd been sleeping on the Murphy bed ever since Paw Paw got sick, and I had her some oatmeal and orange juice on a tray all done up with a cloth napkin like if M'Lea's mother had done it there would have been a rose on there too. And like I said, it was more or less my first dead body, but bang I knew just like that the second I saw her. Which I think shows something, knowing right off the bat like that, like maybe somewhere deep in my brain I remember more about my mama than I thought. There's just no telling what-all your brain'll store up when you don't even know it's there. But I dropped the oatmeal right there in the doorway and my mind went blank and I put my hands on my face and I stood there staring, thinking I'm twelve years old and this is my second dead body counting my mama, while M'Lea's never even had one. And I could almost hear M'Lea's mother saying it's not a fair world, Sylvia. Then I heard myself thinking no, apparently it's not, real calm in my head almost like a grown-up, while outside my body was going crazy, running over to her, shaking her and shaking her, not even feeling real, and my hands could hardly believe a person could be that cold. Made me think of ice tea. I put my head on her chest and I said Memaw, wake up, please wake up, Memaw, and I was begging her so hard I just knew if she was still in that tunnel of light between earth and heaven where you can still change your mind she would have come back, so just in case I was screaming Memaw, come back, Memaw, come back, trying to aim my voice down the tunnel. But I knew all along she was already on the other side. I just knew it.

So I was kneeling there racking my brain trying to figure now what am I supposed to do, only I had no idea whatsoever, which was working me up into a panic. I could feel it coming in my gut the way Memaw could tell when she was fixing to get company, and then sure enough the whole world started getting smaller and smaller and further and further away and the space in between me and the world started getting louder, ringing in my ears to where I couldn't think straight. So I closed my eyes and I focused on my eyelids and I took a bunch of long, deep, slow breaths till my heartbeat quit acting like a heart attack and then I said to myself, Sylvia Grace Mullins, Memaw's counting on you, you got to pull yourself together.

So I started trying with all my might to picture Memaw in the arms of Jesus, glowing with righteousness, no more pain, no more sorrow, walking those streets of gold, because I knew if I could I'd be able to figure what would she want from there. Only I couldn't help it, I just couldn't do it, because there she was, right smack in front of me—dead. Plus I kept thinking if she's really in heaven she doesn't want for anything because that's how it is when you're there, you got everything you need, and then that started translating into she didn't miss me, which worked its way up into she didn't even care, and before I knew it I was saying how could you do this to me. Out loud. Meaning leaving me all alone with only Paw Paw.

I started crying like I was sad but the truth is I was mad too, or maybe stunned is the word, like she'd slapped me in the face. And before I knew it I'd wished I could slap her back. Then of course I wished I could take that wish back, and then right there in the middle of screaming and thinking about slapping, I flew into a panic about how are we going to get her face back to normal. That's how my mind was working, like a fly, darting every which way from streets of gold to slapping to her face. But it was so red, I'd never seen anything so red in my life, and I didn't think there was a makeup in the world that would have fixed it. And the same time I'm also thinking how am I going to tell Paw Paw and make him understand. Because sometimes he was pretty much normal as anybody, but sometimes toward the end he couldn't even follow *Gilligan's Island*. It'd be 12:25 and just about over and he'd say what? What's happening? What's she doing? And you'd have to explain they were trying to get off the island but Gilligan messed it up. And he'd say so they didn't get off? And you'd say no. And he'd get depressed and say do they ever get off? And you'd just say no, Paw Paw, they never do. Then it'd get real quiet and uncomfortable during the song while they'd run the credits and for some reason you'd feel guilty.

So I was thinking all that all at once plus that I was already hungry and would it be wrong to eat before I told Paw Paw and how I shouldn't be hungry at a time like this but I couldn't help it, I was starving for some of Memaw's French toast. I still don't think it looked right for me to be lying over my grandmother's dead body thinking about food of all things in the world, and I like to think if I had it to do over again I'd do it different, but that's what I thought at the time. French toast.

Then I picked up her hand, and that's when she first really seemed like a dead body—cold and eerie and sort of like sex. I mean like there was something I wasn't supposed to know about her but I knew it in my body anyway before I could know it or not know it in my head. And I was kneeling there beside her holding her dead hand, and then I started shaking all over head to toe because I think the truth is I was all the sudden scared to death of her. Scared to death of my own grandmother, that's how upside-down everything was. Also because at first when I'd been scream-ing Memaw come back there'd been tears coming out of my eyes and words coming out of my mouth and I'd been doing everything through my head, but my body hadn't really been in on things, it was just cold as all get-out and numb. And then after I picked up her hand I think my body was shaking because it finally caught up with me, like if it had of been crying along with me when my face cried. You know how you shake when it's a real big cry.

So there I was, I'd already cried with my head and then I was crying with my body and I couldn't think what to think, and then the words from a sermon I'd heard I don't know when flashed into my head. If you really love a brother or sister who's gone to be with the Lord, you'll be praising God with the angels instead of mourning him. That's what Reverend Tutwiler—no relation to the hotel in Birmingham—that's what he says. And it makes sense, if you think real hard about it, because everybody knows Memaw's better off where she is and if you love somebody you want what's best for them. That's what love is. So I tried. I tried right there in the den by the Murphy bed to say thank you, God, for taking Memaw to heaven, sending out prayers as fast as I could make them up, concentrating with all my might on her mansion and the pearly gates and the angels singing and how happy Memaw must be singing along with them, floating around up there. But it was like my prayers wouldn't leave the room and they were spinning around and around me till I actually felt dizzy. And still I just couldn't do it.

Eventually I gave up. I went in the kitchen and made myself some oatmeal and I put in some vanilla flavoring and two spoons of powdered sugar on it and some cinnamon and then I cut up a banana on top—that's how Memaw always did her French toast. I guess I'll miss that French toast the rest of my life. But I did the best I could, and Paw Paw was snoring like an animal, and usually I'd go roll him over but I decided to let him snore that day. So I took my oatmeal outside and sat on the top step to the front porch and stared out at Memaw's chickens, thinking random thoughts like when are we going to throw those old faded chickens away and get some new ones and when I grow up I'm going to have some chickens of my own and some little deer and maybe a little lamb in my front yard plus a birdbath and I'm going to put a life-size Mary and Joseph and Jesus out there at Christmas that light up and every year I'll add one more thing, like a shepherd or a wise man or a donkey. Things like that.

It was a terrible kind of quiet. The oatmeal was making loud squishy sounds in my mouth, that's how quiet it was. I even thought for a second maybe the Rapture came and Memaw got taken and Paw Paw and I got left. Because Reverend Tutwiler says we don't know whether we'll take our earthly bodies with us or get new ones, although I for one hope we get new ones. Paw Paw's was about wore out anyway and mine never was much to brag about. But of course it wasn't the Rapture, which I knew even when I thought it. For one thing, Paw Paw and I would have been taken too because God doesn't make mistakes, and for another thing, when Jesus comes he'll be trailing clouds of glory in the sky, and there wasn't a cloud there. Even though by late that afternoon it was storming bloody murder.

So I ate my oatmeal without a blessing and I tried not to think about the Rapture and I tried to ask myself what would Christ do in this situation, but I kept thinking what would Amazing Grace do. She'd march herself right back in the den, is what—she's not afraid of anything—and she'd walk right over to the Murphy bed and she'd say Memaw, in the name of Jesus Christ of Nazareth, rise up and walk. And Memaw would. And Memaw would make her some French toast and she'd set the table and she'd eat all the French toast she could eat and then maybe go down to the Pell City Medical Center and see if anybody'd checked in overnight for her to heal. She'd walk in the hospital and all the nurses would run over to her and say Amazing Grace, we're so glad you're here, we got a real sick baby. And I'd go heal it, and its mama and daddy would be so happy they'd be crying tears of joy, and the baby would start cooing and laughing, and then I'd go home and eat hot dogs on Wonder buns with chili and cheese and ketchup for lunch with chocolate cake and chocolate icing for dessert. It's not really all that far from what Christ would do. I think he liked fish more than I do, so he might have had fish sticks and corn bread instead of hot dogs. We both like bread. But somehow you just can't imagine Jesus finding his grandmama dead in her bed and calling the funeral home.

But of course that's not how it happened. I finished my oatmeal and I was still hungry because when you're hungry for Memaw's French toast, no amount of oatmeal in the world's going to fill you up, so I opened the refrigerator door and stood there nibbling at things—some strawberry Jell-O salad, some fried

6

chicken, a little bit of chocolate pudding that was starting to go rubbery around the edges—and then I drank some orange juice right out of the carton because there was nobody to stop me, and I was listening to Paw Paw snore while I was drinking, thinking I'm the only one that knows, and this is the last food Memaw fixed before she died, and singing "Amazing Grace," my favorite, in four-part harmony like the Amazing Grace choir in the back of my head. They always sing a cappella on account of how organ music gives me the creeps.

Then I closed the refrigerator and started worrying again about how was I going to tell him and how would Amazing Grace tell him and what was I going to do next and thinking about Memaw just lying there all red in the face. M'Lea would have said it was obscene. That's her favorite word, obscene. I thought about calling M'Lea, only the thought of her saying Memaw was obscene rubbed me wrong. And then I kept thinking about Uncle Mull. I kept thinking somebody's going to have to tell him and Deedee, and it's a harder thing to tell somebody than you might think when you actually start to figure what words you're going to use. Like what do you say first so it's not so blunt. I went so far as to write up a letter in my head, knowing before I even started it I wouldn't send it. It went *Dear Deedee and Uncle Mull, I'm sorry to bother you, and I hope everything is going well for you in Nashville. I am fine. Paw Paw and I are enjoying the cooler temperatures we've had the last day or two. Last Thursday Pell City was the hottest place in the country!* Which was true, we were on *Good Morning, America. I thought you ought to know that Memaw has died.* That's as far as I got.

For one thing, Paw Paw was getting louder and louder, which meant he was about to wake himself up and he was going to call out Mitilene and expect her to come shuffling in there, so I started feeling all panicky like I hadn't eaten anything, and a million things started racing through my mind faster than I could think them. Like run away, she was murdered and the murderer's still here, Paw Paw's the murderer and I'm next, she must have ate some poison food and I just ate the rest of it, call the police, call 911—things like that, until so many crazy things had gone through my head all in barely a second or two that I thought I've went and gone crazy and Memaw's not dead, I just made it up. That's how distraught I was.

And then before I actually made up my mind what to do next, I found myself wandering into the bathroom to look in the mirror and just studying my face, thinking what a nice complexion I have for a twelve-year-old. Memaw always said that. You have a peaches-and-cream complexion. Which makes me prone to freckle. My skin is the best thing about me if you don't count my freckles, and most of them seem to have congregated on my shoulders and back, so my face is more or less normal. Then I opened the medicine cabinet mirror, and the next whole wall was a mirror, so when you put your face in between them you found yourself looking down a million copies of yourself all lined up cheek to cheek, staring at each other—a tunnel of selves. You could make the tunnel curve by moving the medicine cabinet, but I left it still. I was trying to go out of my body and float down the tunnel toward my most distant self. I dragged that out for as long as I could. Sometimes in a crisis things like that help—taking some time out to do something nice for yourself.

Of course sooner or later you have to jump back in the crisis, and when I finally told him about Memaw—because I knew all along that's what I had to do, I was just stalling till I found the guts—and then he didn't believe me. Or he didn't understand. I don't know what, but he just wouldn't accept that she was dead.

He said we'll just let her sleep late today.

I said Paw Paw, it's not that kind of sleep, she's dead.

I had tried to break it to him easy so I'd said Paw Paw, Memaw's gone to be with the Lord.

And he said when's she coming back, like she'd gone to church.

And I said no, Paw Paw, she's asleep in the Lord.

I was trying to think what Reverend Tutwiler would say— he's one of those people who always knows what to say—and these crazy words came out of my mouth that I didn't even know what they meant but I thought surely he'll know. I mean I knew they meant dead, but I wasn't sure exactly beyond that what it means to be asleep in the Lord, how you do it.

He said we'll just let her sleep late, then.

I was all upset and he didn't have his hearing aid in and everything was wrong and finally I said as loud as I could without screaming, Memaw's dead, Paw Paw, she's not going to wake up, she's dead.

Course I felt real bad about that right after I said it, the very minute I said it, because that wasn't how I'd meant to do it at all. And he was just lying there in his bed, not saying a word, and I thought maybe he needs to be alone. I needed to be alone, so I said I'm fixing to get your breakfast, Paw Paw, you want anything in particular?

And he said no, he just barely said no, like he was off in some other world.

So I sort of touched his pajama top, just kind of pet the lapel because I wanted to comfort him but I couldn't think of anything to say, plus I knew he wouldn't hear me anyway, and his hand sort of went up and he patted me on the leg, and I said I think you need some breakfast, and I went to get it.

Then I started fixing his oatmeal and thinking about running away, and I got out that same canister of oatmeal I'd used for Memaw, only I turned it around because I didn't want the man on the label watching my every move, and I was thinking I'd give Paw Paw his oatmeal and then go pack my suitcase and leave. I was making a list in my head of everything I'd take, figuring how much food I'd need and how much underwear and how much babysitting money I had and would I use a suitcase like I was spending the night with M'Lea or tie my stuff up in a bundle and put it on a stick like people who run away in books and I figured I'd just go with the suitcase. Only I couldn't for the life of me think after the packing where I'd go.

Then I came to my senses and I told myself you can't run away. Think about going into a Pac-a-Sak for a Snickers bar and seeing your own face on a milk carton like some sort of child criminal. Plus M'Lea's run away forty times already and she always goes back home. M'Lea says Pell City's smack dab in the middle of nowhere, you can't get anywhere from here.

So I just kept going through the motions of fixing Paw Paw's breakfast, pouring a glass of orange juice from the same carton I'd used for Memaw what seemed like days ago, when I started feeling like my own shadow—all funny and double and not all there. I kept standing there watching myself measuring hot water into a pot and waiting for it to boil and stirring in the oatmeal and vanilla and sugar and cinnamon—just like I'd done for Memaw not an hour earlier. It was so exactly like what I'd already done I even started to think I'd dreamed it all the first time. Like sometimes when I've stayed up late the night before studying or thinking or just couldn't sleep and my alarm comes on, sometimes I'll turn it off and go back to sleep and dream I'm getting out of bed and getting dressed and all that. And I thought what if I dreamed the whole thing and I never made that first oatmeal or brought it in to her or found her dead or any of it and this whole thing is just a nightmare. So I started tracing back to figure if it was a dream then when did I wake up or am I still asleep and if I am how do I wake up, and I thought maybe I sleepwalked out onto the front porch and woke up out there because there was a time out there when I was sort of in a daze. And bit by bit I started undoing the whole morning in my head, and I got myself so worked up and confused that next thing I know I don't know if my own grandmother who raised me from the day I was born is alive or dead.

So I said to myself okay, Sylvia, you're going to have to go check on her, you got to go in there and take another look. Because I had closed the door after I found her, so you couldn't just look from the kitchen, you had to go in there. And I was asking Jesus for help, I was praying so hard and so fast I wasn't even saying individual words in my head except maybe please, God, please, but I seemed to be having a crisis of faith on top of everything else. Because normally I believe in the power of prayer with all my heart—Memaw always said my very existence in this world is a testimony to the power of prayer, and I believe that—but it was that same old thing, that all my prayers kept spinning around and around inside me and none of them were getting out. It was just that kind of day.

Then out of nowhere, almost like a miracle, I started to feeling like Amazing Grace. Not that I could heal or raise from the dead, but I'm stirring that oatmeal, wading around in my head through all those prayers getting fuzzier and fuzzier in my brain, and then boom Amazing Grace gets inside me and takes over and gives me the strength to do what I have to do, so I clear my throat real officially and I feel strong and brave and full of hope like there's been a mistake, and I walk over to the den door and I knock once real soft so as not to wake her up and I say Memaw? Memaw, you all right? And I opened the door and I tiptoed over to her bed, and then I saw her. She hadn't moved.

So I tried not to stare, and I bit my teeth and I said okay, now you got to try to find a pulse. Because that's what people do on TV. But I knew it wasn't going to work. Because she was too cold and too still and too red, and whatever it was lying there in the Murphy bed, it wasn't her.

And then Amazing Grace sort of withered away and I was back to regular old Sylvia. I kneeled down beside her and I put her hand under the blanket and tucked her in like a mama tucking in her baby and I smoothed the covers and tried to cover her ears with her hair, and then I put my arms around her and put my head on her chest and hugged her, hoping one last time to hear the soothing rhythm of her heartbeat, and I said Memaw. I stayed there hugging her, very quiet and very still, listening to nothing.

I don't have any idea what I was doing. I think I might have been trying to get the last little bits of love out of her, I might have been trying to hold on to her for just a few more minutes, maybe that was my way of saying goodbye—I don't know. But I felt like I was trying to get something I needed, and I don't know how this happened, but then sooner or later I was still holding on to her and rocking back and forth whispering Mama. Like a crazy person.

Of course Amazing Grace was far gone by that time, and then in my head I saw a picture of myself falling apart, sort of melting like the Wicked Witch of the West, and I said I have to do something, I have to call somebody. I have to clean up this mess. Because most of the oatmeal had stayed right there on the floor but there were bits and pieces of it from here to kingdom come. And orange juice on the paneling, drops of it splattered on

Memaw's quilt, on the rug. And to tell the horrible truth, that orange juice and that oatmeal were at that second right when I quit rocking back and forth a whole world more of a concern to me than Memaw. Because, well, for one thing, what was she going to do. I mean I had some time. Plus it was like I just couldn't bear to think about her anymore right then, like my brain just had to have a break. But orange juice—I didn't know if it was going to stain, and I couldn't even guess what Memaw would want me to do about her, but there was no doubt in my mind she'd want that oatmeal and that orange juice and that broken glass cleaned up. That's how she was. Clean up your own mess. So I was trying to make sure I'd gotten all the glass pieces and I ended up cleaning under the bed and under the orange crate she'd been using for a nightstand and places that hadn't been cleaned in months, and when I finally got it all clean, cleaner than it had been before in fact, I felt Memaw looking down from heaven saying you did real good, Sylvie. Which was a comfort.

Then I went back in the kitchen and closed the door again and threw away the broken glass and I thought okay, what's next. Call a grown-up. I thought of every grown-up I knew, went through them all in my brain and said no on every one till I got to Uncle Mull, who I finally figured I had to settle on although I could think of some reservations on him, too. Like for starters when he hugs me his beard scratches my face and his jawbone hits my ear and he laughs even when things aren't funny and you can see his gums over his teeth, and Deedee's always hogging the bathroom, making her hair stand up and poof out and go all over the place and putting on lipstick so dark she looks like a vampire and she tries to make us eat health food. But M'Lea's mother is too panic-prone, every little thing throws her into fits and she starts smoking cigarettes ninety miles a minute and she's always walking around like a baby bird because her fingernail polish is wet, and Mrs. Sutherland was still asleep and you just don't want your very next-door neighbor seeing your dead grandmother before she's even been fixed up and still in her nightgown. Plus I didn't want to upset Brother or Will, the baby, who I babysit for every other Saturday morning when Mrs. Sutherland goes to work at the Piggly-Wiggly and who once he starts crying can carry on for hours and everybody on the street can hear him. And I didn't want to call Reverend Tutwiler because he'd already caused enough trouble with asleep in the Lord, and every single adult I could think of was like that—just not right, I mean.

So then I knew I was going to call Uncle Mull, and I said to myself just keep going. Do what you have to do and don't think and bring your Paw Paw his food. So I poured Paw Paw's oatmeal into a bowl and brought it to him and I said here's your breakfast, Paw Paw, but he didn't answer me, so I left it for him on the nightstand and I told myself Uncle Mull will take care of him when he gets here.

So finally I called him and blurted it out, and he said Deedee was at her dance class and could I hold down the fort until she got in, which would put them in Pell City around suppertime.

I said I thought I could, only I had a few questions.

He was acting like this happens all the time, there's nothing to worry about, which set me to worrying even more, and he said shoot.

So I said well, she has a real nice blue outfit she wears to church all the time and I was thinking should I put it on her.

Because at that point she was still in her nightgown and I meant is that the best thing or do you buy a new outfit just for this or does the funeral home provide one, but it seemed to me that somebody like me ought to be the one to put it on her. If there's one thing I knew about Memaw, it was that she wouldn't stand for a man and a stranger on top of that taking off her nightgown and dressing her up for church while she just lay there in her underwear. Memaw didn't even like me to leave my dolls naked.

And Uncle Mull said you just wait, we'll figure out what to do when we get there.

Then I told him about Paw Paw not believing me and wanting to let her sleep late and all.

And Uncle Mull cleared his throat even though he didn't need to and he said slowly but you're sure.

Yeah.

You're absolutely sure.

I said I know what I saw.

And his voice sounded like a kindergarten teacher, all careful and enunciated and sweet, and he said tell me one more time, Sylvia.

And I said a little too loud what else do you want to know, she's dead. Her face is red, her body's freezing, she's not moving or breathing, her heart's not beating, there's no pulse—I don't know how else to put it, Uncle Mull.

By now I was starting to shake again and you could hear it in my voice, and he said all right, calm down, he'd set Paw Paw straight when he got there.

I thought I'd try one more time, so I said I closed the window—Memaw liked to sleep with the window open—but I noticed there's a couple of flies trapped in there and they keep landing on her and I was wondering, do you think I should spray her with Off.

He said I'm leaving here in ten minutes, you just stay put.

So I decided okay, let him do this, I have enough on my head.

And when he got there, I'd barely moved in four hours. I even felt stiff. I'd just sat there at the kitchen table thinking what am I going to do now or what is Paw Paw going to do now or what is Bubba going to do now—because Mrs. Sutherland used to forget to feed him half the time and Memaw would end up feeding him, we had half a fifty-pound bag of Price Busters dog chow in the pantry—or not thinking at all.

And then the whole house got dark in the middle of the day and you could feel a storm cooking up over the lake and gravity pulling at your throat, and Uncle Mull turned on the lights and started calling people and made lunch for Paw Paw and took over like he lived there.

So I said okay, and I didn't even ask if Deedee was coming because I didn't care, I just thought more hot water for us, and I took the rest of the strawberry Jell-O into my room and closed the door and sat on my bed not twenty feet from my dead grandmother, the only thing between us being the wall that held her Murphy bed, and ate.

That was when I first knew what the valley of the shadow of death was. You don't exactly walk through it like in the Bible. You just sit there thinking about something entirely different, like for example what you're going to eat for supper, and it comes and surrounds you and sits on your skin like mist. You even feel clammy, and then it seeps in like poison, like Agent Orange, and you can feel it getting in your bloodstream and grabbing at your organs inside like your heart and your stomach and even your female parts and there's nothing you can do because you're not just *in* the valley of the shadow of death, you *are* the valley of the shadow of death. And it feels like you'll never in your life get out of there.

2

HE WANTED ME TO EAT SOME SOUP, BUT I COULDN'T DO IT. I kept coughing too much and I was too dizzy, and then he started getting frustrated with the coughing only I couldn't stop, just coughing hard, all the way down to my feet.

He was sitting on the bed and his face would blink up and down and he would frown and then he tried to read to me but I kept interrupting him, coughing, until finally he slammed the book shut and threw it on the floor and part of a page ripped out and fell on the bed and I was afraid. Then he went out and I tried to be quiet and put myself to sleep listening to the rain, only he came back in. I had rolled toward the wall, but he pushed my shoulder down so I was on my back looking straight up at him looking down on me and I couldn't tell if he was still mad or not.

Then he had the Vick's Vaporub and his hand was cold on my neck, looking only at my neck, pressing where if I coughed I would choke, but then he looked at my face and he was watching me and I was watching his face watching me and he had pulled down the covers and he was unbuttoning my nightgown. It buttoned all the way down but he stopped before that and then he was still watching me and I was not making a face, and he moved down with his hand and it tingled and he smiled and he wasn't mad anymore so I made myself smile back and he said that feels better, doesn't it.

He kept rubbing and rubbing and it was medicine so he was supposed to so I said yes and I tried not to cough.

Then he unbuttoned another button and he was rubbing my stomach and he said is your tummy upset.

I said nosir and I thought he could feel it beating but he just kept rubbing big rubs and the nightgown was all the way open so just the sleeves and my underpants were on and I didn't move and he kept rubbing.

I said I was supposed to take a multiplication tables test today.

He said you're a smart girl.

I said I know all the way up to the elevens but I have trouble with the twelves.

That's her granddaddy's girl, still rubbing.

It was medicine, he was supposed to because I was sick and dizzy and I didn't feel right.

Do you want to hear some.

Can you do the sevens.

Seven times one is seven.

He is rubbing and his hand keeps touching my underpants, every time now he touches the top elastic of my underpants.

Seven times three is twenty-one.

Then his little finger goes under the elastic at my belly button just for a second just like by accident and then back to rubbing and we are in a rhythm, the rhythm of sevens, and he is still watching my face and I am watching his face watch my face and saying my sevens.

Seven times six is forty-two. Seven times seven is forty-nine.

His fingers go under more and more, under the elastic, and I feel things down there and I start on the eights.

Eight times one.

He was resting on one hand but he straightens up and then both hands are moving, but I don't take my eyes off his face and then my underpants are lowered and I don't move so they won't go any further and then he goes back to my stomach, small little rubs, his whole hand touching my belly button.

He puts more medicine on his fingers and I have finished the eights and gone on to the nines which are easier than eights because there's a trick to nines and it is medicine and I am sick and he is my Paw Paw and I am his girl and I am still on the nines but I'm dizzy and I'm forgetting some but we're still in that rhythm. He puts his fingers gently on my sides and says lift up, just barely says it, and he lifts me and I bend my legs, I let him do it, and I keep saying my nines.

Nine times eight is seventy-two. Nine times nine is eighty-one.

My underpants are down around my knees with the covers and we have not stopped looking each other in the eye and he would never hurt me, he is my grandfather, and I have stopped coughing and I go on to the tens.

3

THAT'S ALL I REMEMBER.

Buddy was out of town, I was sitting in Shoney's by myself and it was raining outside and my hair was wet and I had ordered chicken soup. I had a cough, and when the waiter brought it I was coughing, and there was something about the way he put it down on the table—he was irritated and distracted, and when he set it down some soup sloshed out, and he frowned at me like it was my fault, and then he mumbled something, I think about getting a towel, and he left.

Then my grandfather flooded into my head and I felt crowded, like there wasn't enough room for both of us in there, and I saw the whole scene at once, beginning, middle, and end at the same time like I stood outside of time, like my grandmother said God watches us—except when I got to the tens, and then the picture went blank and I could just hear my voice, my eight-year-old voice, saying ten times one is ten, ten times two is twenty, ten times three is thirty. And the memory was too loud and I couldn't hear anything and I could still feel my grandfather's hand on my stomach and I put my hand there and I kept telling myself he's dead, he's dead, Paw Paw's dead, practically screaming it only not opening my mouth. I had to put my hand on my face to keep the words in. And when I got to ten times ten, it stopped.

So I ran out of the restaurant, and the next day I sent them a check with a note of apology attached. I said I suddenly became ill, and they sent me a coupon for a free meal, which I threw away.

When Buddy gets back in town I tell him about Shoney's.

He says what were you taking.

I say what.

He says what were you taking for your cough.

Buddy, it was real, it happened.

You're telling me you're twenty-three years old and you just remembered this.

Well, it seemed real.

How could you forget such a thing, you're not stupid.

I don't know.

Well, what do you want me to do about it.

I'm not asking you to do anything, I just wanted to tell you. Christ.

He opens the refrigerator and takes a beer. He flips up the top, and the metallic sound of a vacuum filling grates in my ears, but I look at him without making a face. He holds the can out to me as if he's opened it for me, which he hasn't, so I take it. I don't want it, but I'll drink it anyway just to irritate him. He gets another for himself, goes in the den, sits in his chair, and turns on the TV.

He's telling me about the order he got. He just started selling dry walling, everything else he sells is related to the timber industry, and he says dry walling is gravy. It doesn't cut into anything, so you sell the same amount of plyboarding and siding and particleboard and two-by-fours you did before, but the beauty of it is that then you talk them into getting their dry walling from you and hell, you increase every order by ten to fifteen percent with barely any effort. He wishes he'd added dry walling a year ago. He'd be a rich man.

I'm hearing the TV as much as Buddy's voice, standing alone in the kitchen over his suitcase full of dirty clothes, drinking my beer, thinking why don't you ever mute that thing, why do you always have to turn the TV on with the sound all the way up as soon as you walk in the door, is something wrong with your hearing.

He wants to put in a Jacuzzi out back, and this trip just about paid for one. A new builders' supply company just opened in Knoxville, and he talked them into ordering two thousand dollars' worth of unfinished doors more than they needed. They've got a little wormy MBA running the store, and he likes to be told what to buy, you have to bully him around or he doesn't feel like he's getting his money's worth. Buddy lights a cigarette and I bring him an ashtray, go back in the kitchen, and open the suitcase.

All his clothes smell like smoke. Sometimes Buddy's clothes, wrinkled pants with a forty-eight-inch waist and a worn seat drenched in the stale odor of old cigarettes—it's just gross. I don't even like to wash our clothes in the same load. I take out his razor, his dop kit, his shoes, and his belt, then close the suitcase to carry it downstairs to the washing machine. I'm still wearing my workout clothes, and when I get back to the top of the stairs I take them off and throw them down. I walk in front of the TV naked and tell him I'm going to take a shower.

He looks at his watch. When are we eating.

. . .

I take a long, hot shower and try to turn off my brain, just feel what's physically there—hot water, steam, soap, silence, the razor blade on my legs. I run my hand up my legs, feeling for stray bits of stubble. They feel smooth, sexy, separate from me. I think about the razor. I think about taking the blade out and running it across my wrist like I was scanning a credit card, just to see what would happen. It's a dull blade. I draw the line in white with my fingernail. I think about how it wouldn't make a sound. I put the razor down.

I think about taking a bath, thousands of tiny white bubbles popping quietly in my ears. I think about my nipples showing above the water line, pink, my hair pinned up but sort of falling. I look more like Goldie Hawn ten years ago than myself. My toe-nails are painted red. I think about a man sitting on the edge of the tub talking, piling bubbles on me, and I pull him in with his clothes on. Then I fast-forward because I don't know what to do with a fully clothed man in my bathtub, everything I can think of is awkward.

I think about going out drinking and wearing something sexy without a bra and just a little too much makeup and high heels and drinking champagne cocktails with him. I put myself in black lace stockings in a piano bar—not the smoky bluegrass places Buddy and I used to go to but somewhere elegant, with marble floors and Oriental carpets and candlelight and soft music where the piano player wears a tux, and after a couple of drinks I go to the bathtub man's place and we dance a long, slow seduction. He keeps kissing my neck and holding my face with his fingertips in my ears and I drop my head back and close my eyes while he unbuttons my blouse. We don't go to bed until three in the morning, and then we make sweet, sleepy, half-drunken love with the lights on, and the next morning we do it again in the shower.

I'm happily married. It's only a fantasy.

I dry off, pull on jeans and a T-shirt, and go downstairs, gathering my workout clothes as I walk, and start a load of laundry. Then I sit down at my drums, put on my earphones, and lean back into a new artist we just signed, Jake Harris, who I'll be meeting next week. I have his demo tape, and I'm hoping to get to do some of the percussion when he records.

There's something about his voice. He makes you feel like when leaves are burning at dusk in the distance and you think what you're seeing is the sun setting, the day filling up the sky with its passing, and you don't know till you feel the sting in your eyes that it's smoke, and then you think of course. He makes you feel things you can't remember.

Buddy says how can you keep listening to that same damn tape over and over and over without getting sick of it.

I can't explain to him it's not the music itself, it's who I become when I play it. The rhythm takes over your body, the way your heart pumps, your blood vessels constrict, your feet tighten, and you feel it in your eyelids, under the skin on your forehead— it's all run by the songs, and you can't tell whether the music is inside you or you're inside the music because you're both the same thing. Your identities drain out of you separately and pour themselves back into you as one, and you become the soul, the sexuality, of the song. You are the undertow of the music, and for as long as you can make it last, you aren't yourself.

When the tape ends, I start getting a new song—a slow, painful, longing song about being hungry, always hungry. I take off the earphones, get out my father's old acoustic guitar, and start picking out the chords over the sloshing of the washing machine.

Buddy opens the door and yells down when's dinner. For the second time.

I go upstairs, fill a pot with hot water, and start browning some meat. I'm making Deedee's recipe for quick beef Stroganoff, using ground turkey and light sour cream. I stuff the turkey label and the sour cream carton into the bottom of the trash so Buddy won't complain that I'm trying to make him lose weight.

I think about calling Deedee and telling her about Shoney's. I wonder what she'd say.

I think about calling my father, who I haven't talked to in a couple of months, but I decide against it.

The water isn't quite boiling, but I stuff the noodles in, poke at them with a fork.

Buddy's fortieth birthday is coming up in two weeks, so I say something at dinner about having a birthday party for him—six or eight friends over for a cookout—but he doesn't want one.

He says if we have a cookout I'm the one who does all the work, and I'm not going to cook my own birthday dinner.

I say Buddy, I'll do the hamburgers, you just always grab the meat and turn on the grill, so I figure you want to, but if you don't want to do it I'll do it.

He says just forget it.

I say okay, I'll make lasagna, we can have lasagna and salad and garlic bread.

You know what all that garlic does to me.

I say I'll make a loaf of garlic and a loaf with just butter, margarine.

He picks up his plate, puts it in the sink, and walks out of the kitchen.

. . .

My hands are wet and soapy and I'm washing dishes like I do every night, night after night. Like my grandmother did and, I assume, her grandmother did.

It's six-thirty. Buddy's holding his thumb on channel up, and the sound fragments hit me like spurts from a water machine gun. I hate those things, they remind me of semen. If I ever have children, they will never own water machine guns.

I think I might throw a plate against the wall, then scoop up the pieces and dump them in the back yard. Let the archaeologists find them a thousand years from now, put them in a museum. But my ears are too sensitive. I don't want to hear the crash, and that gritty sound broken pottery makes when you sweep it up hurts my teeth. Plus, Buddy'd get mad. What the hell's gotten into you, Sylvia. I've already washed everything but the skillet anyway. I wanted to break a dirty plate. I wanted it to be symbolic.

It was a stupid thought, one of those stupid ideas that flashes in and out of your brain before you even have time to think how stupid it is. I'm just tired.

I scrape the leftover Stroganoff into a cereal bowl and cover it with tinfoil. I wash the skillet, drain the sink, and wipe the countertop with a sponge, leaving little streaks. I look at my plates draining in their rack by the sink and don't remember washing them.

I'm half watching myself do these same mindless domestic rituals and I tell myself this is all there is. It's not supposed to be any better than this. This is what I'm going to do every night for the next fifty or sixty years, this is what everybody does every night of their life, and this is all you get. I feel a new depression moving in over my body and settling down on top of me. My hands start to feel weighted, and the heaviness moves up my arms into my shoulders and neck.

This is all familiar. I always fight it at first, I'd been fighting it since Buddy walked in the door. There's this terrible sense of conflict, and if it doesn't go away within a couple of days, then sometimes I feel like maybe I'll just give up. I'll have a nervous breakdown or go insane or just die. It starts feeling like I'm holding on to my life with my fists, my soul is trying to separate from my body and the whole fight is about keeping them together and it drains you so dry you feel like you don't have enough blood in your body. You start to get weak and your mouth is sticky and you're not exactly dizzy, but you almost wish you were because you're unbalanced, your ears aren't working right, and being dizzy would make more sense.

Then I think I can't do this anymore, I'm just going to let go and see what happens. I'm even curious. I want to know what it would feel like. And when you hear yourself think that way, you know you have to fight it, but it's like a man who's bad for you— there's something irresistible about it, and you get sucked in so you can barely remember why it's a bad idea. And this one comes so hard and so fast I think why go through that whole struggle, just give in now. It'll feel good. You deserve it.

I look in the refrigerator and we're out of beer, so I take that for a sign. I don't believe in signs, but when you get this depressed, you get desperate for the forces of the universe to start working for you, so you take things for signs. You get what you need.

I put away the dishes and go to bed early, but I can't get to sleep for thinking about my grandfather. I'm afraid to go to sleep because I don't want to dream about him. I am falling toward him and I want him to catch me but I can't scream and he doesn't see me coming. He can't see anything. He doesn't have a face. He is reading a newspaper without a face.

I turn on the light, wash my face, and brush my teeth again. I hear the buzz of the TV in the den, the lonely noise of canned laughter. I think what's so funny, anyway, knowing the answer is nothing. I close the door and try to work on my new song, singing harmony with myself in my head, not making a sound.

4

IT'S JUST BEFORE ONE O'CLOCK, AND DARKNESS IS ALREADY gathering. The air, almost salty and sweetly fetid, feels like the Gulf, thick with steam ready to burst into rain.

Uncle Mull tiptoes into the den and stops before he gets to the Murphy bed. I hear him through the wall, and I know what he's doing. He's smelling her. He can't remember the difference between the heaviness of an Alabama thunderstorm just before it erupts and the stale, haunted odor of a dead body. But it's not her. It's the weather, and the lake—a relief. On a humid day you can smell that lake from two miles away. Thought he'd never forget that for a minute, everything smelling like rot. My whole childhood smells like rot.

He goes back in the kitchen to take off his shoes. They're too loud, all you can hear. They sound like he's stomping. Angry, falling-apart sounds echo throughout the house. He opens a window to relieve some of the pressure. The house feels like the inside of a balloon, and his face is sweating. There's no one to talk to, and he struggles to clear his throat. He reminds me of a car that won't start.

He needs a breeze, but the air here is stiff, stubborn. The

whole damn state is stubborn. You'd think after, what, ten years, twelve years—you'd think after all this time one little breeze wouldn't be too much to ask. He rubs his face with a damp dish towel. He's cussing, muttering to himself under his breath. He thinks he's alone.

He'll make a cup of tea, then he'll go talk to me. He rolls up his sleeves, pushing at them in jerks. God knows what he'll say. What do you say to a twelve-year-old. What do you say to your twelve-year-old daughter who thinks you're her uncle who you barely even know. Who makes you uncomfortable as hell. And how do you explain something you don't even understand yourself. Where do they keep the damn tea bags.

First he'll get the body out of the house, then he'll talk to me.

He is so completely absorbed in his own worries he hasn't heard my door squeak open. I know where the floorboards creak and I know how to walk down the hall without making a sound— this from years of pretending I'm a spy, an Indian, a prison escapee. I know how to see without being seen.

He reaches for the phone on the wall and dials his own number. Yeah, it's me. . . . I left a note on the kitchen counter, if you'd just looked. . . . I called you from Huntsville over two hours ago and the damn machine answered. . . . Because I'd already left you a note, and I'd driven two hours, I was halfway to hell, and I didn't think it was asking too much to expect you to pick up the damn phone. . . . Dee, if you just wouldn't wear earphones when you play your drums so you can't hear the phone. . . . All I'm asking is if you insist on driving like a maniac—yes you do, blaring your music where you can't even hear people honking at you, so just let me know when you're home safe so I don't have to be the last person in Nashville to find out when you kill yourself, I don't think that's asking too damn much. . . . I'm not asking you to report your every move, and you know it.

This, I learn later, is their standard fight.

His voice lowers almost to a whisper. I creep closer to the kitchen. I miss some sentences completely, but what I pick up is that in a small, terrible sense it's a relief. For the past twelve years he's known this time was coming, dreaded its coming, and now it's here and soon it will be over with. No, he hasn't told me yet, but he will. Yes, by the time she gets here I'll know. No, not everything, Christ, how could he possibly tell me everything. Just that he's my father and he wasn't driving, it wasn't his fault.

He thinks if I know he wasn't driving it will make some kind of difference.

Then they'll take me home with them, and Paw Paw will go in a nursing home where he belongs. He calls Paw Paw the old man. The old man will go in a nursing home and everything will work out.

I picture Uncle Mull and Paw Paw playing Sorry! and Uncle Mull draws the Sorry! card and sends Paw Paw back to Start. Paw Paw just sits there.

They'll finish the basement for my room. The only other option is his office, and he can't do without his office. He knows a good contractor who'll do it cheap. No, he's not talking the whole basement, she can still keep her drums down there, just the part on the right side of the stairs. It'll work out fine. How much trouble can a twelve-year-old girl be. Deedee and I will get along fine. There's not enough headroom in the attic. No, there isn't, seven feet at the apex. Raising the roof is like adding a whole room, you may as well buy a new house. They'll see how much it would cost. They'll talk about it when they get back.

I step on the loudest floorboard. The hall moans.

We'll see her tomorrow. She promises to drive safely. He hangs up and his hand stays stuck on the receiver.

The grandfather clock in the den sounds, and he casts an angry glance in that direction. It's too loud and too slow, mournful. How the hell did she sleep with that thing going off at all hours, depressing as hell.

The teakettle begins to whine itself into a whistle and he hurries it off the stove. All noise is offensive. Outside it thunders so loudly it startles him, and he jerks and misses the cup, then reaches for the dish towel. Damn. Crumbs all over the countertop, soggy crumbs. No wonder he's seen so many roaches. Huge old mothers. Dammit, who's been taking care of this house, anyway.

The clock is silent again, and it's raining hard. He can barely hear his own feet anymore for the sound of water, water running everywhere. Rain on the roof, in the gutters, pelting the window screens. Even inside the air feels loud and wet, old.

This kitchen is where he first kissed my mother all those years ago, a lifetime ago. This is the room he thinks of when he wonders where he left himself. This is where he puts her when he thinks of her. Not sitting in the Cutlass, six months pregnant with me, her belly button a bump on her T-shirt, her breasts heavy like a grown woman's—the last time he saw her. But here, eating a cake with a fork, a whole lemon pound cake on a yellow plastic dinner plate on this same puke-green countertop, whispering what am I going to do, the terror in her barely shaking fingers making him believe what her flat stomach couldn't. He was just a kid.

I step into the kitchen holding a bowl of strawberry Jell-O, and he's not surprised to see me.

You know I was just a kid when you were born, he says. That's all I was, a little older than you.

He's not the same person anymore, and coming back here is like stepping into an old movie. The kitchen should be black and white. He should be black and white. The gray film outside should be moving in, tinting us, changing us all back.

He's laughing, shaking his head, but nothing is funny. I pick at the Jell-O. He sits down at the kitchen table. He scratches his beard.

Once you get over the grief and the guilt, he says, the hardest thing is living and not living at the same time with who you used to be.

He's not laughing anymore, and I'm afraid he might cry. I've never seen a man cry.

And who you are now, he says, and the difference.

I pretend not to understand. I don't know whether he's talking to me or just talking. He watches his own hands on the table.

I don't know, he says, maybe you never do get over the grief or the guilt, so there's nothing after that.

They can't come get the body until five o'clock, between five and six, and he can't really do anything until my grandmother is out of there. Everything feels wrong as long as she's right there within earshot—eating her food, calling her friends, claiming her granddaughter. She gives him the creeps, casts a shadow over the whole place, like her spirit is as big as the house, hovering over us, watching, disapproving.

Every time he looks at her she looks deader. You'd think there weren't levels of dead—you're either dead or you're not—but she keeps getting deader, and uglier. He thinks she's withering.

He pulls the window closed, lifts the tea bag out of the cup and lets it drip. The first thing is, get the body out of here. He clears his throat and takes a sip of tea. Too damn hot.

He says this place sure could use some new landscaping. That's the first thing he noticed when he drove up. Or at least a paint job. If we're going to try to sell it, we should at least give it a new paint job. Put in a hundred bucks' worth of shrubs, you can raise your asking price five hundred dollars.

He pours the tea down the sink. Last damn thing you need on a day like today is hot tea.

Deedee's coming tomorrow, he says. He throws the tea bag away. You like Deedee, don't you.

Yes.

My mother was just like Deedee in some ways. He was with her that night, the night of the accident. He wants to know if I knew that. He said you're in no condition to drive, Gracie, because she was so hyped up, she was so nervous, almost like she was high. He tried to stop her, but there was no telling her. Not right there on the grounds of the home where if somebody heard them it could ruin everything. She said you got me into this, but I'm driving myself out of here if it kills me. She actually said that —if it killed her. What else could he do. So he thought he'd let her drive until they got out of Mobile and then she'd want to go to sleep anyway—it was three in the morning, and she needed her sleep for the baby. For me. He thought once they got out of Mobile she'd calm down, and then he'd drive. But she had to drive herself off the grounds, and when she had to have something there was no telling her different.

This is what he tells me. I accept that he remembers it this way, but I wonder how my mother would have told it.

My grandparents still blame him, but they couldn't have

stopped her either. And he can't explain to them that he thinks she did it on purpose, that she was trying to kill all three of us. He says you can't tell a person's mother that.

Why he thinks you can tell a person's daughter that, I don't know.

But sometimes when he's here and they're treating him like shit, like an intruder, shielding him from his own daughter and filling me with God knows what kind of crap about him, he just wants to spit at them. Why did they try to send her away, if they hadn't sent her all the way to Mobile, if they had just let her stay there in her own home with them—

He looks at me like he's noticing me for the first time. Well, he says. It's best just not to think about it, he figures. He doesn't really think about my mother that much, except when he's here. And when I'm with you, he says.

He won't look me in the eye. I look too much like her pictures, it's like seeing a ghost. If I were him I wouldn't look at me either.

He looks out the window, walks over to it, says something about the rain, like he's never seen rain before. He doesn't even know how to think of me. He hasn't said my name since he got here. He says it's like we've all been living with lies for so long I've almost come to believe them, and now to think of you as mine— my daughter, my responsibility. Hell, I'm thirty years old and you're practically a teenager. He turns, looks at my breasts. This is crazy. I look at him without making a face. He is suffering, and I'm glad. He says he was only trying to do what was in my best interest. He was too young to raise me, he couldn't give me what little girls need, he had no idea what a little girl like me would need.

I don't say anything.

I was, dammit, he says.

This pain is all I have of him. I want to say something unforgivably cruel. I want to scream I hate you. I've known you were my father for years now, as long as I can remember, how stupid did you think I was, but I waited year after year after year for you to want me, I waited for you to come get me and take me to live with you just because you wanted me, and I made up excuses for you, like you were building a room for me, you were finding a mother for me, you had amnesia, and I believed them, or I half did, and I kept waiting, but I waited too long and now I hate you.

But I don't. I can't get all those words out. I can't think of them. I say you aren't my father. I don't have a father. My father died with my mother in the car accident. I mean it.

He walks back into the den.

I had pushed the wicker rocker into a corner weeks before when I pulled down the Murphy bed. I hate that rocker, the way it squeaks, and nobody has sat in it for months. The right runner is half on the rug, half on the floor, and when it rocks it goes creak-bump, creak-bump. My father sits, rocks, stares. Creak-bump.

We are both too old and too young to be here.

I put my bowl in the sink and go back to my room.

My grandfather is out of bed for the first time today, and I hear the knocking in the wall that means his shower is on.

He thinks of himself as Paw Paw now. My grandmother called him that, and of course I did. He used to be called Ned. I imagine him saying the word into the water and it comes out warbled, strange. It's been a long time since he felt like a Ned. My father still calls him Ned.

I think it is just becoming real to him. He doesn't know why

it took him all day or what he's thought about since I told him—
the whole day has been a blur, and he feels himself finally coming
into focus, finally feeling something. Over the years he has pictured himself at this moment shrieking in anguish, crumpling into
a black hole of loss, but what he feels now is jealousy. She went
peacefully, painlessly. There are worse things. He knows how he'll
go. It'll be a hard crossing, and he wishes he could get it over
with. He always thought he'd go first. She was so much younger.
She was always young.

He lathers his wrinkled arms, his bony chest, his skinny legs,
his withered penis. They hadn't made love that often since the
cancer, but the thought that they never will again comes as a
shock. He feels hot regret pass from his head to his feet, and he
looks at the drain on the floor. He thinks for the first time, I'm not
going to get well. I'm going to die, too. Soon we'll all be dead. He
thinks it without emotion.

He has been betrayed by disease, and he's tired of fighting.
There was a time when the cancer was an enemy, but now he
wishes he could embrace it fully, be devoured by it like a lover,
and its reluctance is all that seems evil about it to him. He wills
his body to die. He wants to lay it down like a burden. He wants
to be a spirit.

He steps out of the shower carefully, steadying himself on
the towel rack, the toilet. He closes the lid and sits down on the
fuzzy seat cover to dry himself. He forgot to rinse off his crotch.
He wipes off the suds with a towel. Soon he's going to need a tub
so he doesn't have to stand up that long.

My grandmother once wanted a tub. They looked into getting one, he even called out a plumber for an estimate, but there
wasn't enough room, so she said it's all right. Went through her
whole life saying it's all right when she didn't get what she wanted

and now she's dead. He wonders if she got what she wanted this time.

Fifty-three years old. Healthy as anybody her age. A little arthritis is all. It's not right. First Gracie and then this. It's just not right.

He folds the towel carefully, in thirds like my grandmother preferred, even though folding it in half made more sense to him. He wonders if he'll go back to folding towels in half.

I close and lock my door.

5

I'D FIGURED DEEDEE'D COME TO THE FUNERAL SO EVERY-
body'd be staring at us, so I went back in the kitchen which Uncle
Mull didn't even notice and I got a whole jar of mayonnaise plus a
box of vanilla wafers and went back in my room to put the mayonnaise on my head. You have to leave it on thirty to forty-five
minutes—that's what M'Lea's mother's magazine said—so I was
sitting there with a towel on my head eating my vanilla wafers and
I said this is a good time to write out my plan.

I've always for as long as I can remember been a planner,
chopping up my days on graph paper into thirty-minute blocks.
Only I couldn't find any graph paper to save my life, which could
have set off a panic any second, so I said to myself Sylvia, just do
what you can, that's all anybody can ask of you, which sounded
like Memaw, and I made myself forget about everything else tem-
porarily and get out some plain paper and start making my own
graph paper and filling in the times. Which helped. Just drawing
those lines, writing those numbers like I'd done a hundred thousand times before. One-thirty still comes after one o'clock, which
still comes after twelve-thirty, which still comes after twelve. I still

find that thought comforting. There's just something about numbers. They remind me of God.

So I'd blocked out all Saturday afternoon and Saturday night and I was starting on Sunday—I hadn't filled them in yet, just drawn the lines—when bang I realized I had no idea what I was doing. I was thinking sweep the porch, straighten up my room, clean the stove, call M'Lea, but I didn't have any idea what you really do when your grandmother dies. Because everything I needed to know was things I'd usually ask her. Like was I supposed to invite her friends over and was somebody going to fix Memaw's hair because I could practically hear her saying I've got to get my hair done before this funeral, I look like a bomb dropped on my head. And how were they going to know what her favorite hymn was—it was "The Old Rugged Cross," and I thought we should have sung it at the service. I thought the part about exchange it someday for a crown would have been a real nice touch. I could just picture Memaw in the customer service line in heaven leaning against this big old wooden cross, and then she gets to the front and turns it in and they give her this huge crown with diamonds and rubies and white fur with black polka dots around the edges and she puts it on and straightens it in a mirror. Then she walks away smiling, trying not to look proud.

I worried about everything. Like what was Uncle Mull doing out there that was making so much racket and was Memaw all moved into her mansion in heaven already and was it a good one and would they let her have a garden there and if they did, how, because there's no dirt, and what do gardeners do up there because there's no weeds, either, or aphids—I think people who garden just about live for weeds and aphids—and had Memaw already found her mother and father and my mother, not to mention Jesus, and was she so happy to see all them that she'd forgotten me.

I had a lump in my stomach just thinking about her. It was about the size of a pecan still in the shell and about as hard. I get them all the time, sometimes only as big and about as squishy as grapes but sometimes they'll be like a fist opening and closing in there, like a mad fist. So as soon as I finished drawing the lines, I felt that lump land in my stomach like somebody'd dropped it there, and I started getting really mad and panicky and upset and not exactly crying but pacing around the room with tears leaking out of my eyes and the lump inching its way up my esophagus and the only way I could keep from bawling was eat vanilla wafer after vanilla wafer and every time I swallowed one try to push that ball of tears back down my throat.

When I should have been worrying over a hundred other things I didn't even know about at the time. I think maybe I just picked up on how my life was fixing to fall apart. I don't go in for ESP exactly—Bo Schifflett, Junior, says it's the occult, and I don't mess with that—but I do think your brain'll find things out and it'll tell your feelings and they'll get all upset but it won't tell your thoughts till later, so you don't know why you're upset. That's what mine does. That's not the occult, though, it's just how my brain works.

Because I was all upset and I had no idea why and Bo Schifflett, Junior, hadn't even heard of me yet and of course I hadn't heard of him either and if you'd of asked him at the time he would have said he was minding his own business making his own plan like anybody does right before the school year starts, but the truth was he was at that very minute plotting the end of the world. Which I credit for Paw Paw's death and for Bo's death and just about for mine. So I don't know, maybe I went into that panic because my brain just sort of sensed all that fixing to happen and was trying to tell me stop. And maybe the panic just got worse and worse because my brain was screaming stop, stop, stop—louder and louder and louder—and I had no idea that's what it was trying to say.

So I just kept going and I sat myself down and I wrote watch *Gilligan's Island* in my first slot and I was thinking I'd have a sugar sandwich for lunch because in the summer Paw Paw and I always watched it at twelve o'clock while we ate and I'd forgot it was Saturday. Paw Paw'd have cornflakes with blueberries straight out of the freezer, and when he was finished with the cornflakes he'd have a bowlful of blue milk and he'd put Cheez Doodles in there and eat them with a spoon like cereal. I'd have a pineapple and cheese sandwich on white bread with chocolate milk if Memaw was home or a butter and sugar sandwich if she wasn't. Every so often I'd make a mayonnaise sandwich.

All that seems like a different life. Sometimes I try to picture myself just sitting in the den with Paw Paw, eating a sugar sandwich, watching *Gilligan's Island,* feeling happy. Only I can't do it. I put some girl in there with him, but she's not me, no matter how hard I wish she was. Then I get a lump in my stomach and I can't make it go away.

Paw Paw got mad at suppertime because there wasn't any mayonnaise, so Uncle Mull put butter on his ham sandwich which he hates and which I'm not too crazy about myself so I can't blame him for not eating it, although if the mayonnaise had of fixed my hair it would have been worth it. Uncle Mull and I ordered pizza. By that time they'd come and taken Memaw and I'd washed the mayonnaise out of my hair and Uncle Mull had put the Murphy bed back in the wall where it hadn't been for months and the den felt too big and empty and I felt all funny about going in there and full of vanilla wafers which is the worst kind of full there is and hungry for chocolate. Because your stomach feels tight and you feel all that sugar running around in your blood making you nervous but you haven't really tasted anything but cardboard. Vanilla cardboard. And I felt hungrier and hungrier and the house felt emptier and emptier and quieter and quieter all night. Even with Uncle Mull and Paw Paw in a snoring contest.

The next day we skipped church which I felt kind of odd about because I had this crazy idea that Memaw would be there looking for me even though I knew she couldn't. Deedee came with enough suitcases to last me for two years and my hair was its old normal self. Nobody even noticed it.

They announced it from the pulpit so everybody swarmed the house, including Mrs. Tutwiler, who brought over a dessert she learned how to make in gourmet cooking school in Birmingham. Nobody there could figure out what flavor it was because it was supposed to be a rum cake only she didn't want to use liquor because of be not drunk with wine but be filled with the Holy Spirit, so she wouldn't tell anybody what she'd put in it instead. She made everybody try it and everybody said how good it was and everybody tried to guess the secret ingredient and she said I'll carry it to my grave and then she was embarrassed that she'd said grave and she looked at me to see if I'd heard, which I acted like I hadn't, and then she left and nobody ate another bite. Eventually little green circles of fur grew onto it and Deedee threw it away.

Other people brought barbecue and cold cuts and cheese and bread and everything you could think of for sandwiches except mayonnaise, so I felt real bad about that and I slipped out and walked down to the Piggly Wiggly and bought some more mayonnaise with my babysitting money plus a Snickers bar. Then I went on over to the hardware store to price chickens. I still had some money left.

We had a mama and two babies in the front yard, but they were so old their faces were just about faded off. We used to have three babies, but when the Sutherlands carried Brother home from the hospital they put Bubba outside, and Bubba cried and cried—Memaw said new baby or no, it's just pitiful to hear that dog moan like that—until finally one day Bubba jumped over his fence and went on a vandalism spree and he turned over our trash can and dragged the trash all over the yard including all Paw Paw's empty Metamucil jars and he knocked over all Memaw's chickens and chewed off the head of one of the babies, and then Memaw went after him with a broom and he tore on down the street with the head in his mouth, terrorizing everybody he saw. We never did find that head. I figure he dropped it down a sewer.

They had everything at that store—pink flamingos, white flamingos, mama geese, baby geese, windmills—everything any yard in the world could ask for except chickens, which was the only thing I wanted. I tried to work myself up into wanting flamingos instead, but I couldn't do it. Memaw said pink flamingos in your yard makes you look like a floozie house. Then I tried the same thing with the geese, but there's something scary about geese, if you ask me. Just as soon snap at you as not, honking their heads off the whole time.

So I headed on back toward home and ate my Snickers bar on the way. Which was the best I felt that whole day, the sun making my hair hot and melting my Snickers bar and me having to eat it fast and then licking my fingers and the wrapper, not thinking about anything but how hot my hair was and was it getting any lighter and had I eaten all the chocolate. Instead of being home where everything was always sadness and pickles.

One thing I don't understand is hearing somebody you know has died and what you do about it is you go out and buy pickles. That's what people do, though. They knock on your door and walk right in and by the time you've gotten to the door to take a look at them they're smothering you and saying oh Sylvia, I'm so sorry about your grandmama, what a shock, what a terrible shock. They might start crying a little bit, and then they hand you a jar of pickles. And you can't even think of their name and you wish they'd leave you alone and you say thank you for the pickles even if you hate pickles with a passion, which I do, and you try to get untangled and get yourself out of there only there's nowhere to go because they've taken over the house. It's like eating solid vinegar.

Memaw wasn't sick. That's why it was a shock. Anybody would have said Paw Paw would have died before her. So I loved my Paw Paw like he was a daddy but I had tried to get prepared in my head for living without him. I thought I had to do that, and to tell the truth it had just about come to a place where I'd thought it would be easier to live without him. I don't know if that's wrong or not, but it's true. But I had never in my born days tried to figure how to live without Memaw.

And I think to this day she died of a broken heart. I think when Paw Paw got cancer she gathered up every ounce of strength and courage she had left in her to fight it, and Paw Paw got ready to drive back and forth to Birmingham for treatment and we all didn't know what to think but we all thought it wouldn't be so bad. I said Memaw, I'm scared to death, but Memaw held my face in her hands and she said other people live through this, Sylvia, and so will we. Then they said they wanted to do surgery and I got scared again, but Memaw said your Paw Paw's a strong man, he's a fighter like you, he'll be all right because God will give him the grace to get through it.

During the surgery, Memaw and I took a walk in a park. She was scared as me and so white her eyes looked like inkblots, so I didn't ask anything. And after an hour and a half of walking around waiting, not saying a word, Memaw said let's head on back. I took her hand and it was cold and she said people live through this type of thing every day and go on to lead perfectly normal lives. And then die, I thought in spite of myself. So I didn't say anything, I didn't even try to comfort her. Because I kept thinking he's gonna die, he's gonna die, and I was afraid I was going to say it, so I didn't say anything.

And sure enough, it turned out they opened him up and looked around and when they were finished and Paw Paw was still asleep, they told Memaw it was splattered inside him like paint, like a bomb had exploded in there leaving little drops of cancer everywhere you turned around. So they closed him back up and they didn't even bother to take out the big tumors, much less the little drops, and they sent him home to die. Memaw said to the doctor, my God in heaven, why? As long as you had him opened up why couldn't you just take out the tumors, you people are supposed to be in the healing business. I can't remember what the doctor said after that.

Then we took him home and she cried and cried every time he went to sleep, and when he was awake she tried to act cheerful and normal and cook food he'd eat and she and I'd sit in the room with him just lying there drugged up and she'd tell me all kinds of stories about how when she and Paw Paw were young and happy. I'd listen but it was really for him. And then she died of a broken heart. At least that's how I see it.

It wasn't just the cancer. It was the cancer on top of my mama getting pregnant on top of her dying and me almost dying and them having to keep my dead mama on life support for two months until I was ready and knowing they might go through all that and I might not make it anyway and the only reason I made it was I'm a fighter and the power of prayer. Which would have to take something out of Memaw.

I've seen pictures of her with my mama before my mama got pregnant, smiling and hugging and their cheeks touching each other in one of them, and then there aren't any for about a year and then there are some of her holding me when I'm a teeny baby, smiling again but not the same, now it's like somebody said say cheese, one two three cheese. Her hair went from black to white that year. I think all that just accumulated and accumulated in her arteries, little bits of sadness she couldn't clean out of her system, and eventually she had so much in there her blood couldn't get through. Only her heart didn't know because she tried so hard to act happy, so it kept pumping the blood out like everything was normal and the blood didn't have anyplace to go so it started backing up in her heart, filling it up like a balloon, and one night it just couldn't stretch any bigger, so it broke.

Because the day I was born, they buried my mama. They cut her open and took me out and then I was alive and she was dead, and I never saw her again. I'm the only person I know who's lived inside a dead body, but I did it for two solid months. That's why I don't count her, though, in my list of dead bodies. Because for one thing there's no light in there usually so I don't know if I actually technically saw her insides or not, and then after I was born, I doubt they let me get a good look at her, and of course I don't remember it if they did. I wouldn't think they would let a baby's first sight be a cut-open dead body.

Sometimes I think about Memaw looking at my mama swollen beyond herself with me, knowing it was going to be the last time she saw her, and then a few minutes later she's holding me, so tiny I don't even seem real, my mama's blood's just been washed off me only I'm still red and I'm wrapped in swaddling clothes, and then her going to the funeral, all in the same day. I wonder what she wore. Because in my mind, when she's holding me, she's wearing a light blue dress, but then at the funeral she's wearing black.

After they buried her, they left me in the hospital for another day or two, and then Memaw and Paw Paw brought me home like I was their baby and they named me Sylvia because that's what my mama told the other pregnant girls in the home she was going to name me, with Grace as a middle name because that was my mama's name and I was all they had left of her. I'd wake up in the middle of the night screaming for my mama's milk and Memaw would fix me a bottle and she'd rock me and we'd both cry ourselves back to sleep, comforting each other. If she hadn't had me to take care of during those dark nights, she didn't know how she would have made it. Memaw told me all that.

But there are certain things you can't ask a person about their own dead child that you can't help but wonder about. Like she was already dead in her brain and they'd been pumping her heart for the last two months, so then did they just cut her open and take me out and unplug her like she was an electric sack? And did they use anesthesia before they cut her open, and did they bother to sew her back closed? Or when they unplugged her and she turned finally completely dead, did that hurt, that last little bit of dying? And did she go into labor, and if she did, if you can breathe and your heart's beating and your baby's growing inside you and you go into labor, how can you possibly do all that while you're also dead? So what if they made a mistake and she woke up from her coma the next day and she was knocking on the door of the coffin, yelling and screaming, and nobody came? Sometimes I think that's what happened, and I think I can still hear little echoes of her screaming let me out.

Another thing is, is it my fault? Because if I were Memaw I couldn't help but think if only it hadn't been for Sylvia. Because obviously if she hadn't gotten pregnant with me—you don't get pregnant every time you do it—then she wouldn't have gone to the home so she wouldn't have been so lonely that she wanted to escape and Uncle Mull wouldn't have gone down to break her out of there and they wouldn't have tried to beat the train and she wouldn't have died. And who knows if Paw Paw hadn't grieved all those years, and if I hadn't looked more and more every day like she did when she died and even grew my hair out long and stringy and braided a little piece down the side for no reason just so I could look like her—because one day he looked at me like he'd never seen me before and he said Gracie, and I felt like I'd won a prize. Maybe if not for all that, he wouldn't have gotten sick. And Memaw wouldn't have died of a broken heart and he'd still go to work and she'd have flowers all the way up the front walk like in old pictures and my mama would have grown up and married somebody better and had lots of babies and they'd go see Memaw and Paw Paw all the time but it would be normal. Not like me, where I just drained the life out of everybody I touched.

Bo Schifflett, Junior, says nothing can kill you until your time comes and God calls you home and then nothing can keep you alive because God has your days numbered since before you're born, and he quotes Scripture to prove it. So the only way you know when your time is, is if you die, that was your time. Otherwise I would say Memaw and Paw Paw both died before their time and I'd wonder if I didn't miss mine and should be dead already.

I never asked Bo Schifflett, Junior, about this, but I think he would have said you can't be born before your time either. Same idea. But I don't know. I look at those babies on TV who weigh two pounds and can fit in the palm of somebody's hand and barely look human, and they always show the mama and she's always real worried and she's got bags under her eyes, and the daddy's crying in public and they ask everybody watching TV to pray for their babies—which I always do. Sometimes I pray so hard I can't stop and I start to feeling like I can't even go to sleep because if I stop praying they'll die, like every sentence you pray is like a breath you breathe into somebody when you're doing CPR, so even if you're exhausted and you don't know if it's doing any good, you can't just stop because even if they're already dead, it would still be like you killed them because you gave up because God knew ahead of time you were going to.

I never asked Bo about this either, but I think CPR and especially how some people are actually dead and then they get brought back to life with it—it's like they did die before their time and then God changed his mind or realized there was a mistake and gave them a second chance. So it makes you wonder.

Because I think Memaw dying like that, and Uncle Mull and Deedee coming down to stay with us and sleeping in the Murphy bed, the very same Murphy bed where Memaw died, just different sheets, and arguing in loud terrible whispers in the middle of the night when they thought nobody could hear them, and me feeling like it was my fault because Reverend Tutwiler says anger is contagious so I knew they'd caught it from me, and the real estate agent coming over, stomping through the house like a pest control inspector and putting a big old brown FOR SALE sign in the yard with yellow letters that made the yard look so funny I went and got Memaw's chickens and threw them away myself, and then all of us moving into their house in Nashville because they had to put Paw Paw on a waiting list because it turns out nursing homes won't take you when you're in the shape he was in, and Deedee saying why the heck do they go into the nursing home business if they don't want people who need nursing care, and Uncle Mull not answering except by blowing his nose, stopping and unstopping it with his handkerchief like it was a harmonica—sometimes you just have to hope it doesn't make you a doubting Thomas to ask yourself if there's been a mistake.

I couldn't hear every word, but I heard enough to know they were arguing about me, and I knew I'd let the sun go down on my anger, and I knew I had to stop before I ruined anything else but I'd tried, I'd just about tried my heart out, and I couldn't do it. Matter of fact, the harder I tried, the worse it got, and I found myself getting madder and madder and sadder and sadder to the point where you couldn't tell them apart. Like I felt sad-mad during the viewing of the body on account of how even though they got her color close to normal I just couldn't stand that little smile she had on her face. Because for one thing it was new. She didn't have it on the Murphy bed and I couldn't help but think how in the world could I have missed it or, worse, how in the world did it get there now if it wasn't there then.

So I stayed sad-mad through the funeral and the funeral party and the two days after when Uncle Mull and Deedee were still there and we still had all that food, and then more or less regular life started happening again all around me only I couldn't help it, I just stayed sad-mad, and I kept getting sadder and madder with every passing day to the point where I thought I might pop.

Months later I said that to Bo Schifflett, Junior. I said Bo, sometimes I feel so sad and so mad I'm afraid my heart's going to explode.

And Bo said you have to get rid of that anger, you have to figure out who or what you're mad at, and you have to forgive them. Bo was wise beyond his years, which was one of the things I loved about him.

So I forgave her. I closed my eyes and I opened my hands and I said I forgive you, Memaw, I forgive you for leaving me. I forgive you for getting old, for not being here when I need you, not being here to listen to me or take care of me or love me or protect me and everything else I can't even think of right now, I forgive you.

And every time I'd get mad about it, I'd do it again. Over and over and over. Because you try to trust God and believe all things work together for good for those who love God and are called according to his purpose and all that, but sometimes you can't help but think if only she hadn't died none of that would have happened with Paw Paw. He would have just died a normal old death like old people are supposed to and I wouldn't have to think about the Rapture and the Slim-fast and the Roach-Prufe milk-shake and Bo Schifflett, Junior, dying, and none of this would have happened.

Of course if you think too much, you start wanting to undo your whole life, and you start unraveling and unraveling in your head just like when Memaw would pull out her knitting row after row till she got back to her mistake, and once you get going on it, it gets easier and easier to the point where you can't hardly stop because you can't for your life figure out what your mistake was. And you know exactly how Lot's wife felt right before she turned into a pillar of salt.

Like first if only Memaw hadn't died but before that if only Paw Paw hadn't got cancer and before that if only I could have lived with Uncle Mull instead of them in the first place. Because one time he and Deedee came out here and they said they were fixing to get married and buy a house and they wanted to get me to come live with them in Nashville like a regular family. That was the first time I met Deedee. So they had all kinds of big talks about it and Memaw cried and Paw Paw sent me over to stay with M'Lea, who lives on the lake in Riff Raff Acres trailer park, and I stayed there two long nights while Memaw and Paw Paw ironed things out with Uncle Mull and Deedee. So M'Lea and I cried and plotted how we'd stay best friends across the miles and write letters every other day in secret code and visit each other every summer and be in each other's weddings. Only I have to admit, part of me was secretly happy. I knew there were worse things in life than getting out of Pell City and going to live in Nashville with your uncle who plays the guitar and wears cowboy boots and blue jeans every day of his life including to church and his wife who works as a receptionist in the recording studio where Ronnie Milsap makes all his albums and who wants to be a drummer in a country-western band and carries a purse that looks like a big piece of Chicklets gum and has actually sat down and eaten dinner at Barbara Mandrell's house. So when I came home I'd already packed my suitcase in my head and I was starving because M'Lea's mother was on a diet and they didn't have any food in the house but Melba toast, which tastes like crackers made out of old rubber bands, and Memaw was cooking lasagna and tunnel-of-fudge cake, my all-time absolute favorites, and not opening her mouth and saying don't ask, only without words, and Uncle Mull'd left without me.

And now Memaw'd left without me and Uncle Mull was

fixing dinner, and my whole life felt like that, turned inside out and folded in backwards on itself, touching in places it wasn't ever meant to.

I couldn't help but wonder if I'd just run away like I'd had a mind to before I even called Uncle Mull and set all the rest of it in motion, if maybe things wouldn't have turned out better. Probably not. Every time M'Lea ran away, she'd come over to our house, and Memaw would call M'Lea's mother to come get her and while we were waiting Memaw'd say M'Lea, running away never solved anything, don't you know that by now. M'Lea wouldn't answer. She'd just sit on the top step to the front porch and clean the lint out from between her toes like that took every ounce of concentration she had, and when her mama drove up she'd get in the back seat and leave without looking at us. Memaw and I'd watch the car roll down the street without saying anything, the top of M'Lea's head just barely showing in the back window, and then we'd go inside and Memaw'd be extra cheerful and I'd try to convince myself it was for M'Lea's own good.

But I don't know. Not running away didn't solve anything either.

6

BUDDY COMES IN THE BEDROOM WHILE I'M PACKING. HE stands in the doorway watching and I don't say anything, I just keep packing. Toothbrush. Toothpaste. Jeans. Shampoo.

He says when are you leaving.

He knows when I'm leaving, we've discussed it a hundred times, so I ask him again if he wants to come.

He says no, if you're going to leave by ten o'clock there's not enough time.

I say Buddy, if you don't want to come, fine, don't come, but don't say you're not coming because there's not enough time to pack.

When are you coming back.

Sunday.

He knows that too. I know what's coming next, but I let him say the whole thing. You work too hard, they don't pay you enough for the work you do, you're just an assistant to a vice president, you're a glorified secretary, you shouldn't be having to travel like this.

It wouldn't be so bad if he didn't say this every time I come home more than ten minutes late, every time I get up early for a breakfast meeting, every time he gets a chance. Halfheartedly, I say my lines: Buddy, it's good for my career to do this, I want to do it, you make a lot of good contacts at these things.

Career. He says it like it's a cuss word. I want you home with me.

Buddy, you knew I was going to do this, why didn't you wait to take your trip until I was gone. He's just back from three days in Atlanta.

He says I had to go when I had to go.

But you have some control over it.

No, I don't.

Some, you do, over the timing.

I keep packing—an extra pair of blue jeans, an extra blouse, extra underwear. I've packed everything I need, but I don't want to stop now. I'm getting mad, but I don't want to fight because I have to leave. I'm thinking I hope you know what you're doing, Buddy. You're taking me for granted, you're treating me like this for the last time, and it's a big mistake. I tell myself don't get so worked up over nothing. Of course he couldn't go to Atlanta for the weekend, it was a business trip, you idiot. I think about my bathtub man. I let myself want him, and I pack a nightgown I think he'd like because he's only a fantasy, and I need a fantasy right now.

Buddy looks at the nightgown and I look back at him, daring him to say something about it. He says are you finished packing.

I guess so.

He closes the suitcase, slides it off the bed onto the floor, and says let's have sex.

I laugh. How can you just switch yourself on like that.

He puts his arms around me from behind and starts rubbing my stomach. He says let's make a baby.

No, Buddy, you know I have to go. I push his arms away, and I feel like I'm unwrapping myself. I can't help but wonder if he's just doing this to make me late.

He says you had time for me to pack, but you don't have time for sex.

Buddy. I close my eyes. He has a point. It would take him fifteen minutes to pack, and we'd be finished with sex in ten. I say Buddy, I'm already dressed, I don't want to mess up my hair.

Fine, let's not mess up your hair, for God's sakes. He picks up the suitcase and starts to carry it to the car.

Buddy, don't be this way.

What way.

I grab my guitar as I follow him. The fight is over for now because we never argue outside, and walking out the door was his way of cutting me off. I look at his back as I follow him to the car. I feel panicked, like he's the one leaving me, and not just for a weekend. He puts the suitcase in the trunk and I lay my guitar down beside it. I tell him there are two casseroles in the refrigerator, and I'm trying to hold his hand. I'm rubbing his arm, trying to leave things on a better note than this. He slams the trunk closed and kisses me lightly, quickly.

I say we'll make love Sunday when I get home.

He says have a good trip.

I hug him and kiss him on the neck. I say I love you.

I watch him in the rearview mirror as I drive away. He lights a cigarette and goes inside, flicking his ashes into the yard.

I get to Birmingham about one-thirty, check into the hotel, confirm Jake's reservations, and eat lunch. I run a few errands to make sure everything's set for Jake's TV interview tomorrow morning and his performance in the afternoon, then I watch some TV and play my guitar in my room.

I don't like being alone. I'm on the tenth floor. I don't look out my window.

Jake's plane gets in at eight-fifteen, and all the way to the airport I think of ways I could slip in the fact that I play drums. I'm too shy to tell David, my boss, because he hates it when people trying to break into the performance part of the business —starvin' Marvins, he calls them—ask him for advice. I'm wondering if Jake feels the same way, but I tell myself he can't be that jaded already. Plus I'm not going to ask him for advice. I'm just letting him know I play the drums, just in case he ever happens to need a drummer, almost like I'm doing him a favor. I'm not at all sure I can pull this off.

I think about shaking his hand when I see him—hi, I'm Sylvia. Hi, I'm Sylvia Reed with Sony Records. I'm Sylvia with Sony. I can't think what to say after that. I'm hoping he won't notice my hands are freezing. I rub them together, breathe on them, trying to warm them up, while the portable hall gets attached to the plane.

People start walking out. A few reunions—mostly businessmen in suits carrying briefcases and a few tourists in loud shirts with shopping bags—but it seems like fewer people hug in the airport than they used to. Most just lower their heads, frown, and leave. Flying has lost its romance.

The plane is late, and a woman is furious. If she's missed her connection to Miami, somebody in management is going to hear about this. I think she's drunk. Why would anybody from L.A. change planes in Birmingham on their way to Miami? It's not a hub. For some reason this bothers me. Why would anybody in L.A. go to Miami? What's the difference?

I'm afraid I won't recognize him or I'll say something stupid or he won't be on the plane or he's already gotten off and I missed him. I should have made a sign that said Jake Harris, but that looks so stupid. Then again, how's he going to know who I am? It could have been a little sign, more like a piece of paper. I should have written him a note last week, told him what I'd be wearing, but it was such a busy week and am I supposed to know a week ahead of time what I'm going to wear?

My hands are still freezing, but now they're sweaty, too. I try to look like I'm not wiping them on my pants, I'm just standing here with my hands on my hips. This is gross. What is wrong with me. I've been in the business over a year now, I've met other singers before. Why I have to turn into such a complete nerd now I don't know. He's a person. He's just a person like anybody else.

He calls out my name in a question, and I'm fluttering my fingers at him, trying to look casual, but I've forgotten what I was going to say. He says you must be Sylvia, David told me you'd be picking me up.

Of course David told him, I knew that. He must have described me, too, and I wonder what he said. Dark blonde hair, blue eyes, or green, he doesn't know, average height. Completely forgettable.

I'm Jake Harris, nice to meet you, Jake says. He shakes my hand hard, and I try to have a firm grip but he's holding me so tight my hand muscles don't work. He says hey, it was great of you to come pick me up like this.

Oh, no problem, glad to do it. I hear myself sounding like Jane Hathaway on *The Beverly Hillbillies* because I'm trying so hard not to sound like Elly May. I've been compared to her before. He lets go of my hand. I say how was your trip.

Oh, fine, you know airlines, I hate to fly.

Yeah, so do I.

Especially alone, he says. I wanted my wife to come, but she couldn't.

I say that's too bad, it would have been fun. I think I might say something about Buddy, that I asked him to come, too, but I don't.

We're walking toward Baggage Claim and there are signs everywhere, but I tell him to turn left anyway. I say you probably know how much David loves your tape, he's very excited about you. I wonder if I sound like I'm kissing up.

Jake says David's the best.

Yeah, he's great.

I think about writing ad copy for Jake. I feel a flush of irritation at Kathleen Turner for ruining the word sultry, turning it into something suggesting silicone lips and an underbite. It's supposed to describe weather, the kind of wet heat that saturates the air and gets under your clothes and wraps itself around your skin and seeps into your bloodstream and makes you weak. But if I say the sultry voice of Jake Harris, I make him sound like an actress whose sweater won't stay on her shoulders.

Jake says I'm really happy to be with Sony, I've heard they take good care of their artists. His voice is the weather kind of sultry.

I say we try.

Jake smiles. I think about his album cover, what kind of photo I'd use if I were in charge of it, whether he'd smile. He has a certain look that reminds me of a young Al Pacino, but I think I'd downplay that, give him his own identity right from the start. His eyes turn down at the corners when he smiles, and he has as many wrinkles as a thirty-five-year-old, although he's only twenty-four. I like smile lines on men—no other signs of aging, though, no baggy knees or withered fingers. No fat. I glance at his hands. They're strong and lean and tan, and he doesn't wear a wedding ring. He also doesn't have long fingernails on his right hand like some guitar players, which strikes me as a relief. I can't stand long fingernails on men, even if it's for their music.

We're waiting for his luggage, and I'm watching the conveyor belt intently, as if I have any idea what his stuff looks like. It occurs to me that what I'm feeling must be because of whatever David means when he says charisma. You have to have charisma more than talent to be the kind of famous Jake's going to be, but he has talent too. This is David talking. Big, David says, he's going to be big, and he rubs his hands together.

Jake hasn't had dinner yet. He says I just couldn't eat that airline crap, and I laugh without trying, as if he's told a real joke.

I say I'd be happy to take you out to dinner, or you might rather just have the hotel send something up if you're tired.

He doesn't want to eat hotel food either.

It's not that he wants to have dinner with me, he just doesn't want hotel food, he made that very clear.

While he gets his luggage I take a deep breath to unknot my stomach, which doesn't work, and try to think of a restaurant. Why didn't I ask the concierge at the hotel, just in case. What is wrong with me. I ask the woman at the rent-a-car counter, and she draws me a map to a Mexican restaurant downtown.

When we get in the car, I grip the steering wheel tighter than I need to, curling my fingers so he can't see my stubby nails.

While he looks over the menu I mention that I've already eaten, a lie I'm not sure why I tell except maybe I don't want to eat in front of him, maybe I don't want Mexican food on my breath—I don't know, maybe it's just that I know I can't eat as long as my stomach is knotted up like this. But he orders a frozen margarita for me, which I'm grateful for because acting relaxed around him is becoming a strain.

Jake isn't nervous. I have the feeling he's never been nervous in his life, and I try not to begrudge him that. I ask him about his music.

He writes his own material, he tells me, which I already knew, and he asks if I know which one David wants to use as his first single.

I don't, but I think his best one is the ballad about the woman who commits suicide, and if it were up to me I'd use it.

He says you like that one, and our eyes connect and I feel the connection in my stomach.

I don't know if it's a question or a statement, but I say yes.

All during dinner we talk around the one about the suicide. It's too filled with raw pain to talk about directly, but I can't leave it alone. I want to know if she was real, if she was a girlfriend or a friend or a wife or what. If she was real, he loved her and he misses her and he's still in pain over her and it's none of my business. I say where do your songs come from.

He says I don't know—something you see, something you read, something you hear or remember or imagine. He's not going to tell me.

I say do you ever feel like they're almost being given to you, like you don't make them up at all, but they just come to you almost fully formed and all you have to do is concentrate and if you listen hard enough you'll have it.

He says you write, don't you. He smiles again and his temples crinkle. He says you're the only grown woman I know who blushes.

．　．　．

After dinner he says he's restless, can we go somewhere and take a walk.

There's a big park where City Stages is going to be, I say, you could see where you're singing.

Have you been there before, is it a nice place to walk.

Yeah, it's okay.

I don't tell him it's near the hospital downtown. I don't say it's where my grandmother and I took a walk while my grandfather had his last surgery. I don't think about holding her hand, so thin I could feel the bones through her skin and so frail I was afraid to hold too tight.

She had stopped wearing her wedding ring because it fell off once in the sink. She was going to have it resized. I don't know what happened to that ring, but I suddenly feel robbed of it. Somebody should have saved it for me, why didn't anybody save it. If I had it I would wear it, I'd put it on a gold chain and wear it as a necklace, or I'd have it cut in two and made into earrings. No, I wouldn't, I would just keep it in my jewelry box. But the thing is, I would keep it. I should have been allowed to keep it. I shouldn't think about this right now.

We pass a liquor store, and he wants to go in. He picks up a bottle of Jack Daniel's and says isn't this what you southerners drink.

I say I'm not much of a whiskey drinker.

He looks at me.

It's just the taste, it's so strong it hurts, I say, it's like swallowing smoke.

But you'll share a bottle of wine with me.

Okay.

He buys a bottle of wine and at the last minute a bag of plastic cups.

We find our way to his stage—there's a plastic banner with his name under the Coca-Cola logo—and we sit on the edge, dangling our feet off the sides while Jake opens the wine with his pocket knife. It feels like a dock, like our toes ought to be skimming the lake. In another corner of the park some construction workers are doing some last-minute hammering. I look at my watch. It's almost midnight, but the festival starts at ten tomorrow morning, so I guess they'll be there until everything's ready.

Halfway through the wine Jake says that song is about my sister.

I don't know what to say. I don't want to pry, but I don't want to look like I don't care. I say wow, I'm sorry—a stupid response, but he doesn't seem to notice.

He says she killed herself three years ago, and I wrote that song about a month later.

I say it's really a beautiful song. It seems like I should touch him or something, but I don't.

He says my father just died a month ago, and now I'm writing a song about what it's like to have lost everybody you love.

I don't know what to say, so I don't say anything.

He's doing most of the talking and most of the drinking, and I feel slightly guilty over the pleasure I take in that, the feeling of power it gives me. He's married and has a three-year-old daughter. They live in L.A., but he's thinking about moving to Nashville for his career.

He doesn't need to, but I don't tell him that.

He asks if I'm married, if I have children.

We slide off the stage and start walking again. He carries the wine in the hand furthest from me. There's a cool breeze, and it's dark and probably not very safe, so I keep wanting his arm around me just to look safer. But he doesn't touch me, his arm doesn't even rub up against me.

I'm being silly, he's about to become very famous, of course he's not going to put his arm around me. And we're both married, we've just talked about the fact that we're both married and he's got a kid.

He keeps talking. His sister and he were both child actors—not stars, just actors supporting their alcoholic mother. He doesn't say why his sister killed herself or how old she was or how she did it, but I wonder if it had something to do with being a child actor and then becoming an adult and not being able to live up to her past. I'm thinking clichés, tabloid headlines—"Former Child Star ODs after Losing Movie Role," "Child Star Shoots Self in Despair over Career"—trying to remember. Only she wasn't a star, she probably didn't even make the tabloids. I'm wondering if Jake's music, having something besides acting, didn't save him.

He started his first band when he was thirteen—the Headbangers. He was the lead singer.

I say you were the head Headbanger.

He doesn't laugh. He's right, it wasn't funny, but if he had said it I would have laughed anyway. He says it was just a garage band.

I'm uncomfortable. I'm uncomfortable thinking about his sister because I don't know how to think of her. I don't know how to talk about her, what questions show basic human concern and which ones would sound insensitive, like morbid curiosity. I don't know what to say. And I don't know what a headbanger is, I don't even know if it's one or two words. It doesn't make sense to me, and I don't know if it's not supposed to make sense, like the

Beatles, or if it's a drug term or if there's something sexual about it, but I'm not going to ask. And I don't know if we're safe.

He had a fight with his wife right before he left to come here, and he's worried about what this album is going to do to his life. We have a pretty good life, he says, and now everything's going to change.

I say yeah.

He and his wife used to sing together. His first band fell apart, but when he was sixteen he started another one, the Studs, and about a year later they brought her in and changed their name to Lisa and the Studs.

This is the first time he's said her name. Always before he's said my wife when he referred to her, and I've wondered if he was abstracting her for my benefit.

She could sing and she's a beautiful woman, he says. Soon after that the band broke up, but by then we'd become lovers.

It strikes me as odd to hear a man call his wife a lover. It's a word Buddy never uses about anybody, and I've never thought of him that way either, it sounds too illicit. I wonder what it would be like to be married to someone who referred to me casually as his lover. I try to imagine Buddy telling another woman that I can sing, that I'm a beautiful woman.

I've lost track of Jake's story. Apparently he and his lover have graduated from high school and started performing together, just the two of them with acoustic guitars, and moved from the proms and parties they played as Lisa and the Studs to nightclubs and hotel lounges, working odd jobs during the days. Jake has been doing a little work for the California Department of Transportation, and Lisa has landed some modeling jobs, which bugs me. Then Lisa got pregnant and they got married, and when she started showing she stopped performing. At first it was just going to be for a while, but then he moved from Top Forty into country, where his career as a solo artist was starting to take off.

He says people started wanting to hear country music, and there just weren't that many country singers out there, especially not in southern California, so I started opening for some pretty big names, making some good contacts. Plus, he says, not too many husband-wife singing teams make it.

He's right. I can't think of any. Sonny and Cher.

He says we both saw I could get more work without her, and she had the baby to keep her busy and we needed the money, but we kept telling ourselves it wasn't going to be permanent and I was singing for both of us then. So whenever I played somewhere she'd get a babysitter and she'd be with me before and after, and during the performance she'd sit in the front row, and it would feel like we were still in it together. Sometimes she'd even bring the baby, and we'd have the whole family backstage.

I'm not sure how aware he is of my presence. I feel like he's answering a question I wasn't ready to ask.

He says we used to write songs together, too, she cowrote "Roller Coaster Woman, Roller Coaster Love"—not one of his best songs, in my opinion. But after the baby came, he says, she just lost something.

There's a long silence, and I think I'm supposed to say something. Maybe he just wants silence. I say I'm sorry, and again I feel like I should touch him, make some sort of comforting gesture, but he might take it the wrong way and I might mean it the wrong way and it could be awkward.

He says don't get me wrong, she's a great mother, but motherhood has somehow consumed her, and the only songs she wants to write now are either children's songs or crap.

I say do you think she's talented.

He shakes his head. I used to, he says, I try to. Sometimes I do, but when I do, I feel like I've accomplished something just by working up that belief. And then I start listening to her, and she has this idea in her head that I should become a children's singer, like some idiot named Raffi, our daughter loves Raffi, you ever heard of him.

I haven't.

He's crap. Totally commercial, not even an attempt at art, and he gets these little vulnerable children and pushes all their buttons and their yuppie parents buy his albums and the children grow up warped, with no concept of what real music is.

He reminds me of heat lightning, all this tightly controlled anger flashing up over hot, stagnant pain and sadness and passion. I'm sounding sloppy. I've probably had more of the wine than I realize.

She resents my success and wants me to make more money, all at the same time, he says, but in a way that's nonthreatening to her, like sometimes I think she'd be just as happy if I'd given up my music too and started working for the DOT full-time. She wants that regular paycheck and group health insurance. He shakes his head. Maybe I'm not being fair to her, he says, I mean when I got this recording contract, she backed off on the Raffi idea and she said she was happy for me. But there's still this barrier between us.

I say I'm sorry. I don't know if he's saying this because it's true or because it's what he thinks I want to hear, but it feels like he's leaving something out.

He says it's nothing. It's just normal tension, I don't mean to make it sound like more than it is.

I say no, I understand.

We come to the fountain in the middle of the park, and Jake

sits on the thick ledge with his back to it. I sit beside him, facing him with my legs crossed. I put my hand in the water. Again I don't know what to say. I'm getting used to this feeling around Jake. It doesn't seem to bother him.

He turns to face me. So is your husband in the business.

No.

Does he want to be.

No.

Be glad.

I'm hoping he won't ask what Buddy does, what he's like.

He doesn't. He says we've talked too much about careers, tell me about the real you.

I hate this question from anybody, but coming from Jake, after all he's just told me about himself, I really hate it. I stall.

What was your childhood like, he says.

I don't want to tell him anything. I want to hear more about him, his marriage, his daughter, his sister, his mother, anything. What would I tell him. There are things Buddy doesn't know. What would I say—that I was responsible for the deaths of my mother, my grandmother, my grandfather, my first love, and for my father's divorce, and there was a time when I wouldn't have been too sad if I'd been responsible for my father's death too. I'm not going to tell him this.

It was pretty boring, I say, really, just your basic childhood.

Nobody's childhood was boring, he says.

Almost nobody's was, but mine was, I say. I was being cautious with the margarita at dinner—I kept thinking this was part of my job so I had to act professional—but now I want to be drunk.

No, it wasn't, he says, what's your happiest memory, or your saddest.

I feel plain, flat. He's had dinner at Planet Hollywood and I took him out for Mexican. I look around. We're about five blocks from the hospital where my grandfather had his surgery, and I can see what I think is the top of the building.

He says everybody has some story worth telling.

I don't want to insist that I'm as boring as I feel, but I can't think of anything. The same year Jake starred in a bubble gum commercial where he blew up a bubble and flew around an animated set, I missed two weeks of first grade with pneumonia. That's all I remember from that year.

I ask him what his father was like.

No, we're not talking about me right now, he says, what was your father like.

This is my fault, I shouldn't have brought up fathers. He's in landscaping, I say.

But what was he *like* when you were a child.

Well, he was kind and gentle, I say. He worked hard. He loved me. This sounds like a normal answer to me, it sounds credible.

Did you grow up in Nashville, he says.

Apparently he bought it. No, I grew up in Pell City, Alabama, it's about an hour from here.

And you moved to Nashville when you decided you wanted to get in the business.

If I could think fast enough, I would tell him now that I play the drums and I write songs, I play the guitar a little, not as well as I play the drums, but well enough to write songs, and I sing. I want to sing backup, and I moved to Nashville after, what, after somebody, some record company executive, heard me singing in Pell City, and I'm just working for David until I get my break, but I could play the drums when he records, I've listened to his demo tape a thousand times and I know exactly how they ought to sound, I know I can do it.

But I'm not a good liar. I don't have enough nerve, and I can't think fast enough, I can't reinvent my life over and over like good liars do. I've taken too long to answer the question.

He says when did you move to Nashville.

I was twelve.

And your father got transferred here?

No, it wasn't that.

I don't know how to stop him. I can't close up and refuse to answer after everything I let him tell me. If I didn't want things to get this personal, I had no right to listen to what he said, but I did, I drank it in, I wanted to know everything he was willing to tell me and more. I still want to know more. I want to see pictures of his daughter, I want to know her name, I want to know where his father was when he was growing up, what his mother's like now, if she ever got treatment for her alcoholism, what happened to her when his sister killed herself, whether either of his parents was musical, where he got his talent, how he learned to write like he does.

He says your mother then?

What?

Your mother got transferred.

No.

Then what, why'd you move to Nashville when you were twelve? Heat lightning again, just a little flash of irritation.

I'm not cooperating. I give up. I moved to Nashville, I say, because my grandmother, who I'd been living with since I was born, died, and my father and his wife lived there.

He says hey, I didn't mean to pry, I didn't mean to make you say anything you didn't, weren't comfortable—I'm sorry.

He feels so bad, so awkward, that I want to tell him more. Maybe to show him I trust him, maybe because he's emanating a kind of sensitivity and I think he'd be a good listener, I don't know why. He's been holding the almost-empty wine bottle between his legs, and I reach for it. We've left the cups somewhere, so I drink straight out of the bottle, watching his reaction while I do it. He smiles, but I can't see his laugh lines in the darkness. I take another drink, a long one this time, and I think I see surprise in his face, but I don't care. He doesn't say anything, and I wonder if it's because he can't think of anything to say. Now he knows how I've felt most of the evening. The bottle is empty, and I hand it back to him. He puts it on the ground and looks at me like he's wondering what I'm going to do next. I'm wondering the same thing.

I uncross my legs and turn my back to the fountain, lean back on my arms, and look up at the stars. There aren't many out tonight and I think about commenting on that, but I don't because it sounds like a drunken thing to say. Also romantic. No, a lot of stars would be romantic, no stars are just drunk. My head is spinning. I wait as long as I need to, and Jake is patient. I like that about him, but I tell myself not to mention it. Also, he's a good dresser, but I won't mention that either. Telling somebody something you like about them is also a drunken thing to do. I'm making up these rules as I go along, but they strike me as very wise rules. Don't mention stars or other people's positive qualities. Also avoid walking. I haven't had that much to drink, not really, but I've never felt so drunk in my life.

I moved in with my father when I was twelve because I had to, I say. I didn't have anywhere else to go. It was the first time he'd acknowledged he was my father, even though I'd known it as long as I could remember, so when I got there I was hurt and angry and feeling abandoned and he was trying to make up for lost time, which made him overprotective, mostly because I think he was scared to death I was going to end up like my mother.

I stop. Jake doesn't ask how my mother ended up, but I think I've said too much. I'm telling it half to see if it sounds true, half because I think Jake feels slightly self-righteous because he had an alcoholic mother and he suffered as a child, so I want to show him up—I was just as abused as you, so there. I don't know why, but I'm mad, and I feel like throwing all this in someone's face, and he's the only person around. At the same time I feel bad for him, I want to show him I understand, we come from the same kind of pain. That still doesn't explain it. Maybe I've just had too much to drink so my mouth is out of control. I should have eaten dinner.

There's an awkward silence while I'm thinking this through. The construction workers seem to have moved closer and picked up some speed. Their hammering is louder and more insistent and it's getting inside my head.

He says how big is this park.

I don't know.

He says let's walk some more. He throws away the empty bottle.

We come to a tennis court and we sit down on the pavement, which is still a little warm. It was a hot, sunny day. I wonder if it's possible for pavement to retain heat that long, but this is a thought that has never occurred to me sober, so I don't mention it. He lies down, three feet away from me, and I wonder how much he's feeling what he's had to drink, how much of what I'm feeling is because of what I've had. I wish we had another bottle of wine. We haven't spoken for several minutes. I'm sitting with my legs straight out in front of me, leaning back on my hands, looking at the nonstars again. My head feels heavy. Holding it up is taking some effort.

Were you happy before you went to live with your father, he says.

I'm not sure.

What do you mean.

I mean I was a child, were you happy when you were being raised by your alcoholic mother, it's not a yes-or-no question, there were times you were and times you weren't.

Were your grandparents alcoholics.

No.

Now I'm irritated. These are very personal questions and I don't know how not to answer them without being rude and I can't be rude to him because I still can't shake my sweet southern upbringing, I guess, and I think he senses that and he's taking advantage of it. Also, whatever else we're developing tonight, we have a business relationship, and he's got a lot more power there than I do. I need him for my career much more than he needs me. I feel like I'm swimming and my feet suddenly can't reach the bottom.

He says what were they like.

I'm stalling again, panicking, searching my memory for anything worth telling, and he thinks I'm being coy. He's told me the whole story of his life, and if I don't tell him something I'll offend him. I've been pretending I was more sophisticated than I am, I've tried to make him think I'm a real songwriter and I do this all the time—go out drinking with singers and songwriters, get drunk and lay open my heart—and now I don't know what to do.

He sits up and lights a cigarette and I can tell he's irritated. I feel heat lightning about to erupt, and I start telling him about my grandfather, the Vaporub. It's the only thing I can think of.

While I'm talking he lies back down. I'm trying to explain I've just remembered all this without saying so because I'm afraid he won't understand how I didn't remember it for all those years. I don't understand it myself, so I can't expect him to.

I don't know why I'm telling him this. I haven't told Deedee or my father—I don't think I'll ever tell my father and I wish I hadn't told Buddy—so why am I telling this to a stranger. Maybe because he's a stranger. Maybe I'm telling him for the same reason other people tell their life stories to the people who sit next to them on airplanes—because they have a captive audience who'll never be able to confirm or deny anything that's said so they have to take them at their word. Maybe I'm that desperate for somebody to listen to me. I've always felt scornfully sorry for people like this. Maybe I've just had too much to drink. I don't hold alcohol well. But I get to the end, and I have to stop and say that's all I remember, it's fuzzy after that.

He sits up. Why didn't your grandmother stop him, he says, where was your grandmother, where was your mother.

I don't know, my mother was dead, and I don't know where my grandmother was. Now I wish I hadn't told him. He's emanating anger and I don't know what to do.

He says wasn't there anybody you could tell, somebody to protect you.

I don't know. I didn't know what it was at the time, I thought it was normal. I thought there was something wrong with me.

Did he do it again.

I don't know how to answer, it's too new to me. Something dark tries to flash into my brain, a hand, elastic. I feel things in my stomach. I close my eyes tight to push it back out, and I think I shake my head.

He says I'm sorry, I shouldn't have asked that, but it makes me so fucking mad, what people do to their children. If anybody came near my daughter, if anybody laid a finger on her, I'd kill them. He's grinding his cigarette out.

I close my eyes again. I can't think of anything to say. There's a long silence. I feel embraced by his anger, dressed in it like silk. For the first time in a long time, I feel safe.

I lean back on my hands, look up at the sky. I feel small and vulnerable and I want to be held and the night suddenly feels very dark. He lights another cigarette and I inhale and hold it in my lungs. I don't know what brand he smokes, but it's different from Buddy's, sweeter, and it smells like death. Not cancer or rot, not a dead body, but death itself. It's comforting. He's looking at the sky too, and the silence between us soothes my skin like a bath.

I wonder if I should have told him, but since I did I wish I had another drink.

I think about what I'm wearing—a pink short-sleeved cotton sweater with a floral pattern woven in and pink leggings. My panties are pink cotton bikinis, not particularly sexy but not as bad as some I have. My bra is plain, functional, white, hooks in the back. I don't let myself think why I'm thinking this.

He says we should probably get back to the hotel, and I agree. He helps me up—a gesture I think of as southern, also charming. Also necessary. His hands feel warm and strong. I want to watch them play the guitar.

On the way to the hotel we don't say much, and I wonder if he'll try to come in my room and if he does what I'll do. But he doesn't. He walks me to my room, but he doesn't lay a finger on me, and he shakes my hand when he says goodnight as if we've just had a normal business lunch.

· · ·

I go into my room alone, double-lock the door, drop my clothes in a path to the bathroom, and turn the shower on as hot as it will go. I take off my watch and my jewelry, put it all in a glass, and step into the shower. I had too much to drink, I shouldn't have had so much to drink in a business situation, it was stupid. I'm scrubbing myself with a washcloth, watching my skin turn pinker and pinker, almost red. I shouldn't have told him all that. It was stupid, just plain stupid. I wish I had my loofah sponge. What was wrong with me. I'm rubbing myself raw, I'm sick of all this dead skin, why do I have to have dead skin, why do we have to live with parts of ourselves that are dead. It's gross. Same with hair, why do I have to have hair all over my body, it's just disgusting. I'm shaving my legs for the second time today. I wish I could have my legs waxed or, even better, electrolysized, but I'm too scared it would hurt. I just hope he's drunker than I am, that in the morning he'll have forgotten large portions of our conversation. It's possible. What is wrong with you. Are you trying to sabotage your best shot at getting some session work, you want him to think you're neurotic, you want him to think you're a drunk. I wish I could throw up.

I think about making myself throw up.

It would be so easy. I'd feel so much better, cleaner. I think it would clear my head, I'm not thinking clearly, and then I could start tomorrow with a clean slate. I look at my stomach, smooth my hands over it. Throwing up is the closest I know how to come to undoing the past.

I pull open the shower curtain and look at the toilet.

I tell myself don't do it, Sylvia, don't even think about it, close the curtain.

Just this once, one time won't hurt anything, and it'll probably keep me from being as hung over.

No.

All I'd be throwing up is margarita and wine, I'm just trying to get the poison out of my system.

You're so stupid, you are so fucking stupid.

It would be so easy. And it would be healthier than digesting all this alcohol.

I look at my toothbrush. I've never liked the idea of sticking my finger down my throat, I'm afraid I'll get it on my hand. But a toothbrush is okay. A toothbrush would do just fine. Then I could throw it away and buy a new one in the hotel gift shop tomorrow.

Stop this, Sylvia.

I could even charge it to my room, so Sony would pay for it. I take some inexplicable pleasure in the idea of David paying for my toothbrush.

Stop. Don't even think about it, it's a dangerous thing, and it always starts with one time. Close the curtain.

I close my eyes. I let go of the curtain. I wash my hair, scrubbing my scalp with my fingernails. I scrub my whole body again, starting with my face and working down methodically, in case I missed something before. I can't get clean.

I step out of the shower and feel myself sweating as I dry off. I close the lid of the toilet and try not to look at it. I comb my hair, brush my teeth so hard my gums bleed, take an Advil—Buddy always takes one when he's trying to ward off a hangover. I pull on a T-shirt because I don't feel like wearing the sexy nightgown I brought and crawl into the king-size bed.

Just go to sleep, just sleep it off. Don't think.

It's too quiet. I go back into the bathroom and put on my wedding ring. I turn off the light, but it's not dark enough, and I lay a towel at the bottom of the door, then grope my way back to bed and get in. I'm used to being in a double bed with Buddy, and all that space makes me lonely. I line up the extra pillows beside me in the bed, but I need something heavier. I put my guitar on top of the covers, then underneath. I add my suitcase. I want to be crowded.

I used to do this with stuffed animals. I'd lie in my single bed, and my grandfather would tuck the sheets around me all the way down my legs. I could look down my body and see a mummy. Then he'd say which animal do you want, and sometimes I'd just want my camel, but sometimes I wanted all of them and my dolls, and he'd pile them on, and I'd try to sleep very still to keep them from falling off. He'd kiss me goodnight on the forehead and leave my door cracked with the hall light on. In the morning the animals would be on the floor.

He was a good, kind man. He was always gentle to me. He would never hurt anybody, couldn't.

I can't be remembering right.

I wish I hadn't told Jake. It gives him power over me. It makes us intimate in a way that we're not.

I can't sleep.

7

YOU CAN TELL WHEN YOU GET TO TENNESSEE. THERE'S A sign—WELCOME TO TENNESSEE, THE VOLUNTEER STATE, which I thought meant they'd volunteered to be a state where the rest of us just sort of had to because we lost the Civil War—but also things change. Little torn-up barns and stuff, and it gets hillier. Only it's more than that. It just feels different, like a foreign country. I kept thinking I wonder if this is what England feels like since they speak English in England but it's still foreign. They speak English in Nashville too, of course, except Nashville mothers say hookup instead of carpool. That didn't really affect me, though, me not having a mother. Once I started school, Uncle Mull or sometimes Deedee just came and got me in the afternoon. We didn't call it anything.

All three of us were in the car, Uncle Mull and me in the front seat and Paw Paw asleep across the back, snoring. Deedee'd left a couple of days earlier because she had a mean boss and she'd said she'd try to get the house ready for us. So I was sitting there next to Uncle Mull with my eyes closed, and I kept thinking what am I supposed to do and then I'd think what would Amazing Grace do.

Amazing Grace is from when I was eight. I was sitting in the Three Sisters' beauty parlor reading *Star* magazine while Memaw had her hair done, and I came across a page full of pictures of those little children who have some disease that makes them die of old age, and I looked at this little boy not any bigger than me, only he was bald and more shriveled up than Paw Paw, and chills went all the way through me and my hair stood up on my arms. It was as good as a burning bush. And I said Lord, that's my call, I got to heal those children. And before I knew it I had myself all done up in my head as Amazing Grace, child faith-healer, and I was traveling around the world with the Amazing Grace choir, healing all the children who were dying of old age and going on TV telling everybody about the love of Jesus everywhere I went. So every night for a year I asked God for the gift of healing and I claimed every verse in the Bible I could think of about how God always answers prayer and if you ask God for it he'll give it to you and if you trust in the Lord he'll give you the desires of your heart. So I don't know what went wrong. I guess I won't know till I get to heaven and my eyes are opened. Because I never did get the gift.

And while I was crossing the Tennessee line, counting cows and trying not to listen to Paw Paw snore, it occurred to me as a fact that at twelve and a half, having already become a woman, it was pretty much too late to be Amazing Grace, child anything. Which still makes me a little sad to think about. But still I couldn't help thinking what would Amazing Grace do.

Then my mind started wandering over to Jesus. I was starting to feel kind of sorry for Jesus, having a daddy who would let him die for a bunch of strangers. I was thinking about Deedee having gone to get the house ready and how that was like Jesus saying I go to prepare a place for you and how me leaving Pell City was like him leaving Nazareth and how his real daddy being in heaven was like my real mama being in heaven. I kept telling myself he knew how I felt.

It didn't work, though. *I* didn't even know how I felt.

When we got off the highway, I pretended to wake up and I started looking around. We went by some neighborhoods with houses so big you could get lost in them. Then we went by some big ones only it would have been easier to learn your way around, but we kept going. Then we came to some that were closer to Memaw and Paw Paw's house size-wise and I thought that would be better because I'd be used to that. But we just kept going. And then Uncle Mull said, very cheerful, this is our subdivision, and we turned.

The houses looked like toys, all yellow and pink and baby blue, and I was wondering which one was his and how he ever remembered which one it was. I thought why don't they put something on the door or in the yard so you could tell. Chickens, for example.

Uncle Mull said this whole subdivision used to be a cow field.

I said what happened to the cows.

Uncle Mull said they became Big Macs.

I looked at him without making a face.

He said I'm just kidding, bad joke, I think they moved them somewhere else, maybe to Alabama.

I knew they were dead.

He said I'm sure they're fine, I was just kidding.

But he wasn't.

He said that's why there aren't very many trees, though. Because of the cow fields.

He was right. I didn't see one.

He said I wish I'd had this landscaping contract, whoever had it should have planted some trees.

I thought why don't you just plant your own tree.

Then we were pulling in the driveway and Uncle Mull said well, here we are. He was honking *bump bada bump bump, bump bump.* Paw Paw woke up so fast I thought maybe he'd been faking it too.

I got out and went to the trunk for my suitcase and Uncle Mull said leave that, I'll come get it later, and Deedee'd run outside and left the front door open so flies could go in and she was helping Paw Paw get out of the car. That's all that was happening, come to think of it, but it felt like when you have a dog running around in circles barking. I wanted my suitcase. I thought about pretending there was a dog and it was Bubba and Memaw'd be saying shoo, you nasty dog, and Bubba'd just go crazier, barking all the way down the street. I didn't have much heart for it, though.

Right before we went in the house I took one last look at the street, trying to place myself. I started thinking how when you're doing turns in ballet, you're supposed to pick out something like a little dot on the wall at the other end of the room, and your body goes around and around but you keep your head focused on your dot and it's supposed to keep you from getting dizzy. I always took too long deciding on my dot, though, and when it was my turn I'd just start spinning around, hoping I didn't fall down. That's how I felt at Uncle Mull's front door, like I was looking for something to help keep me standing up, only I couldn't find anything.

The house smelled like Worchestershire sauce, and Deedee set Paw Paw down on the sofa and opened up the windows and nobody was saying anything except Uncle Mull. He was running around pointing at the sofa saying now here's where you'll sleep for now, Sylvia, but it's just temporary, until we get things straightened out.

I said yessir.

He said hey, if you ever want a midnight snack it sure will be convenient.

I said yessir. There wasn't even a door between the den and the kitchen, just a place in the wall. I didn't tell him I wasn't allowed to have midnight snacks, I just said to myself, well, now you are. But he was laughing like it was funny so I didn't know if I really was or if it was a joke.

Then we walked down the hall, me following him like a dog, and he said and here's the bathroom and I had to go look in the bathroom and say uh-huh so he'd know I saw it. I needed to go, but I didn't say so. I had the feeling if I did he'd stand right there at the door and say good afterwards.

Then he said here's where your grandfather's going to sleep for a while and then this will be your room.

He was pointing at this little room with a desk in it and no bed and no room for a bed. So I looked at him and I looked at the room and then back at him. I hadn't cried at the funeral or the funeral party or when they put the FOR SALE sign up or any of it, but I was looking at Uncle Mull's desk and thinking how I'd forgotten to feed Bubba before we left, and all the sudden I started to worrying so hard and so fast about Mrs. Sutherland forgetting to feed him too, and Bubba just getting skinnier and skinnier to where you could see his ribs through his fur and him looking for us to feed him and nobody being there, and finally him starving to death, and I threw myself into such a panic over Bubba that I burst into a fit of crying. Couldn't stop to save my life, just crying all over head to toe in convulsions like a crazy person.

Deedee brought me a glass of something, some kind of fruit juice that wasn't orange juice, and she put ice in it which Memaw never put ice in orange juice, and I drank it fast trying to swallow everything even though I needed to go to the bathroom and that just made it worse. I could feel one ice cube hitting my lip up to my nose. I think cold things feel good on your skin when you're crying that hard. When I was finished they were staring at me, and I wiped my nose with my hand. Then Deedee got me a paper napkin, but it was too late. Then we all just pretended I hadn't cried.

Before long we were laughing about something, I can't remember what. I like that too, though—laughing when you still feel like crying. I like the way it makes you go tight, like there's two of you and one of you's trying to get away and the other one's trying to pull you back in and your muscles turn into ropes.

Deedee said the bed was supposed to be there yesterday but she'd called that morning and they guaranteed it would be there by five o'clock.

Uncle Mull said I guess we better get this desk out of the way, then.

Deedee said okay.

He said I guess we ought to put the desk over there and the bed here, pointing.

Deedee said no, the bed has to go there and the desk has to go here, exactly opposite.

Uncle Mull looked at her.

She'd already measured and it had to go where she said, there was no other way, the way Uncle Mull wanted to do it wouldn't work.

Uncle Mull held up his hands and opened his eyes extra

wide, and then they started moving the desk to where Deedee'd said.

Uncle Mull said dammit, this thing weighs a ton.

Deedee acted like it didn't weigh anything except you could see in her fingers it did. She wasn't making a sound, like if she did she would grunt.

Then they got it to the wall Deedee'd said and when she put her end down she banged the wall where it made a little dent and Uncle Mull said dammit, Deedee.

She didn't say anything, she acted like she hadn't heard him.

I went in the bathroom. I tried to go away in my mind, but I couldn't think of anyplace to go. I've always done that—separate my head from my body and go away in my head. Like once I was sitting in church when the air conditioner was broken, everybody fanning themselves, even the choir, and the preacher had sweat pouring down his face like tears and he kept mopping himself up with a white handkerchief, and right there in ninety-something-degree heat I made myself get chill bumps. I just put myself out there in the North Pole with my sleigh dogs and my fishing pole and my igloo and the wind whipping my hair every which way, snow in my eyelashes and my nose running and it freezing solid on my lip, and I was getting redder and redder and colder and colder—and next thing I know I'm back at church and the sermon's done and the choir's singing the benediction and I've got chill bumps. I've just always been that way.

And then there I was, my body as far away from Pell City as I'd ever been, and I couldn't get my mind out of that bathroom to save my soul. That was the thing about that house. There was nowhere to go.

When the bed got there we were all sitting around in the

den. The doorbell rang and they both jumped up and Deedee said that must be the bed and Uncle Mull said yeah, it's probably the bed. So I said probably so. Paw Paw didn't say anything.

The men set it up in the study with Deedee telling them what to do which I didn't think there was room for it but which somehow there was. I could hear somebody in my head saying the Lord provides but I kept thinking maybe I just hadn't seen right the first time. Then I kept telling myself, hearing myself tell myself, God is everywhere, even Nashville. Only I had this feeling in my stomach like I'd left him in Pell City with Bubba, and I knew this didn't make sense either but I kept thinking about God starving too. And I could hear somebody in my head—I didn't know if it was the same person who was saying the Lord provides or somebody else—but I heard somebody say every breath of life is a gift from God, and I kept thinking if I left him in Pell City, he's not here to give me the breath of life and I could drop dead any second. I started breathing funny, thinking every breath might be my last and hoping it was, but then Deedee looked at me so I stopped.

When the men left, Deedee tore the plastic off the mattresses and put on some sheets, and Uncle Mull went and got Paw Paw and helped him get in. Paw Paw was acting like he was ninety-five, like his feet were cast in cement. I just watched the whole thing like I didn't know how to change sheets or take care of Paw Paw or anything, I was just a child. I went back in the den and sat down in front of the TV. I didn't turn it on, though, because I couldn't figure out how. They had remote control.

Then Uncle Mull came out and closed Paw Paw's door real softly. I didn't say you don't have to be quiet if he doesn't have his hearing aid in, I just sat there.

Then Deedee said well, Sylvia, and there was something about the way she said it that made me want to tell her I'm twelve, not five, but I just looked at her. She wore big, dangly earrings. She said we've got to figure out where we're going to put your clothes.

I looked around. I said that's okay.

She started to touch me but then didn't. She said we could buy you a clothes rack, but she didn't want to, I could tell. Buy was the loudest word.

I said that's okay.

She said well, if we could just get you a chest of drawers or some shelves or something.

I said it's okay and she acted like she didn't hear me. I could feel another one of those crying fits coming on, my face was getting hot, and I said Deedee?

She looked at me.

Can I have some more of that juice?

She practically ran into the kitchen, I could hear the ice clonking into the glass before I knew what was happening and she said Sylvia, this is your juice now, you don't have to ask for it, this is your home, isn't it, Mull.

And then he was in there with her and he said yeah, and I went in there too to get the juice. At Memaw's you could eat anywhere but some houses you're only allowed to eat in the kitchen and I didn't know. I drank it slow, kept the glass at my mouth even when I wasn't drinking to cover up my face. I tried to go away so Amazing Grace could take over, but it didn't work. I wondered if I'd left her in Pell City too, but I told myself don't think about that right now, she'll find you.

When I finished drinking I was still there by myself and Deedee was saying to Uncle Mull in her most cheerful voice

Sylvia and I were just trying to figure out where to put Sylvia's clothes, weren't we, Sylvia.

He looked at me.

I said yeah.

He said well that's great, good, that's real good. His skin was tight on his face. You could tell how the cartilage of his nose was shaped and his eyelashes were blond. There was something about his face. It looked naked.

I looked out the window, but the window didn't have a curtain on it like it was naked too, so then I just looked at my own clothes, the ones I was wearing.

Deedee was still on the clothes. She thought maybe we could find something in the basement and she started going down there, her feet making crash noises on the steps, and Uncle Mull and I followed her. I wanted to go last, I was going to stand on the steps so I wouldn't have to go all the way into the basement on account of how basements give me the creeps, but Uncle Mull held the door and did after you with his arm like he was polite, so I had to follow Deedee. She kept talking. Maybe we could get some of those corrugated storage boxes or she thought she saw something last week, week before last, that would work at K mart but she didn't really look at it because you know.

I was thinking Deedee thought I had more clothes than I did. I could have kept them all in my suitcase easy and I wanted to. That was when I realized I was thinking about running away. I hadn't made a plan yet, but in a way it was more serious because sometimes you make a plan to do something instead of doing it, and I was just going to do it.

That's also when I first saw her drums. They were blue with glitter on them, and just a little glitter in swirls like stars or like galaxies, not covered solid with it like things that aren't real, and the tops were white that you could just barely see light coming through them even though there wasn't any light, like certain kinds of typing paper, and you could see in the middles where Deedee'd played them the most, like the sounds had left scars.

I walked over to them, afraid to touch them, and nobody was saying anything and Deedee handed me her drumsticks and I looked at her and she said sure, go ahead. So I sat down inside them and you could hear my moving in the drums like I was surrounded by the hollow sounds of echoes, everything I did or was or ever had been echoing in the drums like ghosts.

I didn't do anything, though. I wanted it all to happen only in my head because Uncle Mull and Deedee were watching my every move and I wanted it to be private.

So I just sat there in the echoing quiet, and I liked how my hands felt holding the drumsticks and I liked how the drumsticks felt in my hands, how when they touched the drums you could feel the sound go up the wood into your fingers and your wrists and your elbows into your brain all in a split second like two lightning charges up your arms, traveling the speed of sound, meeting in your head with a bang.

I liked how I felt when I sat there—like I was bigger than myself, and light, and I could make sounds people could hear far away. I touched the drums and they made the sound of Deedee's feet going down the basement steps only they turned it into something ancient, like tribesmen sending messages, and I kept tapping soft and slow and feeling the rhythms spread themselves out inside my body. I felt like I was one of those messages, and every time I tapped the drums I sent myself a little further away.

· · ·

I couldn't eat dinner that night. I didn't know what it was. I wasn't even sure it was food, I was having to take that on faith. Plus we hadn't said a blessing and I had this thing about blessings, like if you didn't say one your food might be poison. I tried to say a silent blessing in my head, but I was having trouble.

Uncle Mull said you don't have to eat it, Deedee why'd you have to try to force-feed her this kind of crap on her first night here.

I took a bite and swallowed fast. I said this is good, but it was too late.

Deedee was looking at Uncle Mull like he was a demon in a devil suit, and then she put down her fork so hard everything on the table felt it and Uncle Mull said Dee long and slow with the same sounds you'd make to say I'm warning you, and I wasn't finished swallowing the first bite but I took another one and another one trying to show them it was okay and then they were screaming at each other, so loud I thought even Paw Paw could hear.

I didn't know what to do. Memaw and Paw Paw never had a fight in my life. Whatever Paw Paw said Memaw and I did, so what was there to fight about.

I went outside. I wanted to take a walk, but I was afraid I couldn't find my way back.

I sat on the stoop outside their front door, tearing apart a leaf, and listened to them fight. They kept jumping around, fighting about everything including dinner and me living with them and Paw Paw living with them. Uncle Mull didn't want to fight in front of me, and Deedee wanted to know how they were ever going to fight if not in front of me, they had no privacy anymore.

I quit listening. I put my chin on my knees and covered my

ears with my hands and I just kept wiggling my wrists, listening to the sound of my hands on my ears like waves. I found out if you do your hands in little circles on your ears, fast on the down part and slow on the up part, it sounds just like the ocean.

Eventually Uncle Mull came outside. He wasn't mad anymore, just tired.

I wasn't mad either. I'd been mad, thinking about my mama being alive, about everything being normal, and then thinking about Memaw which always made me sad-mad, but by the time he got out there I was just tired too. I felt heavy, like the air in Nashville was too thick. I thought maybe it was pollution.

He sat down beside me and he creaked on the way down which was a long way because he was very tall. He was also skinny. He reminded me of a skyscraper in Birmingham from when Paw Paw had his surgery. I didn't say anything, but I wondered if it hurt him to bend his legs and if not, why'd they make so much noise. I'd been trying not to listen to the fight, but I'd heard some things, like he'd promised to put Paw Paw in the first nursing home that would take him once they sold our house in Pell City but they couldn't afford it until they sold it. I was thinking maybe he was going to tell me they were going to have to send me away too, like to an orphanage, and he wasn't saying anything because he was trying to figure out how to say it. I was thinking when he told me I'd be very grown-up about it and say I think that's the best thing for everybody. Then, in the middle of the night, I'd run away.

Only I hadn't figured out how to get out of the subdivision. But I'd find a dog to lead me out, a great big huge dog who'd also protect me and when I got tired he'd let me ride on his back, and we'd go to the highway and then we'd hitch a ride with some really nice man whose little girl had just died and he'd want to adopt me. I'd have curly hair and rosy cheeks and I'd be smaller so you couldn't blame him. But I'd say well, sir, it's a tempting offer and I thank you kindly, but I've got to go live with my best friend, M'Lea. And it turns out the dog was Bubba and he'd missed me and he'd followed my scent all the way to Nashville and he'd take me back home and Mrs. Sutherland would be there waiting for us. She also wanted me to live with her and she and M'Lea's mother were going to have to fight it out but meanwhile she'd cooked up a big dinner with hot dogs on Wonder buns with chili and cheese and ketchup and chocolate cake with chocolate icing for dessert.

Sooner or later Uncle Mull said I guess I'm pretty much of a loser in the father department.

I was wearing sandals. I was looking at my feet. I said it's okay.

That wasn't what I meant, but I'd already said it, and I don't believe in taking things back, so I didn't say anything else. I wanted there to be firecrackers or something, but it was quiet. It was a hot night but I felt cold. My toes were dirty. I was hoping it was too dark for him to see my toes.

We stayed out there a long time trying to think of something else to say. After a while I quit trying and just sat there. What I found out was, the longer you sit somewhere the more you hear. Like at first it had been quiet, but by the end I could hear crickets and distant traffic and people's air conditioners turning on. Somebody's car door slammed and the engine turned on and they drove away. Other stuff inside my head like my heartbeat. It was like lying on M'Lea's dock looking at the stars. The longer you stayed there with your eyes open, not focused on anything, the more stars you'd see. We'd seen falling stars lots of times, which always gave me chill bumps, and once a meteor shower, which was the most beautiful sight I ever saw, like a whole universe tearing itself apart without making a sound.

I said could we call M'Lea and just let her know I'm okay.

Uncle Mull said sure we can, you want to call her now.

But I knew if I did I'd start crying again, so I said no, tomorrow.

When we went inside it was bedtime, and Deedee'd already made me a bed on the sofa. She said is this going to be okay with you.

I said yeah, yes ma'am.

She said don't call me ma'am.

I'd meant it nicely. M'Lea'd told me northerners don't like to be called ma'am and I'd thought to myself M'Lea thinks she knows everything. And then it turned out to be true.

Uncle Mull said it's just temporary.

I said this is nice, thank you.

Deedee said yeah, but even for temporary maybe we could get a sofa bed. She looked at Uncle Mull.

He said maybe so.

I said it's okay.

She said we could even rent one.

He said maybe so.

Deedee said well, goodnight.

Uncle Mull said goodnight. He leaned toward me and I thought you're supposed to kiss your father goodnight but I was afraid I wouldn't know how and I put my hands on my face. His hands jerked, and he said goodnight again.

Deedee said sleep tight.

I thought maybe I was supposed to say don't let the bedbugs bite, but I just said night.

Finally they left.

Their house was like their outside. There weren't enough doors, and the longer you listened the more things you could hear. Sounds I don't know what they were—creaks and thumps, things moving. I thought if I believed in ghosts. I curled myself into a ball so I'd all be on one cushion and tried to pretend I was deaf, which didn't work. Then I laid myself out flat on my back, folded my hands, closed my eyes, and pretended I was dead.

8

I'M WAITING FOR JAKE WITH THE MOTHERS OF THE BATHING suit models who go on after him, sitting in a plastic chair in a closet-size room trying to block out the sound of the mothers so I can hear him on the monitor. He sings the suicide ballad, and it gives me that feeling like when low-frequency thunder rolls across your diaphragm and echoes in your kidneys.

I tell myself I'm studying everything he does because I'm learning. This is a person who knows how to be a star.

When we get in the car to leave the TV station he asks me if I have any plans for the rest of the morning.

I say yeah. This is my chance, this is the perfect opportunity to let him know I write songs and play drums, and all the sudden I'm embarrassed to tell him. He's just so good, so professional. His performance reminded me how far out of my league he is. But he's quiet, waiting for me to say something, so I tell myself Sylvia, if you don't say something here about your music you're a fool. This is your best shot, and if you don't take it, you'll always wonder what could have been. I hate myself. I say I'm signed up for this songwriting workshop, it starts at ten.

You write songs, why didn't you tell me you wrote songs.

I did tell him, and I don't know whether to feel relieved because I can assume he's forgotten much of what I said last night or offended that I sat there across from him at dinner and told him flat out yes, I write songs, and now he's forgotten, which if he'd assumed I had talent, if he'd assumed my songs were any good, he'd have remembered.

Or maybe what I'm feeling is just nerves, a combination of nerves and a hangover. Maybe I don't remember last night as well as I think I do, either.

Anyway, he's interested now, so I tell myself forget it, the reasons he's forgotten I told him last night are a moot point.

He says he'd really like to hear some of my work.

I don't know.

Come on, one song, play me one song.

I can't.

Yeah you can.

No, I can't, I've written like fifteen songs and only finished one, I just can't do endings, that's why I'm going to the workshop.

What are you thinking they're going to tell you in the workshop.

I don't know, something about endings, I guess.

Why can't you finish your songs.

Because they never say what I'm trying to say, I get frustrated.

That's art, Sylvia, there's no trick they can tell you in a workshop to fix it.

I guess. I feel embarrassed, amateur.

He says will you play one of your fragments for me.

Well, I've got one that's pretty much finished, it's just not—I don't know, it's missing something.

Can I hear it.

Okay, if you play something for me.

Deal.

I think about singing for him. I think about having sung for him and six months from now he's at the top of the charts, doing all the late-night talk shows, and I'm in my bed at home watching him on TV realizing the song I played for him was crap.

I'm sitting on his bed watching him open his guitar case. He offers his guitar to me, but I say you go first.

He plays half a ballad about fading, faded love, and I watch his hands moving over the strings like water.

He says he's not finished with it, he's still working on it.

I tell him it's perfect, and I don't ask him if it's about him and his wife.

He hands me his guitar. It's a Martin, and I'm intimidated. I don't want to smudge it with my fingerprints. I look at my hands, willing them not to shake. My fingers feel cold and stiff, and they aren't curving right. I strum it to see if it needs tuning, which it doesn't, but I'm stalling.

I'm not going to tell him I don't feel good enough to play his guitar. It's just a guitar, a hollow piece of wood. I've played a Martin before, once.

I try to pretend I'm alone, that it's my guitar. I try not to think about him looking at my mouth, my hands. I don't look at him while I play.

He acts like he loves my song, but I can't believe him. He's just trying to get me into bed, he's trying to make up for asking too many personal questions last night, he's just being nice.

I say you don't know what I mean, about how it's missing something?

He says it's a good song, Sylvia, you just need to play with it some more.

You think so?

Yeah, write out the words.

I write them down and they strike me as inane—*I know you don't love me no more*—but I hand them to him. He plays it through the way I've written it, then again, changing the key, adding *no, I know you don't* a couple of times, singing the chorus an extra time in the middle and fading out with it at the end. When he plays it, it sounds like a real song.

I say it sounds sadder that way.

He says it's a sad song, I hope it's not autobiographical.

It's not, I say.

Good.

Do you think it's too sad? I don't want to cross the line over into pitiful.

He says it's not pitiful, it's beautiful.

I say it's beautiful the way you sing it, I like the way you end it with *I know you don't.*

He says you're not writing hymns, Sylvia, you don't have to tack on a chord resolution and sing amen to be finished.

Yeah, but I just have this bad feeling, like it's always less than what I wanted it to be.

That's why you write the next song. You keep trying again, knowing ahead of time you're going to fail if success or failure is measured by how perfectly you say what you're trying to say, but you just hope you'll create something good or beautiful or true anyway.

You feel that way about your songs.

Yeah, I do.

I'm suddenly aware of my hair, and I think it's a mess. I comb it with my fingers and put it behind my ears.

I'm not religious, he says, I don't pray or anything and I usually don't talk much about God, but sometimes I feel like what's right in a song, the possibility of creating something beautiful out of the imperfection that comes with being human and the way sometimes it's the imperfection itself that makes the song beautiful because that's what makes it true, that's how I understand God.

What do you mean.

That's grace.

I touch my neck. I feel embarrassed talking about God.

He stands up and calls a friend of his, Miller, a vice president at RCA who's going to be at the workshop, and tells him he's heard me and I'm great, he's got to hear me. He hangs up and tells me it's up to me now, break a leg, and it feels like a warning.

I say thanks.

He says don't thank me, it's a good song, you've got talent.

I say stop looking at me.

He says I like looking at you.

I say you're making me self-conscious.

I don't know if Miller is a first name or a last name—I don't usually call men by their last names without saying mister in front of them—but he comes up to me after the workshop and starts pumping my hand, telling me how much he loved my song, how much he wants to see more of my material, and he says Jake and I must come up to his suite for a drink around six. This is the first time I'm sure he's Miller.

I say thanks, Miller, we'll be there.

He tells me his suite number, looks at his watch, and says he has to run. He's literally running out of the room. Six o'clock, he yells from the door.

I smile and wave, but he's already gone. The sneers of the other workshop participants are hovering over me, and I get my guitar and leave as quickly as I can.

I drop off my guitar in my room and head over to City Stages, eating a barbecue sandwich as I walk and keeping my eyes open for Jake. I make my way to his stage, where he's already running a sound check. He's all business, he's barely even friendly, and I'm intimidated again. I ask him if I can do anything for him, but he says he likes to be alone before he performs, so I get a diet Coke and wander around, listening to other musicians, people-watching, killing time before Jake's concert. I'm trying not to think.

He draws a big audience and he has great stage presence. He doesn't have or need a live band, just his guitar, but I play the drums for him in my head anyway. I stand at the front of the crowd right by a speaker for the whole performance, where his wife would stand if she were here, and I let his music enter me and I let part of myself slip out so there's more room.

After the performance my ears are ringing and I'm clapping, everyone is clapping, but he's looking at me, and I yell at him you were wonderful. I resist the impulse to do a thumbs-up. He smiles and his temples wrinkle and he's back to himself and he signs a few autographs and puts his guitar in its case.

When the crowd breaks up I congratulate him again, but he doesn't want to dwell on how great he was. I like that. I ask him to meet me in the lobby a little before six to go to Miller's suite.

He says so the workshop went well.

Yeah, I did the song the way you played it and it went fine. Good.

I say I'll tell you about it later, I've got to get a shower. I don't tell him I have a headache and I feel a bad depression coming on and it's everything I can do right now to fight it.

He says me too, I'm worn out.

We walk back to the hotel through a maze of braless girls in tight T-shirts. I can't figure out why he wants to be with me.

In his suite Miller is a different person. He's wearing a silk bathrobe and his chest hair staring me in the face makes me uncomfortable and he won't put down his drink or his cigarette or his cellular phone and he won't sit down. It's what people call salt-and-pepper, that chest hair. Thick pepper with a little salt. His constant movement makes me nervous but also relieved because I have a feeling he's not wearing anything under the bathrobe—just chest hair all the way down. He keeps pacing and telling jokes I don't get and calling us babe, calling everybody he talks to on the phone babe. There's a phone that came with the room, a regular phone with a cord, and if he would use that he wouldn't be doing all this pacing because if he did he'd trip on the cord or tear it out of the wall, and I think why can't you be still and use the phone that came with the room like everybody else. I can't place his accent, but it's not southern. It's a little bit nasal, irritating, intimidating, and I have this strange protective feeling about the South, like Miller doesn't belong here. I hate this attitude.

Miller and Jake are talking insider music business, the gossip part of which reminds me of my grandmother's beauty parlor, and I'm drinking a glass of white wine and smiling idiotically and feeling desperately bored. I don't know what's wrong with me. This is my fantasy. I'm sitting in a beautiful penthouse suite, I didn't know they had rooms like this in Birmingham, and here I am sitting in one of them with a professional singer and a vice president from a major recording company, both of whom are interested in my work, and all I can think about is getting out of here. I want to take another shower. I have cigarette smoke all over me and I want to wash it off. I want to throw up. I want to work out, then sit in a steam room and sweat the impurities out of my system until I'm limp.

I want to eat a chocolate cake, a whole one with icing, all by myself, a tunnel-of-fudge cake like my grandmother used to make. I used to have that recipe, and somewhere along the way I lost it. I wonder if I could remember it. You put a whole box of icing mix right in with the cake mix and something like two or three cups of pecans. I want to be in my own home in my own kitchen making a cake, feeling the heat from the oven on my legs, hearing the distant laughter of Buddy watching TV in the next room.

Jake is schmoozing expertly and I hate him for how well he does it. He's dropping names, laughing. Whatever situation he's in, he always knows exactly how to act. He's an actor, how can you ever know an actor isn't acting? I think why are you doing this, don't you have any loyalty to David, to Sony? They're talking about David, and Miller doesn't like him. He's hesitant at first, but when he sees that Jake and I aren't going to defend David, his jokes at David's expense become crueler. We all laugh. After my first glass of wine, I laugh as much as either of them.

Miller notices me for the first time since we've been there. He pours another glass of Scotch for Jake and another glass of wine for me without asking whether I want it and says he thinks I'm quite a talent, he wants to know how long I've been writing.

I say I guess I started when I was fourteen.

Miller says fourteen, which means tell me your story, I think.

I say my stepmother let me use her drums and my father gave me his old guitar and taught me a few chords, and their marriage was starting to fall apart and they fought all the time and I felt responsible for the fighting because it was usually about me, so I'd go in the basement and close the door and get out his guitar, and because I didn't know any songs, I'd make them up.

Miller has sat down for the first time. He's wearing some kind of pants, gym shorts or pajama bottoms or something, under the robe. Both of them are looking at me, and the attention makes me uncomfortable. When their arguments got to be really loud, I say, I'd put James Taylor or Patsy Cline on my stepmother's earphones and play the drums, trying to drown them out.

This is all wrong. I'm being too serious, I should say something funny, but I'm not a funny person. Jake and Miller aren't southerners, and I feel very southern around them—naive and unsophisticated—and I don't know what's expected of me, and I don't know what their attention means. I keep talking, trying to change my tone. They'd be yelling, I say, and I'd be downstairs banging away—no wonder our neighbors hated us—and then when my stepmother moved out, that's when I was fourteen, she left me the drums, probably because I'd practically ruined them anyway. I give up and stop.

Jake says do you still play the drums.

Yeah.

He says did David tell you I'm looking for a drummer, do you do any session work, does he know you play.

I'm just starting out, really, I mean professionally, so I haven't told David yet because he's sort of suspicious of people trying to—

Starvin' Marvins. Miller interrupts me. We all laugh at

David's expense. Miller takes a drink. He looks at me. Can you read charts, he says.

Oh, yeah, I say, I read charts.

Have you worked with other musicians, can you communicate with them.

Yeah.

Jake says yeah, she's great.

Then Miller turns serious and takes my hand. Stand up, he says. I do. He turns me around, nods for me to sit back down. I do. You're great looking, he says. You've got a great body, and if you spent two hours with my hair and makeup and wardrobe people you'd be a knockout, and if you play drums anywhere near as well as you write, if you can anchor a band like I think you can from knowing you one afternoon, there's no stopping you.

I don't know how to take this. Is he drunk or high, he has had a lot to drink since we've been here. Come to think of it, so have I. How long have we been here? Is this show business b.s., like saying let's do lunch? He could offer me a contract, he could make my career for me if he decided to, but he's just saying there's no stopping you. Doesn't he know how many people out there can put together a song and play an instrument, or do you get to a place where you're so insulated from all that that you actually start believing everybody who deserves to make it makes it?

I should be thrilled. I don't even deserve to make it. Jake does, when Jake writes he feels connected to God. When I write I feel like I'm the only person in the universe who exists.

This is all wrong. I've been trying to get this kind of attention from David, from anybody, for a year now, but now that I've finally got it, it's not enough. It's just a teaser, and it makes me mad. Like what is the crack about my hair and makeup supposed to mean? I don't always go to a lot of effort for my appearance, but at this moment I look as good as I know how to make myself look. Maybe he's just showing off, he finds me attractive and he wants me to know how much he could do for me if he wanted to, emphasis on if. Or maybe this is just how he is with everybody, this is Hollywood, love you, babe. Maybe he's just using me, he's doing Jake this favor because what he really wants is to sign Jake for his next album. I don't know how to read any of it, I don't even know how to read Jake, he's acting so differently now from last night. Jake and Miller are insiders discussing me, the outsider, like I'm not there, and even though what they're saying about me is what I've dreamed of industry insiders saying, it makes me feel vulnerable. It also makes me feel dumb, like I don't know the difference between a seduction and a rape.

I think of Buddy, flicking his ashes into the yard, and I hear Jake last night—*I don't know what success is going to do to my marriage. Up until now we've had a pretty good life.*

Miller gives me his card. He's holding my hand, and part of the tension I'm feeling is sexual. If I ever need anything I have to promise I'll call him. Right. He writes his home number on the back of the card.

Maybe I'm imagining things, I'm developing some sort of complex where I think I'm more attractive to men than I am, like maybe it started with my grandfather and I made the whole thing up with the Vaporub and then last night with Jake I thought he was attracted to me too, I actually worried about what I was going to do if he asked to come to my room, but maybe I made that up too and it meant nothing to him. It obviously meant nothing to him, he didn't even remember I write songs, he just wanted somebody from the label to buy him dinner, and now I'm imagining Miller is attracted to me too. Right. This guy could sleep with any rising country music star in Nashville, probably has. He could be gay for all I know. Come to think of it, he's paid Jake more attention than he has me. What am I thinking. He said I needed two hours' worth of makeup and hair, and I think he's attracted to me. What is wrong with me.

I don't know, but when I'm with Jake I feel so pretty, I feel like I'm in a slow-motion hair commercial. This is stupid. But I really feel it, like my hair catches the sun and the air is so clean the whole world almost shimmers and if I wanted to I could do the splits in the air and I'm barely real. And I can't help but wonder if I'm not projecting what I feel onto Miller, if for the first time in my life a man in that kind of position finds me attractive because for the first time in my life it's conceivable to me that he would. What am I doing.

Miller looks at his watch. He's back to the way he was in the workshop. What is wrong with these people, always changing personalities, you can't count on any of them. He wishes he could take us to dinner, but he's already got another commitment and he's got to take a shower, he's never been to such a sweltering place before, he can't figure out how people who live here can stand it. He wishes me the very best, thanks Jake for discovering me, and goes into his bedroom, dropping his bathrobe behind him as he goes. He has the hairiest back I've ever seen.

Jake and I sit there awkwardly, look at each other and smile, finish our drinks. I put Miller's card in my purse. I say are we supposed to go? I'm whispering.

Miller is singing in the shower, and he's a terrible singer.

Jake doesn't know. For the first time since I've known him he doesn't know what to do, and I like him for that. We look around the room.

Jake says let's go out and celebrate.

Okay, what are we celebrating.

For starters, you've got one of the most powerful people in the business interested in your work, he says.

And you were fantastic today and the crowd loved you, I say.

Miller's shower turns off. Jake takes my hand. Let's get out of here, he says, and he opens the door.

We have a big dinner with a bottle of wine. When our meals come, Jake says why didn't you tell me about your music, what kind of work have you done?

I don't know. I shake my head, look at my food, poke at it.

He says I mean your work with other musicians, who've you worked with, we probably know a lot of the same people.

I bite off half a hangnail, take a sip of wine, smile. I try a line of his. We've talked too much about work, don't you think?

Sylvia.

Jake.

What's going on with you?

He shouldn't know me this well, he shouldn't be able to tell something is wrong. Buddy wouldn't. Yes he would. I'm not sure. Jake is smiling, almost laughing at me.

You haven't worked with other musicians, he says.

No.

Can you read charts?

I chew on the other half of the hangnail. I watch the woman at the next table struggle with a piece of lettuce. It's too big, and she can't fit it into her mouth.

Sylvia, Jake says.

His eyes remind me of Einstein's, the way they turn down at the corners. He has that same romantic disheveled intelligence and sadness and sensitivity, plus long eyelashes and great hair. I wonder if his daughter got his eyelashes.

He says my name again.

Can you teach me?

God. He shakes his head, takes a drink, crinkles his temples. God, Sylvia. When he says my name it sounds like a caress.

Is that a no, I say, but I know it's not.

Everything is getting mixed up.

After dinner we're walking to my car and I'm wondering what's going to happen next and he says you grew up around here?

Yes, about an hour from here.

Show me, he says.

Tonight?

Yes.

You want to see Pell City?

Yes.

Why?

I just want to know what kind of place could have produced such a beautiful, talented, fucked-up person.

I say you don't know what you're asking.

Yeah, I do, I want to see it.

You Californians, you think there's something exotic about small southern towns, you've seen too many movies, but Pell City couldn't be any more boring.

He says believe me, I don't expect it to be exotic.

I say I didn't mean exotic exotic, I just meant—I don't know.

What did you mean? He's laughing at me and I think I hear affection in his laughter. I fuss at myself for making that up. He's gently mocking me, and I don't know how to take it.

I say I just meant you think it's going to be strange, weird, something different, I don't know what you think, but if you think it's worth driving an hour to see then you think there's something there worth seeing, and you're just wrong, I'm telling you it's a boring place, nothing ever happens there.

There's an edge in my voice that surprises me, and I decide to back off. Let him go there if he wants, what do I care. Neither of us has to do anything tomorrow.

I let him drive. He's had more to drink than I have, but he seems more used to it than I am, and he weighs more. So I'm sitting in the passenger seat and he's in Buddy's place—whenever I'm in the passenger seat, Buddy's driving. I push that thought out. He hasn't touched me, this is just platonic. As far as Jake's concerned I might as well be a man, we're just taking a drive. He wants to see the South. Let him.

I can't decide how to sit, and I finally decide just to sit regular, but I feel self-conscious. I'm too aware of my hands, and I don't know what he's thinking. I lead him to the highway. I'm nervous, and I don't know why—if it's him or that I haven't been back there in so long, eleven years. I'm beginning to wonder if this was a good idea.

He turns on the radio loud and rolls down the windows. I'm feeling a sense of dread in my neck and trying to push it down to my back so it won't get in my head.

I close my eyes.

You can smell the lake before you see it. I smell myself as a child playing on the sand with M'Lea, the warm, coppery smell of sunburned skin that hasn't turned red yet, the itchy stench of a dead fish on the bank, its exposed eye attracting flies. M'Lea's dog after he got into the fish, the mothballish smell of wet fur. Sweaty old men, my grandfather fishing, the clean, brown, gritty smell of dirt from the jars of worms he'd buy.

You open a jar of worms and you can't see anything but dirt, live dirt, black and squirming, and you feel out a worm in the movement and you shake it off and you get this terrible pleasure out of skewering it on the fishhook, wrapping it around and stabbing it again. It makes your grandfather proud. Nobody thinks you're a sissy.

We'd go down to the public dock and I'd carry the worms, and I must have fished, but what I remember now is the smells— the sour smell of warm beer and chewing tobacco on other fishermen's breath, dead fish on ice, mostly catfish but sometimes a bass or two, and later the greasy smell of fish frying. Bologna sandwiches with American cheese and mayonnaise on white bread and the fishy way my hands smelled while I ate. Sun-weathered wood, and algae, which I thought was seaweed. The loamy smell of my feet. Grape Nehi, or orange when the bait shop was out of grape, and chocolate chip cookies my grandmother made with the chips melted from having sat out in the sun. The sweet, silver, salty taste of blood if you pricked yourself on a hook.

He's cleaning the fish, tossing heads and tails around, showing me the eggs, smiling. His hands are bloody with thin, rusty-looking fish blood. Look, Sylvie, this one was pregnant. I feel ashamed, embarrassed at the idea of my grandfather looking inside a pregnant animal. It seems wrong to kill a pregnant fish.

I'm feeling overwhelmed. I need a goal. I say we should try to find Riff Raff Acres, it's a trailer park right on the lake where my best friend, M'Lea, used to live.

He says Riffraff Acres?

Yeah.

Riffraff?

I'm embarrassed. What kind of jerk would name someplace Riff Raff Acres, and what is wrong with me that this thought has never occurred to me before. That was just what it was called.

I begin to see my childhood through Jake's eyes, and it looks bizarre. It's grotesque in the way a traffic accident involving bearded ladies and two-headed men would be. You'd hate yourself for wanting to watch them get out of their cars, stretch their necks, and exchange insurance information, but you could hardly stop yourself. That's why he's here.

I want to find it, to show him it's a normal place with normal people. It could be in California.

But they've put up condos, or I can't remember where it was. We can't find it, anyway. I wonder whatever happened to M'Lea, and I feel stabbed with a terrible sense of loss for her. I should have invited her to my wedding. I should have called her mother and asked about her. I wonder if she's married now, if she's changed her name, if she has children, if she's happy. I wonder if she ever thinks of me.

Jake wants to see the house where I grew up, and I don't want to argue with him. We've come this far, we may as well.

We find it, and I'm pushing down memories like when you're trying not to throw up. It's been painted a different color, it looks greener, but it's dark and you can't see it that well. Whatever color it is, it was painted a long time ago, maybe right after we sold it, and it's not well kept up. I'm glad it looks so bad. I hate that house. Also, by California standards it might be considered a large house, and I think Jake resents rich people. I don't let myself feel anything else. I think this time next year he'll be rich, and then things will change. I think about how much the house would sell for in Nashville, I think what color I'd paint it—white or maybe pale yellow. Then I turn it blue. Anything but green, why would anybody have painted it green. It's the color of vomit, it's an army color, it's a combat house. It's obscene, M'Lea would say. I'd paint it white, and I'd put a swing on the front porch and ferns, big hanging ferns, and flowers all the way up the front walk. Who are these people who live here and what right do they think they have to let the house go like this. How much would it cost to give it a new coat of paint and mow the grass. Why do people buy houses they're not willing to keep up. It would break my grandmother's heart to see the house looking like this.

I suddenly miss her between my eyes with a piercing clarity, I mean I feel her absence there, and it is a physical pain. I think how when I was a baby she'd rock me to sleep in the middle of the night, each of us using the other as a substitute for the person we really needed. You take what you can get. I learned that early.

I could break down and cry, I could start shaking, I could scream, but I push everything down. I rub my forehead. I don't look at my bedroom window. I barely look at the house, I'm focusing on the numbers in my head, how much the house is worth in dollars and cents, how much it would cost to paint it. We don't get out of the car, and after a second I say let's go.

Maybe I'm not hiding my feelings as well as I thought, because he drives off quickly, as if he's spooked too. Maybe this house just does that to people.

There's a park where you can go to swim, and I suddenly want to see it and I remember how to get there and I lead us to it.

The parking lot has a new gate that's locked, but we park on the street and climb over the gate. We walk toward the woods and there's a fallen log and I say watch your step, the first thing I've said since we got here, and I hear my voice tremble and I wonder if he does. We go into the woods.

It's darker now, and we walk along a path under some trees toward the lake. We walk as close to each other as you can without touching—we have to, it's a narrow path—and we don't say much. The cicadas are louder than I remember, and the air pulses so hard with their primitive music you can feel it in your legs. I'm wondering if they have cicadas in California, if he knows what they are. Their rhythm lulls me, comforts me, and gives me a headache at the same time.

He says you know you scare me.

I say I scare you, how could I possibly.

We keep walking.

He says I just don't think you know what you're doing.

I'm a fool. He thinks I'm naive, he's been with Hollywood actresses and famous singers and his wife is probably incredibly sophisticated, she used to be a model. My hair is too long and I'm wearing pink and I'm wondering if anybody in Los Angeles wears pink, and he thinks I'm a southern belle and I'm suddenly aware of my accent and I can't think of anything to say and I hear myself saying what do you mean even though I don't want to know what he means.

He says you're a beautiful woman, I'm told I'm an attractive man, we're alone here in the dark.

He stops talking, although his voice implies there's more to the sentence, and I can't believe what I'm hearing. I feel like I'm swimming and I don't let myself think and I don't know if it's true but I hear myself asking, you think I'm— then I can't think of the word. I don't know whether I want to know if he really thinks I'm beautiful or if he thinks I'm naive or if I really want to know anything about what he thinks of me. I can't think what to tell him. We keep walking. He doesn't answer.

Then all at once his hand touches my wrist and I slide my hand into his and he says stop for a second only it's almost a question and he pulls me toward him and I lean into him and then he's kissing me and I'm kissing back and his arms go around me until I'm inside him, losing myself, and I've been wanting this for as long as I can remember, but I still can't believe it's me, kissing this beautiful, talented, dark, married man, the first man besides Buddy I've kissed since Bo, the first man I've ever kissed who had a child. He tastes like licorice.

I'm in his arms, and we're kissing soft and passionate and long the way married people don't bother with anymore, and he's kissing my neck and he's a better kisser than the bathtub man and there's a part of me that wishes I could die now, doing this without ever having had to think about it.

He leans back to look at my face, then caresses my forehead, moving my hair, and he kisses me again. He looks at me, studies me as if I'm beautiful.

I take his hand and lead him to a platform jutting out over the water. I'm standing in front of him, and he's holding me from behind, watching the moon on the lake, and I close my eyes and my leg starts to tremble. His fingers slide onto the small of my back as he turns me to face him, lowering his hands, pulling me to him. My arms go around his waist, they go all the way around like they can't with Buddy, and our bodies are pressed flat against each other, there's nothing separating us like with Buddy, and I feel him swelling low on my stomach, and my leg won't stop shaking. It may be getting worse, and Jake has obviously noticed, but he seems to like it. At least he sees some humor in it. He's laughing that same gently mocking laughter, but I'm not making up the affection in it this time, and he says almost like he's in awe of me, you're trembling, and he kisses my fingers one by one and I realize my hands are trembling too.

I say now I'm the one who's scared.

He kisses me again. He says there's nothing to be afraid of, I'm not going to hurt you.

I believe him.

9

I FELL IN LOVE WITH BO SCHIFFLETT, JUNIOR, AND JOINED the Rapture Club my first day at Nashville Christian Academy.

Bo always said Sylvia, you can be a missionary or a mission field, and I think with Memaw and Paw Paw and all he decided I was a mission field ready to be plowed and that's why he gave me all that attention. But at the time all I knew about Bo Schifflett, Junior, was that he asked me to be the secretary of the Rapture Club my first day at Nashville Christian, before I had a chance to be an outcast, which is the thing I feared most in life, and I loved him for it. And all I knew about mission fields was that my whole life I'd heard missionaries in Sunday school say we've just come back from the mission field, and boys and girls, it's ripe for the harvest. And I'd think well, after all these years why don't you just go on and harvest it. Thinking it was this great big field where missionaries just kept planting things and planting things, year after year after year, which I figured the food was for poor people, and then right when it was ready to harvest they always came to our church to ask for money instead.

That's the difference between them and Bo. Bo didn't try to raise support and he didn't have any slides from foreign countries or stories about funny things that happened on the mission field because the people there don't know English, but he saw his mission field and he decided it was ripe, and he went after it with a vengeance.

Like my first day at Nashville Christian—I was trying to open my new locker and it turned out they'd given me the wrong combination, but I was getting all frustrated and thinking about my legs hanging out of my dress because you have to wear a dress there and my knee socks when the cheerleaders were all wearing pantyhose, a thought that hadn't even occurred to me until that day, and feeling fat and dumpy, and Bo Schifflett, Junior, comes up to me like he doesn't even see my clothes because he's looking at my soul and says hey, Sylvia Mullins, just who I need. He already knew my name. And he introduced himself and I thought I'd turned into Cinderella just like that. I could feel my cheeks flaming, and I said what do you need me for, Bo, and I thought I was ready to die.

Which if I'd have dropped dead right at that minute, I would have had a good life. A pretty good one.

But I see Bo asking me to join the Rapture Club as a turning point which things had been going a little bit downhill up until then because of Paw Paw having cancer but we thought he was going to get well and we were going to come out of that okay, and then Memaw died and Paw Paw started getting worse fast but at least I had Uncle Mull and Deedee, at least there was a way everything still might have worked out. But when I told Bo I'd join the Rapture Club, I think that downhill slope got a little steeper. And then Paw Paw died and it got much steeper. And then Bo died and it turned into a cliff.

But he said I want you to join my Rapture Club, Sylvia, and he said my name like it was beautiful. For a while there he about had me convinced it was, and I was starting to prefer Sylvia to Grace. That's how he was. Whatever he said or whatever he even thought, you would just believe it and start thinking the same thing. I still don't know how he did that. I think it was just a gift he could use for good like Billy Graham or evil like Jim Jones, and I think by the end he'd used it for both. But he said he was going to be the president and I could be the secretary and this was the most important club I'd ever be asked to join because God had revealed to him that the Rapture was coming before the end of the year and our job was to tell the masses and make sure they were ready.

I said sure, Bo, I'll do it, just like I would have said I'd go cow-tipping or witnessing in the airport or anything else in the world he'd asked me to do.

And he said he was glad to have me on the team, and he shook my hand and sent what felt like glitter all the way through me and then he left. Which I'd never known a fifteen-year-old who goes around shaking people's hands, but I thought well, people just do things differently at Nashville Christian Academy than they do at St. Clair County Middle School, which was the truest thing I thought that whole day.

I also thought if this is the end of the world that explains a lot. Matter of fact, in a way it was a relief. Because there were a million things about the idea of living through Paw Paw dying that worried me, but the only thing about the Rapture that really bothered me at the time was the thought of Jesus coming when I was taking a shower. Because you don't want to be caught when you're having an affair or robbing a bank, but I didn't want to be caught naked either. I still don't. Bo said we won't be embarrassed on account of we'll be glorified, but I take fast showers anyway.

Bo said the Rapture Club would meet in Mrs. Tinkler's room during football practice every Wednesday because his daddy being the coach, he had to stay after school anyway, and it would be Bo and me and eleven other Rapture Watchers and all the Rapture Watchers would be girls on account of how all the boys at Nashville Christian Academy played football except Bo because he was too little. Plus he had delicate bones. Both of which I think were thorns in Coach Schifflett's side and which I think Bo knew.

Coach Schifflett liked to put his arm around Bo Schifflett, Junior, and say here's my living breathing proof your sins will find you out, and then he'd tighten his arm around Bo Schifflett, Junior's neck which he was very strong and his arm was so big it covered Bo's whole face. Plus Bo's neck was just about the skinniest neck I ever saw. If you looked too hard at it you'd feel guilty like when you stare at somebody's wart, where Coach Schifflett's neck was so big around he couldn't hardly fit it into his shirts. So he'd hold Bo's neck and I'd think he's gonna break Bo's neck without even trying, he's just gonna snap it in two. And if Marylou Manderberry or any of the cheerleaders was around, Coach Schifflett'd wink at them. It made you shudder. And you couldn't for the life of you figure why everybody just laughed like it was funny.

Because the last thing I need is my sins tracking me down and finding me out. Sometimes you got to ask God's forgiveness and forget about them and hope they forget about you. Though your sins be as scarlet he will wash them white as snow and cast them into the furthest sea, and you just hope they can't swim.

Of course, that plan didn't work for Coach Schifflett. He came back to America thinking he'd left his sins on the other side of the ocean, only Mrs. Schifflett, who wasn't Mrs. Schifflett at the time but I don't know her other name, she tracked him down and she brought Bo Schifflett, Junior, with her and she made him marry her. Bo likes to think if his mama had of waited on the Lord a little longer and Coach Schifflett would have had time, he would have gone back and got them on his own, but that's how it happened. She tracked him down and made him pay and they got married and she and Bo moved in with him and I don't know the whole story but at some point she went crazy and she wouldn't talk to anybody but Bo and she'd only talk to him in Vietnamese.

It wasn't that bad a crazy, though. Not then, anyway. It got worse after Bo died. But anybody can think of worse things that could have happened to Coach Schifflett for doing what he did than getting a wife like Mrs. Schifflett and a son like Bo Schifflett, Junior, out of it. Because it's not like she would run around naked or kill anybody. She just wouldn't talk. She'd come to football games and she'd sit there wrapped up in a million sweaters and blankets and she wouldn't look at anybody but Coach Schifflett and she wouldn't talk to anybody but Bo and she wouldn't know when to cheer and you'd have to wonder why she even bothered to come.

One time Mrs. Tinkler was sick and Coach Schifflett had to monitor her study hall and he spent the whole study hall cleaning the erasers by banging them on the walls. Just kept walking around the room banging erasers on the walls, leaving little white rectangles. And he liked to read the newspaper holding it up in front of his face and when he was finished he'd put it down and he'd have pencils hanging out of his nose. It was funny. But I can imagine if you were married to him how it might drive you crazy.

Coach Schifflett was a star football player in high school—he tells his testimony in chapel every time they can't find another speaker—and then he got a scholarship to play at Alabama for Bear Bryant who was a great man even though he drank and who was like a father to Coach Schifflett. So people were talking about

Coach Schifflett winning the Heisman trophy which he never did because Bear Bryant was a team coach, not a star coach.

Only then he got hurt and joined the army or the marines or one of those groups and he got sent to Vietnam, which is where he met Mrs. Schifflett. And he did all kinds of bad things there including drugs and heavy metal music, and he was mad about not playing football, so he was making all the wrong plays and it was the fourth down and he had ten yards to go and he was ready to give up and punt. And then one day when he was hung over, God came to him like the great coach of life and said join my team, which Coach Schifflett did, and God saved him and turned his life around and made him a winner and now he counts his salvation as more valuable than a Heisman trophy and he figures if that's what it took for God to get his attention, it was worth it.

So he came home and got a job coaching football and started the football ministry which means he leads a Bible study in the boys' locker room after football practice every so often—I guess they take showers first, I don't know. I hope so. It doesn't sit right, the idea of having a Bible study while you've got other people's blood on your clothes. If you ever walk by the boys' locker room after practice all you can hear is them yelling, calling each other dogs, snapping each other with towels.

Men who used to be on drugs have the best testimonies of anybody, and former athletes are the next best, so you can imagine how good Coach Schifflett's is. Plus he tells jokes in there too, so it's funny.

If my mama had of lived through the train wreck but still almost died and then had to go through years of painful physical therapy, or if she'd been paralyzed for a while and then later miraculously healed and if God had spoken to her in the hospital and told her to have a ministry with pregnant teenagers and she'd ended up witnessing to thousands of troubled girls and saving that many babies' lives from abortion, she could have had a pretty good one.

You have to do something really bad and then suffer for it and triumph over it with God's help and turn it into a ministry if you want to speak at chapel at Nashville Christian Academy. I've done something really bad—I made the Roach-Prufe milkshake—but I haven't suffered enough for it and I'm not going to make a ministry out of it and I wouldn't tell a bunch of strangers about it for a million dollars, much less the people at Nashville Christian Academy. I don't think they pay you anything, though, because you're just supposed to do it for God's glory. But even if I did, which I won't, I still can't think of any jokes I would tell. You have to tell jokes.

One time we had this TV minister's wife all the way from California who is very famous, and she told us how she wanted a log cabin and she prayed for it and claimed it in the name of Jesus, and then one day she noticed that this little house she passed every day on the way to church that was covered with siding was really a log cabin underneath. So she looked up the owner and bought it just like the Proverbs 31 woman and she had it moved to her back yard and took off the siding and fixed it up, and now they call it the GAP House for God Answers Prayer, and she has her quiet time there every morning. Which everybody at school said was a miracle and the Women of God Club, which I'm not in, it being mostly cheerleaders and that type, they decided to study her book, *The Spirit-Controlled Woman*, after they finished the one they were on.

Maybe this was a sin because of bad attitude, but that one left a little ache inside my chest, like a hole in my heart. I couldn't stop thinking how come I can't be as rich as a TV preacher, and how come the things I need can't be things you can buy. Because if I were and they were, I'd have a whole lot more answered prayers. So I don't count her in my list of people with the best testimonies, which Coach Schifflett is still the very best.

It wasn't a real hole. Some people have real holes in their hearts, only it's usually babies, and they die. But I know how they feel before they do.

There wasn't a war or anything, it was way after the war, and I don't know what he did over there, but I think it had something to do with looking for people who'd been in the war and got lost. I don't know whether he found anybody, but I doubt it. Coach Schifflett is a lot of things, but if you had a lost relative in Vietnam he's not exactly the person you would want looking for him.

I think if I were Bo Schifflett, Junior, I would have wondered if my daddy had had more of a choice about this instead of just made a mistake and then decided to do the right thing, would he have wanted me.

Like sometimes Coach Schifflett called Terry Roberts, the quarterback, son. After school that first day I was waiting outside the gym for Uncle Mull to pick me up, and Bo was standing around on the sidewalk trying to get some other Rapture Watchers, and the football players were heading out toward the field for practice, and Coach Schifflett said son. Terry turned his head and said yeah, Coach, and Bo Junior just stood there frozen like he couldn't hear, like he wasn't even there. Then Coach Schifflett threw a football at Terry and said start running drills, I'll be right out. It just made you shiver.

I walked over to Bo and I said Bo, are you okay?

He waited a minute and then he said you're from Alabama, right?

I said yeah. I still don't know how he knew that.

He said you ever feel homesick?

I said I guess so, maybe.

He said I know how you feel.

I said what are you homesick for? I didn't know he was from Vietnam at the time.

Heaven.

I looked at his eyes. They were so brown they looked black.

He said I think we all feel homesick for heaven because that's where we really belong in our hearts. This earth is just a ball on the chains on our feet.

I didn't say anything. For one thing I didn't know what balls on chains on feet were. Uncle Mull pulled up right about then, and I said see you tomorrow, and I left.

That's when I decided to buy the Slim-fast. Because I wanted to be Bo Schifflett, Junior's girlfriend, and I wanted Coach Schifflett to think Bo had as skinny and pretty a girlfriend as Terry Roberts had, and I wanted Coach Schifflett to say something crude that I didn't completely understand and wink at me and then hit Bo on the rear end.

Later, after I found out about Bo's mama, I started wondering if what I was really homesick for wasn't my mama and what he was really homesick for wasn't his. Not that his mama was dead, but once you're crazy it's never the same.

Bo Schifflett, Junior, wasn't the only one. There was this whole group of people including grown-ups who were holding Bible studies going through Isaiah and Daniel and mostly Revelations because there's a blessing for anybody who reads Revelations, and they'd bring in clippings from the *Tennessean* whenever they found something that fulfilled a prophecy. They were keeping a scrapbook to leave behind after the Rapture so the pagans could figure out what happened, and they'd paste in every article under the passage from Scripture that had prophesied it, which prophecies were being fulfilled every day of the week.

Bo said it was like watching a jigsaw puzzle being put together, the first piece being that Israel had become a nation because God had said not one generation would pass from the earth after his people were brought together before he came back. Plus there were earthquakes and wars and rumors of wars and Russia, a nation founded on atheism, distributing nuclear weapons to their godless allies everywhere and threatening to take over the world. Bo said Russia was the bear in Revelations, and helicopters were the giant metal locusts, so he said Russia's going to drop the bomb on Israel from a helicopter and the trumpet'll blow and that'll be it. Bo said the mushroom cloud is the clouds of glory, and Jesus'll be sitting on top of it on his throne and first the dead in Christ will rise up out of their graves and off the bottom of the ocean and join him in the air and then all the live Christians will go and then we'll all live in the peaceable kingdom for eternity.

Bo went to this Bible study every Tuesday night where they'd tell him all this stuff and he'd come to school the next day saying did you watch the news last night. Nobody ever had, but he'd tell what happened, and he'd say that was prophesied two thousand years ago. He'd even give the Bible reference and quote the verse, and Coach Schifflett would just mutter durn fool, durn fool, and shake his head.

So none of the football players or cheerleaders or Women of God went in for it, and Marylou Manderberry said Bo, *my* Bible says he'll come like a thief in the night, you won't know the day or the hour.

And Bo's ears turned red and Bo said well *my* Bible says we are not in darkness, that that day should overtake us as a thief, so if you want it to overtake you like a thief, that's your problem, but my Bible says watch and be sober, so that's what I'm doing. Bo said you can't be distracted by people like Marylou Manderberry when you've got a call from the Lord.

So I believed Bo because he was getting his information straight from God, which is more than Marylou Manderberry claimed, and I started thinking about the idea of never turning thirteen, never graduating from high school or getting married or having children, which kind of made me sad sometimes and a little bit scared others, which I knew was a sin because you're supposed to want Jesus to come back more than anything, that's what you're supposed to be living for.

But I couldn't help it. For one thing I'd seen a picture of Armageddon, where the battle that destroys the world is going to be fought—Bo showed us one time in a Rapture Club meeting—which nobody can tell me that's not worse than seeing a snake cross your path in terms of shivers. It's a big field like a Civil War battlefield only everything's dead like winter, except there's no snow, nothing like holly, just death, just end-of-the-world, nuclear-war death. You look at it and you can feel the earth decaying in your stomach.

So I worried about Armageddon, but I also worried about the actual Rapture. Like what would it feel like to be yanked off the face of the earth and catapulted into the heavens. Because I don't even like how it feels when an elevator starts and it takes a second before your insides catch up with your skin and then they come too fast and you feel your brain bump against your skull. And how was every Christian from the whole history of the world going to fit on the mushroom cloud, and what if you fell off, and what about the dead in Christ, what if they'd been cremated or cut in two. You start thinking about it all and you can't hardly stop.

I couldn't stop. I'd wake up in the mornings thinking the Rapture came and God forgot I moved and I got left, or it's coming today and Uncle Mull and Deedee aren't born again and they're going to hell. Every time I pictured Uncle Mull and Deedee they'd be weeping and gnashing their teeth and dog-paddling around in the lake of fire, and I'd start sweating.

I just had this worry-ball inside me I couldn't get rid of, and my arms felt heavy and my head felt dark, like something was weighing down on me or the air was too thick. I felt like I was walking through the valley of the shadow of death, and you couldn't get out from under the shadow because it was all over you and around you and trapped inside your body like your own mortality, so there was nothing you could do. I was afraid maybe I felt that way because I wasn't ready for the Rapture when Bo had said our mission as the Rapture Club was like John the Baptist, the voice crying in the wilderness prepare ye the way of the Lord. Only I was afraid to tell him I didn't really know what that meant, how you do it. All I could think besides pray and memorize Scripture was lose weight.

So I'd try to drink those Slim-fast milkshakes as often as I could stand it, as a drink or as pudding or frozen, every different way you could, which Memaw wouldn't have allowed but which Uncle Mull and Deedee didn't even notice because Deedee's band had started getting more jobs and she'd be out until one or two in the morning half the time and supper just turned into a fix-it-yourself type of deal.

Only it wasn't working, I was still fat as ever. And I'd stand in front of the mirror sucking my stomach in till I felt dizzy, and I'd do sit-ups and jumping jacks till I felt like I might pop, and then I'd get on Deedee's scales, and still nothing. I knew I was running out of time if the Rapture was coming before the end of the year, and I told myself he's gonna come like a thief in the night, you might be naked or you might be just in your underwear, and if you're still fat you're gonna be sorry.

So I started making myself throw up. I could almost hear Memaw saying desperate times call for desperate measures, only I couldn't think of when she'd said it. Sometimes it scared me how fast she was fading from me, like how I couldn't close my eyes and see her face anymore. And then I'd think I'll see her again in just a few months when the Rapture comes, and when she sees how skinny I'll be by then, she'll be proud as punch. I could see that one easy, Memaw hugging me and then holding me out at arm's length and saying you've turned into a beautiful young lady, Sylvia, I'm just proud as punch. Then she'd hug me again, practically smashing my face.

So every morning I'd have a strawberry Slim-fast for breakfast and then throw up and every night before bed Paw Paw and I'd have a chocolate Slim-fast for dessert only then I'd go throw mine up. I thought of it as a double whammy.

At first it was hard to make myself do it. It hurt and I'd make these awful noises so I'd have to leave the water running just to feel private. But I knew my body was a temple and I thought God deserved better than a fat temple, and I thought he was helping me because throwing up got easier and easier, to the point where I hardly even had to try. It wasn't exactly like Amazing Grace was there—she wouldn't stand for throwing up—but it was sort of like I'd turn myself into somebody else like I used to do with her. Because I'd drink the Slim-fast and then go into the bathroom and there'd be this time where I wasn't myself, where I wasn't real, and then I'd sort of lower myself off the ceiling back into myself and by the time I finished brushing my teeth, I'd be back to normal.

I didn't tell Bo any of this, though, because it kind of scared me. Sometimes I was afraid I was going crazy, and Bo said we're not to live in fear, if you live in fear you're being ruled by Satan. But sometimes I was afraid Bo was going crazy too.

Bo had quit studying because when we get to heaven our minds are going to be perfect and we'll know all this stuff anyway. But I couldn't bring myself to stop because Uncle Mull was spending so much money on tuition. So Bo was memorizing the Bible like crazy, he'd finished Matthew and Mark and he was on to Luke, and I was trying to do my homework and lose my weight and memorize John and take care of Paw Paw and make Uncle Mull and Deedee like me and convert them to Christ and prepare myself for the Second Coming. I wanted to get myself meek enough to inherit the earth, but I wanted to inherit the earth so bad sometimes I thought I was being greedy, and I don't think you can be meek and greedy at the same time. So between all that I couldn't hardly sleep at night.

The first meeting of the Rapture Club, Bo said he wanted to memorize the whole Bible between the thirteen of us. He said the days of Tribulation were coming and the Communists were going to take over and burn all our Bibles and make us read the Communist Manifesto, and they were going to turn our churches into Communist training grounds and brainwash our children and wage the biggest, most ruthless, most devastatingly thorough war on the morality of this country you've ever seen and we had to have the Bible memorized so that when they burned them all up we could come back together and write it back down.

I started getting this panic spell, and I said Bo, couldn't we just hide some.

He looked at me like I was crazy.

But I was afraid I'd have to memorize the so-in-so begat so-in-so's, so I was willing to risk something with Bo to get out of that, plus I thought even if I did memorize them, I was afraid I'd get them wrong and I didn't want the whole responsibility for the survival of one thirteenth of the Bible on my head. Plus, what if I did it and then the Communists killed me with a nuclear bomb before I had a chance to write it down? So I said couldn't we put some in a bank vault and bury some in our yards and hide some in boxes in our attics and send some to the mission field and surely if we hid enough of them one or two would survive.

Bo turned white. He was getting mad, so no matter what he said that was the last I was going to say about it, and he said Sylvia, you're either for us or against us.

And then this long long long silence, everybody afraid to break it while my head was spinning like he'd hit me, and finally I said I'm for you, Bo.

He nodded his head like he forgave me and then he looked at the other girls and said be watchful, the evil one is going to try to stop you at every turn.

I didn't know if he was talking about me or Satan, but I felt like crying, so I prayed dear God, please don't let me cry in front of Bo, and he didn't. Before, I never would have thought to bother God about something like that, but people at Nashville Christian Academy believe in carrying every little thing to God in prayer. Like Marylou and her mother, every time they go to the mall they pray for a parking place on the way there, and God hasn't let them down yet. She shared that the day the Women of God gave the chapel program.

Bo said we can't hide the Bibles anyway because the Communists are already watching every move we make, they have big satellites and huge computer files on every one of us, they're reading our lips right now. And then he walked over to the window and opened it and said like he was talking to somebody standing right there, but you're not going to conquer. We've put on the whole armor of God, the breastplate of faith and righteousness, the helmet of the hope of salvation, and if God be for us, who can be against us? You may smite us on the heel, but we will crush you on the head.

That was from the Bible, but at the time I thought it was from Coach Schifflett. It was the kind of thing he'd say in a pep rally.

Then Bo closed the window and walked back over to us and sat down and said let us pray.

We bowed our heads and closed our eyes like a reflex, only I couldn't help it, Bo was praying for strength to fight the good fight to the end, asking God to crush the enemy, and I'd never had an enemy in my life and I started picturing crushed enemies and I started to get scared. And all the other Rapture Watchers—there were only three, Bo was still waiting on God to tell him who the other eight should be because he'd asked Marylou and all the cheerleaders and the Women of God and about fifty other girls and they'd all said no—but the other Rapture Watchers were saying yes, Lord, every time Bo said something, and I opened my eyes and peeked at them and every one of them had their foreheads all crinkled like they were trying to solve a math problem and their fingers clutching each other so tight you could see white on the rims of their fingernails, and I said in my head so nobody could hear it please, God, please keep me safe, and I didn't know if I meant from the enemy or from Bo.

Then we were finished praying and Bo said even so, come Lord Jesus, and we all said amen. Then we sat there real still, like we'd prayed so hard we were worn out.

• • •

Deedee made dinner that night, which was unusual for her. Whereas Memaw always made big dinners with two vegetables and homemade rolls or biscuits and meat—Memaw wouldn't think about serving dinner without meat—Deedee hardly ever cooked meat, and when she did it was always something strange, and only when Uncle Mull would say Dee, I can't stand it, I got to have some red meat. Then she'd make it but she wouldn't eat it and she'd be all snippy about it and you wouldn't want to eat it with her watching.

But this time she was acting real nice, too nice, and after dinner she said Sylvia, you want to go shopping?

Well, it had never in my born days occurred to me to shop on a school night, but while she was saying that she was picking up her purse and getting out her car keys, so I said okay even though I knew I'd have to stay up late memorizing my verses.

But Deedee wanted to buy me some dresses for school, which I needed because people at Nashville Christian Academy wear the fanciest clothes I've ever seen in my life and I told Deedee you should see what Marylou Manderberry wears, I don't think she's planning on wearing the same thing twice all year.

Deedee said we can't compete with the Manderberrys but we can do something.

So we went to the mall and found a parking place fast without even praying for one, and the first thing we bought was bras, which Deedee wears black ones, old-lady ones, and I was afraid she might try to make me get one like hers, but somehow she knew better, and we got two just alike, white with teeny pink bows in the middle, just like Marylou's, which was the happiest

I'd felt since Memaw died. Except when I thought I'd like to tell Memaw I'm wearing a bra now and I knew I couldn't. I thought about asking God to tell her but obviously I didn't want to talk to God about bras, him being a man, so I figured probably my guardian angel told her. I'm pretty sure my guardian angel is a lady, but I've never tried to talk to her because I think it would be too much like praying so it would look like idolatry. So I said thank you to Deedee and I wasn't just being polite, and for the first time in my life I felt like I loved her. I didn't tell her, though. She's not the gushy type.

So everything was going fine, but then Deedee wanted to get me some clothes, only she likes the strangest clothes. When I'd try on things like Marylou wore Deedee thought they were boring, so I got what Deedee wanted because she was paying for them. But when I got to school the next day I felt like I was wearing a costume, and I wished I could disappear.

I kept trying to fit in at Nashville Christian Academy and wear Deedee's costumes, which is two things it's about impossible to do at one time. I sort of wanted to do my hair like Deedee's too so my hair would go better with my clothes and I had this crazy idea that Bo might like it that way, but I didn't know if wearing spikes on your head was allowed at Nashville Christian.

One thing I was learning was that God is pickier than you might think about what people wear. Like Marylou Manderberry said the Proverbs 31 woman wore linen and purple, which was the color of royalty, and she'd quote the verse about consider the lilies how they grow, they neither toil nor spin yet Solomon in all his glory was not arrayed as one of these, which means if God is in control of every aspect of your life including what you wear, which if he's not there's a problem, then you ought to wear nice clothes. When she said that about the purple, I thought if only I'd have known, I could have had a purple bra. Deedee loves purple. I thought I'd ask for something purple for Christmas if the world hadn't ended by then.

I was learning all kinds of things. They've all gone there since kindergarten and their parents got married there and their grandparents are buried there, and things make sense to them that don't to other people. Like you have to be crazy about the football team because we play some secular schools which always beat us like thirty-five to nothing but it's a witness to them. And if anybody on the football team gets injured playing football you say bless his heart, bless his poor little heart, and some people form little prayer huddles right there on the sidelines until he gets up and then they yell praise the Lord. Only some football players, if they get injured another way, like two of them were in a car wreck and some people said there was an empty beer bottle in the back seat, and when Marylou Manderberry heard about it, she shook her head and said God's trying to speak to them, only she made it sound like if there's anything in the world you never want to happen, it's God trying to speak to you.

Pretty soon after the bras, word got out that I came from a secular school in Alabama and my whole family's dead. Which somehow seemed to account for my clothes because people stopped looking at me like God was trying to speak to me and started looking at me like bless your heart.

That was the first time I'd ever thought of St. Clair County Middle School as secular. I wasn't even sure what it meant other than bad, but I was starting to feel like I was not just Bo's but the whole school's missionary project, and I didn't know whether to be grateful or mad.

I didn't tell Deedee, though, because I was pretty sure it

would make her mad. She wasn't too crazy about Nashville Christian Academy. Any little thing would go wrong there and she'd be off on a tangent about institutionalized sexism, and I couldn't help it, my mind would just start lining up the sexists in jail. They'd be wearing striped prison uniforms with ties pinching their necks red and they'd all have big mustaches like Coach Schifflett and there'd be four or five of them, all standing there holding on to the bars with pitiful looks on their faces. Sometimes one of them might be holding a steel cup or a heel of bread. It made me feel good, picturing those sexists all locked up together, having to share one little toilet. Sometimes I'd put Paw Paw and Uncle Mull in there with them, and that made me feel good too. I don't know why. It was probably a sin.

Deedee and I were getting along okay ever since the bras, but Uncle Mull wasn't getting along with anybody. It was a recession, and Deedee said don't worry about him, men just get that way about money, but I worried anyway. And Paw Paw was getting worse by the minute. I said I think we ought to go get checked to see if we've caught it, and Deedee kept saying cancer's not contagious, you're not going to get it, Sylvia. Only I couldn't help but wonder. Because sometimes it seemed like that whole house had cancer and was eating holes in itself, everybody rotting from the inside out.

It was that dead hot of the middle of September where you have to keep reminding yourself that fall's just around the corner because you can't hardly stand the heat another day, and Paw Paw'd be asleep with his mouth open looking like he was dead only without covers. And Uncle Mull would sit there watching TV in his undershirt and gym shorts, eating Doritos in a daze like he'd never seen a TV before, and he'd get mad every time Deedee turned on the air conditioner because she thought he was made of money. And Deedee'd go down in the basement and put on her earphones and play her drums hour after hour, drowning out everything and everybody in the world.

You couldn't hear what she heard, all you could hear was the drums. But that beating would go inside your brain and transform itself in your ears into nights full of thunder and heartbeats on monitors, nails being hammered and footsteps running down docks. I'd lie on my sofa bed, and Deedee's drumming would go in my body and I'd open my pores and hear through my skin, everything getting hot with the hearing, my feet and my kidneys and my hands and my face and even my female parts, and I'd lie there sweating, perfectly quiet and perfectly still, thinking about Paw Paw and God and the Rapture and Bo Schifflett, Junior, and throb.

1 0

I'M GETTING DRESSED FOR THE BIRTHDAY PARTY AND I CAN'T decide between pants and a skirt. I have my black stirrup pants and a straight black skirt laid out on the bed and I'm standing in front of them in my top and underwear, staring at them blankly.

The TV is on, as always, and I don't know whether Buddy or I turned it on. Some celebrity is getting married for the fourth time—a big wedding with a white dress. I feel jealous. I want to fall in love four times before I die. I want four men to fall in love with me.

There's a commercial about a couple who've been married fifty years and never had their prescriptions filled anywhere but Harco. I think what's wrong with you people, you're eighty years old. Lighten up.

I go with the skirt. Stirrups make me think of a gynecologist.

Everybody at Buddy's birthday party, all our friends, are his age. They're Buddy's friends, they've known him longer than I have. They knew his first wife. When they talk about the past they pretend she didn't exist.

One of them has knee trouble, and he makes everybody be

quiet so we can hear it bend. We do, and we all laugh. It's an athletic injury, he says, it's bothered him since high school. I don't say how come nobody my age has these things. I don't say anything.

They bring over black balloons and a sign that says OVER THE HILL and they think it's hilarious. They think everything about getting old is hilarious because they don't think they're old. I hope I die young.

It's 1992 and I'm already tired of the nineties.

I didn't get rich off the greed of the eighties. I barely experienced the eighties at all, I was just trying to survive. I was an unwelcome visitor in my father's house that whole decade, and now that I have my own job and my own money, I want to make my own decisions, do whatever I want. Sometimes I think by the time I'm ready to settle down into comfortable monogamy and drive a minivan and recycle my trash, it will be the next century.

When Buddy was my age it was 1975.

Everything I did with Jake and everything I want to do with Jake wouldn't have seemed so bad in the sixties or the seventies, even the eighties, but now even *Cosmopolitan* has articles about not having affairs.

We didn't have an affair. You have to make love for it to be an affair, and we didn't.

He wanted to on the lake. I was sitting on the rail, and he was standing facing me, at first beside me, then in between my legs, I opened my legs to let him stand there, and he put his hand up my skirt and I put my arms around his neck and we were kissing and I was somebody else, somebody beautiful and thin and sexy. It was warm, and he touched my thighs with his fingertips, and his calluses felt tickly, and I wondered if he could feel me through them. Then he pressed his palms against my skin and I felt my tendons tight like strings and he moved his fingers over me and I felt hollow and I wanted to. I was breathing his breath and it felt like if he breathed my breath and wrapped his arms and legs around me and came inside me, I would melt into his skin and disappear, and I wanted to. I was closing my eyes so I could feel myself disintegrate, and it was starting, my bones were going limp.

And then I heard my voice like it wasn't mine saying Jake, we can't.

He said yes, we can.

I was saying no, we can't, and he was fingering the elastic on my panties, touching me almost by accident, and I was leaning into him.

He said your body's saying yes.

I said my body doesn't always know what's best for me.

He said it knows this time.

I couldn't answer him.

He said let's go swimming.

We don't have bathing suits.

He said we don't need them. And he touched me softly, so gently it hurt.

I said what if somebody saw us, what if we got caught.

Who cares.

I do.

Nobody's going to see us, Sylvia, the gate's locked, we're completely alone.

I looked at the lake. It was black with a white surface and it was still, just barely quivering, and it looked deep. I was wondering if there was slime on the bottom, if there were snakes, thinking about my feet touching slime, touching snakes. Then Jake touching me and his hands hot and the water touching me and its hands cold, moving inside me, hot against cold, making thunder.

I jerk his hand out of my skirt, close my legs, and stand up. I can't look at him. I say no, Jake, we're both married.

Long silence. I'm pressing my temples.

Okay, Jake says. He's ready to go.

We walk back to the car, and he's withdrawn. It's awkward and quiet and I haven't been fair and I feel bad for that but I'm frustrated too. What did he expect? Even if we weren't married, this would be our second date. I wouldn't make love to anybody on a second date, what kind of woman does he think I am? Plus it's not even really our second date. Last night doesn't count because I didn't know it was a date, I thought it was business. Part of the time I thought that—I don't know what I thought. And what if I said yes? Does he have condoms with him, did he plan this last night, before we'd even kissed? Or was he thinking of not using condoms and leaving me to deal with whatever happened after that alone? I'm not the one who's not being fair, he is, and it's arrogant of him to make me feel this way. He's not even a star yet, he hasn't even recorded his album, and it's already gone to his head.

We get in the car and he looks at me expectantly and I don't know what to say.

He says well?

I say yeah?

He doesn't know how to get out of here. The irritation in his voice grates in my ears.

I tell him go straight. We drive the bumpy road in the dark, the trees overhead blocking out the starlight, and the only sound is the gravel under the tires. Finally I say take your next left, and my voice sounds funny.

We're heading toward the graveyard where my grandparents are buried. We have to pass it to get back to the interstate and I feel irresistibly, morbidly drawn to it. I say do you have any interest in old country graveyards?

He looks at me.

I put my hand on the seat.

He touches me.

We're reading inscriptions in the starlight, and every time we move from one tombstone to another he takes my hand to lead me there, then lets go.

I think he wants to kiss me again, but he's being patient, gentle, waiting for me to be ready. I could kiss him just for that, but I don't because I like being pulled open like this, unraveled by desire. I feel myself being pushed out of my body, taken over, and I want it to happen slowly so I can remember every second of it. I want to find out what it means to be consumed with passion.

My mother and my grandparents are buried here in a far corner, and I get quick flashes of my grandparents' graveside services—folding chairs, a hot tent, I can't breathe, sweat on my neck, on my back, heavy, pushing me over and I can't straighten myself out and it is not the first time. I think of my mother and I think that was not the first, nothing ever is. Then I see my grandparents in their coffins, decomposing, and I'm coming apart and I put Jake's arms around me so he'll keep me together and he pulls me close and I lean my head toward him and I'm holding him too tight for him to kiss me and I think about the Rapture and the last time I was in a graveyard at night, the night the Rapture didn't happen and Bo Schifflett, Junior, died, and don't think about Bo, don't think about the past, all you have is here and now, all you are, and I taste his neck and he's salty and I taste his ears and he feels scratchy on my tongue. He takes my face in his hands and he's kissing my ears and my hair and the back of my neck, kissing toward my throat, and he unbuttons my top button, kissing me there, and I am nothing but what he touches and he touches me everywhere, he kisses my eyelids, my eyelashes, and if I let myself go I would disappear, so I'm holding on to his arms and his elbows and shoulders as his hands move over me.

He unbuttons my blouse, kissing me the whole time. He unhooks my bra, and I watch my breasts appear in the moonlight, and they are startlingly white. I watch his fingers touch them, then I drop my head back and close my eyes while he cups my breasts in his hands and kisses them. I feel my blouse pulling out of my skirt and his hands move over my back and he says you've got a strong back and I say do I, and he says I can feel your muscles, I didn't expect that, and he's shaping my back muscles into existence, I could be whatever he wanted me to be, and then he's kissing my stomach, he's on his knees kissing my stomach with his hands reaching up caressing my breasts, and my legs are trembling again and I have to sit down and we sit on a long marble slab near the feet because I don't want to sit on the words.

An image of the dead body lying six feet below us flashes into my head and I try to push it out. I look at the date—died five years ago. Five years and three and a half months. It would have to be all skeleton by now. It probably doesn't even smell anymore.

Jake lies on his side, propping himself up on his elbow, and I'm lying beside him, unbuttoning his shirt, and I become pleasantly aware that in this position I look like I have cleavage. He moves his finger down my cleavage and I put my face in his chest and his chest hair tickles my face and he's kissing my head and my hair falls on his shoulder and then I'm lying on top of him and his finger goes into me and I'm starting to disintegrate again and I have to stop.

It's too much like death, like Bo's death, like something I can't name, but it isn't right. I suddenly feel very sober and cold. I slide off him and he reaches up my skirt again and I say no again and he turns away frustrated again.

I'm afraid. This is a dangerous game, and I want to stop. I say I'm not trying to tease you, I told you we couldn't make love and I thought you accepted that.

He sits up. I thought you changed your mind, what do you want?

I want to make love with you, I think you know that, but I can't.

Why not.

I told you. I sit up and look away.

He touches my face. Look, he says, the infidelity has already occurred.

Don't say that.

It has, be honest with yourself.

I hear myself sighing. Okay, yes, some kind of infidelity has occurred, but it hasn't been consummated. I look at him.

He rolls his eyes. You're drawing arbitrary lines, let yourself have some pleasure.

I'm having some pleasure. I touch his hand.

His fingers intertwine with mine and he looks in my eyes. Well, have some more. He touches my breast softly, carefully. Life is short, he says, and he glances at the engraving on the tombstone we're sitting on.

Jake, I've never wanted anything so much in my life, but I can't.

Why.

Because. I cross my arms. Because it's dangerous—emotion-
ally, mentally, even physically, maybe also spiritually, although I
haven't thought about myself in that way for a long time.

I'm not going to hurt you, Sylvia.

Not on purpose, you're not, but you can't help it.

He's stroking my hair. I've never known a man this gentle.

When you have sex with somebody, I say, you give part of
yourself to them, you become a part of them.

He's quiet. He listens to me. I want to become part of him. I
think I would be safe if I were part of him. He's stroking my hair
and my back, my muscular back. I feel warm and safe and good
and strong and uncomplicated and I like his hand on my back. I
like the cool marble under my legs and I like the dark hot air on
my arms like sheets and I like how he tastes. I would like to be
married to him and feel this way forever.

I think his wife probably feels safe.

I shake my head. It's that you're married, and if I make love
to you, I don't know. I'm afraid I'll lose some of myself. I'll become part of you and then we won't be together so I'll be living a
fragment the rest of my life and I'll never be whole.

People do it all the time. He's drawing little circles on my
arm with his finger.

I know that.

All the time.

That's not relevant. I'm not talking about what sex is or does
to other people, I'm just saying what it does to me. Other people
didn't grow up the way I did, other people didn't, don't— I can't
finish. I'm getting confused.

Is your husband faithful to you?

Yes.

He doesn't answer.

I say you don't believe me.

No, it's possible that he is, Jake says.

He is. I pick up a pine cone and start tearing it apart. Is your wife faithful to you?

Yeah, she's satisfied.

I feel suddenly angry like a hot flash, and I don't even want to anymore. I throw the pine cone away and look at him without making a face.

Okay, Sylvia, he says, and he stands up, offers me his hand.

I stand up, hook my bra, and button my blouse but leave it untucked. We walk aimlessly in the quiet, our hands in our pockets.

I'm feeling too many things. Our feet are too loud and I can't breathe right and I'm hot and why isn't he touching me, do I have to have sex with him just to get him to hold my hand, do I have to have sex with him just to keep him from being mad at me, was it all a trade-off and now I owe him something and he's mad because I'm not playing by the rules and it was all a transaction and if you don't get what you paid for you take it all back. Well, it's not fair. Nobody ever taught me those rules, I didn't know how to play, I didn't know what I was doing and he knew I didn't, he knew before I did, and he should have told me, he owed me that much. If I owe him this he ought to have owed me that.

I stop and turn toward him. I'm holding my arms and I feel my fingernails in my triceps. I say you need to understand, I'm not trying to tease you or treat you badly, I've just never done this before.

Done what.

This, any of this. I can't look in his eyes.

How many lovers have you had? He's holding me again.

None. Well, one—my husband.

He smiles. You're kidding.

I'm embarrassed again. I can't look at him, and I start walking. How many have you had? I've never asked anyone this before, and I don't know if this is like pillow talk, if it somehow excites him to talk about other lovers, or if it's how you do things now, if you have to interview each other to see how likely you are to get a disease.

More than one, he says.

Lots more?

You would probably think it was a lot. He's holding my hand.

I'm running numbers through my head. What is a lot. Two, four, twelve, a hundred. I don't say anything.

He says it's been a while, though.

How long.

He's thinking. I'm an idiot. I just asked him to think about his last lover who no matter what she was like was better than me.

He says at least three years.

So not since your daughter was born.

His eyebrows move. I don't think he's made that connection before. He doesn't answer. It's also been three years since his sister died, but I don't say it.

Does your wife know.

No.

What would happen if she found out.

She'd probably take our daughter and leave, I don't know.

You wouldn't try to get her.

I'd want her, but she's got things she'd use against me, she'd get her.

Like what.

Well, if she was leaving me because of an affair she'd start with that, but I've also got a record.

A record.

It's sealed, I was a minor, and it was nothing, just possession of pot, but she'd use it to prove I'm an unfit father.

She could destroy you, you'll be famous by then.

Yeah, I guess she could.

So why do you do it, why give other people the power to destroy your life.

They won't.

How do you know, how do you know I'm not going to start calling you at home, how do you know I'm not going to call her.

You're not.

Well, no, I'm not, but how do you know.

It happened once before, actually, and I just told her it was an obsessed fan.

I don't say anything.

I've got fans, you know, he says.

I know.

He says so you don't want me to send you roses next week.

I put my hands on my face.

I'm just kidding, he says, just kidding.

You're scaring me.

He says Sylvia, I'm not going to hurt you, I care about you.

I don't know what to say. I care about you too sounds so lame. And I'm still worried. I can't get comfortable, I'm too aware of my joints. I think I'm going to have arthritis when I'm old. I say you're really not afraid of your past catching up with you.

Maybe I should be.

I would be.

The graveyard is giving me the creeps. We're coming near the section I think my grandparents are in, and I have this feeling like static in my brain. I push it out. I'm getting a headache.

I say maybe we should get back to the hotel. I wonder if I should clarify that I mean back to our separate rooms, but I figure I'll cross that bridge when I come to it.

When we get to the highway he tells me his first sexual experience —he was fifteen, he was visiting his grandparents in New Mexico, and his mother found him in the desert in the back of a pickup.

It is pillow talk, I don't need to know this, not the details. Not any of it. I feel intimidated. I've never known anybody who's been to New Mexico, much less had sex there. When I think of New Mexico, I think of a coyote on a big rock in silhouette against an orange sky above the month of October. I've never even known anyone who had sex in a truck.

I want to know if it hurt, why they didn't get out and do it in the sand. I want to know what it would feel like to make love in the desert.

He asks for mine.

My wedding night, I say. I feel like a cliché.

How long did you date before you got married.

It's hard to say when we actually started dating, maybe a year.

You dated a year, you were together a whole year and you didn't—how could he keep his hands off you that long?

I say I was fatter then. A stupid answer and not the reason, but the question embarrasses me. It makes me feel fat, and I can't think how to explain it. I've never known anyone you had to explain the idea of being a virgin on your wedding night to.

And was your husband a virgin too.

No, he was married before.

How old is he.

Forty.

Forty—so he came of age during the sixties.

It's not like he was a hippie or anything, I say, and I sound defensive. I say how old's your wife.

Jake says she's my age, actually she's four months older than I am.

Anything he says about her is more than I want to know. I don't want her to be real.

Jake asks what attracted me to Buddy.

I don't know. He's a wonderful man, I say, very kind and gentle and hard-working. He made me feel safe. I think about asking him what attracted him to his wife, the model, but I don't want to hear it.

You dated for a year and you never slept with him and then you married him, he says, how would you know whether he'd be any good.

I know you would be.

He doesn't answer.

I say I think you take the next exit. We're staying in the Civic Center Sheraton, and we follow the signs.

We pull into the hotel parking lot and my stomach relaxes a notch. He walks me to my room, and I unlock the door, then turn to look at him, trying to say no with my eyes so I don't have to actually say it.

We don't have to make love, he says softly, I just want to sleep with you.

Jake— I look up and down the hall. It's empty, but this is hardly private.

Beside you, sleep beside you, Jake says.

Jake.

What.

I'm already taking home more guilt than I know how to handle tomorrow, and I can't wake up with you and go to bed with my husband on the same day.

He nods. He understands, I guess. Or he's resigned himself to it. He kisses me on the cheek. Goodnight, Sylvia.

I barely have the energy to wash my face and brush my teeth before I fall asleep.

He calls me the next morning, and we go down to breakfast together. He's affectionate and kind, but I'm flustered and can't enjoy it. I didn't take off my makeup last night and I want to look unforgettably beautiful but my eyes are puffy.

He says we'll see each other again.

I nod and stir my coffee. I keep adding things to it—cream, sweetener, more cream, more sweetener—because it's too hot to drink and I want to be doing something.

He says are you going to be okay?

I think so.

Then he gets serious, like he's in a business meeting or he's a coach talking to the quarterback on the sidelines. He says the thing is, never admit anything to your husband.

Oh, I won't.

They'll believe anything, any outrageous lie you come up with they'll believe because they want to.

That sounds sort of cruel, I say.

What's cruel about not telling somebody something that will just hurt them?

I didn't mean it like that, it just sounds sort of calculated.

It's not, it would be cruel to let them find out, it would be cruel to throw it in their face, it would be cruel to give them the opportunity to picture something that would haunt them the rest of their lives, so you don't let them know.

I won't. I can't decide whether to be grateful or mad. Of course I'm not so stupid that I'm going to go home and tell Buddy what I did. But then again, I don't know what I am going to tell him, and maybe I need this.

Even if you're in a big argument, he says, and you're really mad and you just want to hurt him, you don't let go of this.

I wonder why he's telling me all this, if it's to protect me or him, but I want to hear it.

You're a strong, beautiful, intelligent, talented woman, and you might have a hard time, but you're going to be okay.

I don't know what he's talking about. I look at him without making a face.

He says we'll see each other again. He's sure of that.

His plane leaves in an hour. I offer to take him to the airport, but he's already called a taxi. He kisses me on the cheek, signs the check, and is gone.

When I got home from Birmingham I was sick. My body ached and my head ached and I felt heavy like I was breathing gravity. I took aspirin and went to bed and I told Buddy I'm just exhausted, I've been working too hard. He believed me and left me alone.

I don't know what it was, if I was punishing myself or trying to withdraw from the world because I couldn't deal with it, but I didn't want Buddy to touch me until I could get Jake's touch off my skin, and I couldn't do it, I kept feeling Jake's hands through the sheets, and everything reminded me of him—salt, heat, water, the smell of pine, the smell of my own hair, darkness.

Sometimes I'd think God was making me sick to punish me or to warn me, trying to speak to me. Then I'd say you sound like Bo Schifflett, Junior, stop it. Then I'd think no, you skipped dinner, you got drunk, you walked around downtown in the middle of the night breathing all that pollution, you barely slept, then the next night you were halfway undressed lying on a cold marble slab, and you got sick. You would've gotten sick if you'd done the exact same thing with Buddy. It's just science.

But I wouldn't have done the same thing with Buddy. Which is part of the problem.

I got well just in time for the birthday party and threw myself into that. In one day I did with the house what would usually take me two weekends—I did all the floors and the bathroom, washed the front door, cleaned the oven, changed the sheets, did the laundry, washed the walls in the kitchen. I made a homemade cheesecake and enough lasagna to feed thirty people even though we only invited eight, and I bought five bottles of red wine and made a big salad and ran around all night pouring wine and water and passing bread and clearing dishes.

When the last person walked out the door at twelve-thirty, Buddy went to bed, and I washed all the dishes by hand and mopped the kitchen floor and watched *Steel Magnolias* on HBO while I worked on the carpet a little where somebody had spilled some beer. When Julia Roberts died, I felt good and I cried so hard I could feel pink welts on my face. I fell asleep in Buddy's chair with the TV on and stayed there all night.

The morning after the party Buddy won't move. He's lying on his back with his hands behind his neck, staring at the ceiling. I think he's hung over, so I bring him two Advil and ease myself into bed, still stiff from the chair, my spine facing him. I'm almost asleep when he says I'm forty years old. There's something in his voice like gravel.

I open my eyes. I say forty's not a big deal, chronological age doesn't mean anything. It's what we used to tell each other when we started dating. I was nineteen and he was thirty-six.

He says I'm forty years old and forty pounds overweight and childless. He's speaking slowly and his voice is tired. I sit up and look at him, my elbows on my knees and my face in my hands. He says housing starts keep falling. Sales aren't what they used to be. He's looking at the ceiling, talking into the air, like I'm not there. He sighs and yawns at the same time. He just needs some sleep. We both do, that's all. He says my whole life hasn't turned out like I thought it would. He shifts his mouth.

I can't find any compassion. I say well, Buddy, what'd you think it would turn out like. I don't mean it sarcastically. I really want to know, because I don't know another building supplies salesperson whose life isn't exactly like his.

He closes his eyes.

I say why don't I make some breakfast. I get out of bed.

The next week we have four of the worst fights of our marriage. I work as late as I can every night, wishing Buddy would go on a little business trip, maybe to Memphis or Chattanooga or Knoxville, he usually does well in Knoxville, just a night or two to give the tension a chance to unwind. But I don't suggest it because it would just start another fight, and we're both too tired to keep this up. Buddy sleeps in his chair every night, and I lie in bed listening to him snore, resenting him for it.

On Sunday we start fighting as soon as we wake up. Buddy

came to bed in the middle of the night and I say something about him hogging the covers and it goes from there. We're yelling, slamming doors—it's one of the worst fights we've ever had, and it's over covers.

I sleep in the middle of the bed and he has to scrunch all the way to the edge and I make up the bed so sloppily that there aren't any covers on his side.

I sleep in the middle because he weighs two hundred and thirty pounds and as soon as I get in I get sucked into the hole he's made there and I've been wanting to buy a new mattress, sometimes I can't believe I'm sleeping on the same mattress he slept on with his first wife just to save a few hundred dollars, but every time I bring it up Buddy says no, every time I bring up any improvement for the house Buddy says no, so all our stuff looks like crap.

He says somebody has to look after the money, somebody has to keep you from spending us out of house and home, and I for one refuse to apologize for not being as vain as you are, for not wasting fifty dollars a month, for example, on a health club membership.

I am not vain and it is not wasted and you'll admit that when you have your heart attack.

Shut up about the heart attack, Sylvia, I'm forty years old now, it's not funny.

I'm not trying to be funny, I'm trying to be healthy, and I'm trying to get you to be healthy.

You're self-centered and vain, is what you are.

I'm not vain, Buddy, don't do this.

You wouldn't be vain if you could see yourself drool in the middle of the night.

Oh, fine, you want to complain about what people do in the middle of the night, you can talk about your own snoring.

I do not snore.

You do too, I should record you, I can't get one good night's sleep for all that honking and wheezing, I feel like I live at a truck stop.

I do not.

You do too, and you do it because you're overweight.

Get off my back already.

Buddy, it's a medical fact, I'll show you the magazine article. Overweight people snore sixty percent more often than regular people.

I don't care what your stupid man-hating magazine says.

Fine, then listen to me, I'm telling you you snore, and if you'd lose some weight you'd feel better, you'd look better, you could do your job better, sex would be better, we'd both sleep better.

We argue all the way through breakfast—I can't eat, but I make him eggs and pancakes with syrup and sausage and orange juice and coffee, and I practically throw it at him and he sits there and shovels all that food into his mouth, yelling the whole time. I'm so upset I can barely get down my coffee, and he's eating more food in fifteen minutes than I eat in two days.

We fight all morning until three o'clock that afternoon and Buddy's been eating on and off the whole time—three bologna sandwiches, all made by me and all without so much as a thank you, Popsicles, brownies, milk, an apple which I wash and cut up for him and which he dips into the peanut butter jar, which means that next time I open it there are going to be little dried-up apple remains in there that make me feel like throwing up, more brownies and milk until we're out of milk and I'm not going to have any for my coffee tomorrow unless I go to the grocery store tonight.

He could cut down so easily, and he won't even try. He could have turkey instead of bologna, plain apple instead of apple with peanut butter, one brownie instead of four. He could exercise.

Then I tell myself okay fine, he can do anything he wants, he can't hurt me. I never eat peanut butter anyway, and black coffee once in a while is not going to kill me.

I haven't had anything to eat all day, I've barely slept all week, and I'm yelling at him about Popsicle wrappers on the counter and the goo they leave even after you throw them away, so if he could just wipe the counter with a sponge, two seconds, tops, is all I'm asking, but no, and he never takes out the trash and our whole life is turning into garbage, we live in a dump, look at the back yard, what is all that crap, how many months has Buddy been promising me he's going to clear out the back yard.

What the hell's wrong with the back yard.

What do you mean what's wrong with it, look at it, open your eyes and take a look at it, take a look at our whole life, you don't see what's right in front of your face.

Yes I do, there's just nothing wrong with the back yard.

Buddy, look at me, what do you see.

It's a normal back yard.

Fuck the back yard, look at me.

He stops. He looks at me. I never say fuck. Slowly, he says what in the hell, Sylvia. He's shaking his head. He drops his hands and looks away.

I say Buddy, look at me, look at how I'm changing, how I need different things now. I'm not the helpless, innocent child I used to be.

He's recovered, and he's mad. He says I know that, you don't think I don't know that, you think the sweet, meek little teenager I ate cookies with not too many years ago would hand me this kind of crap over some weeds in the back yard.

He keeps yelling, but I'm yelling on top of him. Listen to me, Buddy, I'm trying to tell you I feel like a different person now. I look in the mirror and it strikes me as odd that I look familiar. I listen to myself speak and I don't recognize my own voice. I look at old pictures of myself and I may as well be looking at pictures of a stranger, I feel absolutely no connection—Buddy, shut up and listen to me, I'm telling you something important.

He's stuck on the yard. He mows that damn yard every Saturday morning like clockwork. He starts dreading it every Thursday, but he does it for me. He couldn't care less about the damn yard, but he fertilizes it, he mows it, he trims the hedges, all for me, all because of my obsession with the yard. Whatever I want I get, but am I willing to give him the one thing he's asked for—a baby, a family, the most normal, reasonable request he's ever heard of for a forty-year-old man—hell no. We've got a better yard than half the people on the street, and we're the only couple on the block without children, but he's agreed to put that off because I say I'm not ready for it. But hell, what more do I want, I'm just impossible to please, he doesn't know why he even tries.

Buddy, forget the yard, I'm talking about my identity, I'm trying to tell you who I am.

Are you about to start your period.

God, Buddy, what do I have to do, what can I say, what do I have to do to get you to understand.

You're about to start, aren't you.

I'm getting madder and madder and louder and louder. I can't hear myself and I don't think he hears me either. He's not listening, he's yelling too—every other night I'm out there with the sprinkler, watering the grass, which makes it grow faster, which makes him have to cut it that much more often, but what do I care. He never listens, what do I have to do to get him to listen, I could run around naked, I could catch on fire, I could scream and weep and gnash my teeth and he wouldn't listen—and then the world starts getting smaller and smaller and Buddy gets sucked farther and farther away from me, and I'm still yelling about him not listening, but I slowly become aware of a noise, a physical noise forming a barrier between us, and I can't hear him, I can barely see him through the thick fog of noise and I don't think he can hear me. I'm yelling as loud as I can, my throat hurts I'm yelling so loud, only I can barely hear myself over the noise. I think sharp pains are shooting through my stomach because I'm doubled over with them holding it but I can barely feel them because this noise insulates me from myself like snow in my head. Then it's making loud flashing pictures, shapes and dots and swirls like paisley, and the sound is clear like a bell and fuzzy with static at the same time, and it pulses on and off, in and out, and I can't see and I can't hear and I can't breathe, I can't even feel my own stomach pulling me down to the floor.

And then I'm lying on the floor crying, wailing some terrible awful sound, the only sound that can break through the paisley blizzard in my head and reconnect me with myself, and I close my eyes and I keep moaning like an animal until I can hear myself doing it, I can choose to do it, and I do, I keep wailing until I begin to feel myself again.

I don't know how long I do it because the snow in my head is blurring my concept of time, but I moan until I can feel my face and I can feel tears pouring down it and I'm moving down a tunnel toward myself and the noise inside my head starts to melt and the shapes start breaking up and disappearing like grease in a dishwashing liquid commercial and I feel my stomach and the sharp pangs bouncing around inside it, and I curl up and I hold myself and I keep crying, I'm crying and shaking and I can feel my tears cool on my face.

I'm coming back together, and I gradually become aware of Buddy holding me, Buddy petrified of me, holding me and rocking me and not knowing what to say, calling out my name, so softly I can barely hear it. Sylvia. Sylvia. Calling me back.

I know I have to relax, I have to give my stomach a break before it tears itself open, and I put my face in his shirt and the soft, protective roundness of his belly and I let him rock me back and forth, his arms thick and warm around me, and I listen to my name and I try to feel connected to it.

I try to relax my brain, but when I do I get dizzy and I feel like I'm about to be flung into another universe, like my brain is winding up, spinning, about to let go, and I try to reel myself in, I try to hold on to Buddy, to anything, to keep from floating off into space and never coming back. I tell myself it's necessary not to let go, don't let go, Sylvia, it's important. But I don't care. I don't care if my brain lets go and sends me hurling into another dimension of reality.

I'm suddenly keenly aware that there is more than one reality, and we may be missing something by living our whole lives in this one. I'm being initiated into higher knowledge, I'm having a spiritual experience, an epiphany, and I'm suddenly filled with an almost overwhelming sense of peace and contentment and clarity of mind, like you must be in heaven when you realize what's really important and how trivial all your problems on earth were and for the first time in your existence you let go of yourself and relax. And I realize all my problems would be solved if only I were dead.

I hear myself moaning very softly, but I've stopped wailing

and I've stopped crying. I become aware of my hands, and they are fisted onto Buddy's shirt, grasping so tightly my fingernails are digging through the cloth into my palms, and I let go of him and I look at my palms and I see four little smiles imprinted on each of them, all in a row, and it strikes me as almost unbearably funny and I burst into laughter, laughter mixed with tears of exhaustion, and I laugh and I laugh until I'm empty.

And finally I'm empty, wonderfully and completely empty. I've wanted to be empty all my life, and now I am and it's everything I always hoped it would be. I feel like I've been released from bondage, like this earth was a ball on the chains on my feet, and now I'm free and there's no connection so there's no pain because I don't feel a thing. I don't even feel empty, I feel absolutely nothing. And I don't care about anything. I don't care if we stay married, I don't care if we get divorced. I don't care if I die, I don't care if I live, I don't care about food, about my body, about my job or my career. I don't care about Jake. I'm not hot, I'm not cold, I'm not hungry, I'm not full, I'm not lonely or happy or scared or sad. Nothing matters, so nothing hurts. I just want to sleep. I just want to be left alone and sleep.

I'm vaguely aware of being lifted up, moving, then Buddy tucking me into bed, smoothing the covers over me, and I drift off into the soothingly familiar territory of quiet nightmares.

Jake said you'll have other affairs, and you'll make love with the next one.

But I said no, this is a once-in-a-lifetime thing for me, you'll forget my name, but I will carry you with me to my grave.

He said then at least give yourself the pleasure of making love to me.

Sometimes I think he was right. I should have made love

with him in the graveyard. I should have let him spend the night in the hotel with me and made love with him again the next morning. I should have done my whole bathtub man fantasy with him, except I would have let him take off his clothes before I pulled him into the bathtub. How much difference would it have made?

This is part of what depresses me. I used to think I lived in a world that had some kind of moral order to it, where if you had an affair you'd be throwing yourself down some dark terrible hole you couldn't dig yourself out of, nobody could dig you out. Like you'd get pregnant or get AIDS or his wife would find out and hire an assassin for you, or you'd die in a car accident with your lover and you'd both be burned beyond recognition. Or your husband would find out and leave you right when the affair was breaking up and you'd lose your job and the house and the kids and the dog, you'd lose everything, and you'd end up wearing a hairnet halfway down your forehead and an orange apron, making French fries at K mart. But something.

And maybe I even sort of wanted that. Not K mart, just something. Because I wasn't happy with my marriage and I was afraid of what I thought might be happening with my career and afraid at the same time that it might not be happening at all and I couldn't think of anything to do about any of it, so maybe I thought what I was doing with Jake was going to send my life out of control in a direction I'd never thought of before, and maybe I thought that was what I needed.

And then nothing happened. I went back to Buddy, Jake went back to his wife and daughter, and nothing happened.

Another thing that depresses me is the realization that I'm not in love with my husband.

. . .

It wasn't always this way with Buddy.

After Bo Schifflett, Junior, died I closed down and started eating everything in sight and I built a cocoon of fat around myself so nobody could touch me. I was growing breasts but there was something wrong with breasts. Breasts make men lust and lust is sin and the wages of sin is death and Bo Schifflett, Junior, lusted after me and he was dead and my grandfather lusted after me and he was dead and my mother lusted after my father and she was dead and who knew who was next. So I kept eating but there was something wrong and I was growing hips and thighs and everything else to hide the breasts, but it didn't work, nothing worked, I couldn't control my own body.

Bo said your body is a temple, you have to take care of it, and I knew that, I knew you have to exercise and don't drink and don't smoke and wear nice clothes and brush your hair a hundred times every night, and it is terrible to be fat and ugly, it's a sin, and I knew I was fat but I had to be, I couldn't be skinny or pretty or any man who loved me would die.

And the fatter I got the less I looked like myself and the less I felt like myself, so it was like I wasn't the one who was fat. I wasn't even the one who was living my life. I was in disguise and there was another, more beautiful, lovable me that nobody knew, hidden away or asleep like in fairy tales, but if they did know me they would love me but not because I was pretty so they wouldn't die. And meanwhile I felt safe, tucked away there inside myself.

And four, five years after Bo, Buddy was the first man I let near me.

He couldn't have been more different from Bo. He smoked and he drank beer and he cussed and he was old and for all I knew he'd never even heard of the Rapture. And he was big. My grandfather had been skinny and my father was skinny and Bo Schifflett, Junior, had been so skinny that I didn't trust skinny men anymore, so compared to them Buddy seemed bigger than life, and I liked how small I felt around him, protected. He was my friend, and he was so wrapped up in his divorce that a romantic relationship didn't even occur to me as a possibility.

He used to come over to see my father when his wife would leave him, and I'd always be making desserts and my father didn't like sweets, but Buddy and I would sit at the kitchen table and eat together. He'd talk about his wife, and I liked it that he was vulnerable but that I couldn't possibly hurt him because his wife had already destroyed him, and I wouldn't have to do or say anything, and Buddy would just keep talking like I was barely there, which is exactly how I wanted to feel.

Three years passed—Buddy got divorced, I graduated from high school, got a job, and started taking some courses at MTSU —and one night when my father was out of town on business Buddy came over. He was standing at the front door, and I said my father's not home. I'd been making cookies and the buzzer on the oven went off and I went to take them out and he came in and we were alone for the first time and I said would you like some cookies. I put them on a plate and turned off the oven and we sat down at the kitchen table and we talked about cookies and school and the weather and I had a bluegrass band on the radio even though I almost never listen to bluegrass, but he said do you like bluegrass?

I said yes.

He said there's a good bluegrass band playing at the Bluebird Café tonight, you want to go hear them?

That was all it took.

Sometimes I think we fell in love because we were both wounded, and when either of us looked at the other we saw something we wanted somebody to see in ourselves. And sometimes I think I fell in love with him because he took care of me in the way I'd always thought my father should have and didn't, and he fell in love with me because I needed him in a way his wife didn't anymore, and he needed to be needed.

Sometimes I think that's not love, I've never been in love, and I'm afraid I'm one of those people who doesn't know what love is.

Once we started dating, his wife called me a few times. She said some rude things, warned me not to fall for Buddy, and I got some strange mail, mostly newspaper clippings about messy divorces. It scared me, but she was the one who left him, and I knew he would have gone back to her in a second if she'd said one word of encouragement. But the phone calls bothered me anyway. He asked her about it—cussed her out about it, actually— and she said it wasn't her, but who else could it have been.

Sometimes I think he called her to see if she still cared. So when she said it wasn't her, that's what made him so mad.

Monday morning Buddy brings me hot tea with lemon in bed. He left the spoon in the cup and I can't stand the shriek of stainless steel on stoneware. Also, I have to have coffee, if I don't I'll get a headache. But I don't say anything. I take the spoon out, lick it and put it on the bedside table, and drink the tea.

I seem to have made some kind of impression on him last night. He's careful and sweet and solicitous and he wants to know how I feel and his words sound tender and overenunciated.

I feel okay.

He wants to know if I feel like going to work today.

Yeah. Why wouldn't I go to work.

He's sitting on the edge of the bed. I don't like to have conversations with people sitting on the edge of the bed. He's sitting, I'm lying, he's dressed, I'm in my nightgown, he's doing all the talking and I'm supposed to be listening—it's all wrong.

He's already ruined one marriage, he says, and when we got together he thought he was being given a second chance with his life and he's not going to blow it this time. He's been going through a hard time, turning forty and trying to figure out if he's really doing with his life what he wants to do and trying to take off some weight and give up cigarettes, and he hasn't worked through everything but one thing he's sure of is that he wants to spend it with me.

I look at him. His forehead is messed up.

He says he has to admit he doesn't understand everything I need, but he's trying like hell to, he's really going to try to be here for me now, if I'll just give him the chance.

Sure, Buddy.

I have to get ready for work. I put my hair up and take a shower. So Buddy's going to be here for me now. I lather my stomach, my breasts, my arms, my neck. What the hell is that supposed to mean. I don't need him here, I don't need him now. Where I need him is too far away and too long ago for either of us ever to reach. I spread my toes and wash my feet.

I get dressed, put on my makeup, fix my hair, make some coffee.

Buddy apologizes for not making coffee.

I tell him it's okay, the tea was nice.

He says I should have known.

No, I liked the tea, I just—

You always drink coffee.

Buddy, stop.

I leave for work early and take the long way to give myself some time alone. I turn on the radio, then turn it back off.

How could I explain to him. Where would I start. It's just that I'm so tired of it all, sick of it. I get to where I hate to hear the words vinyl siding, and he goes on and on about it. He can't understand why anybody in their right mind would want to put that kind of crap on their house when they could have pressed wood. The vinyl siding people are lying to the American public, telling them it's cheaper. Cheaper than what. Nobody thinks long-term in this country anymore. He's obsessed with it. And he's the same way with gas prices, always commenting whenever we pass a gas station—it's up a penny, it's down two cents. Two gas stations across the street from each other charging five cents' difference for the same gallon of gas, now who in their right mind wouldn't cross the street for the lower price.

Who cares. If you don't think just like Buddy, you're not in your right mind.

He never cleans out the ashtray in my car, he never does the dishes, he never takes out the trash, he never does anything in the yard without bitching about it for three days before and three days after. He never tells me I'm beautiful.

Jake kept saying you're a beautiful woman, you have a beautiful body, and every body part, he'd say the skin inside your thighs, inside your elbows, is so soft, and he'd kiss my wrists and tell me I have beautiful wrists. Every inch of me he told me was beautiful I believed him. He even thought I had beautiful feet. I've never felt so beautiful before, I didn't know it was possible to feel that beautiful.

With Buddy I can fix my hair and put on makeup and a sexy dress and he won't even notice. And if I say how do I look he says fine. He hates my feet.

My grandfather always said I was beautiful. I miss my grandfather.

I miss my grandmother. I miss my mother. I miss M'Lea and M'Lea's dog and M'Lea's mother and our old next-door neighbor, Mrs. Sutherland, and her babies, Will and Brother, and their dog, Bubba, and Amazing Grace, and I feel a terrible, physical longing inside for someone I've lost and can't even remember. I have big gaps in my memory, months at a time I can't recall one event from.

When I get to work, I call Deedee and ask her to have lunch with me.

She says today?

I say yeah.

She says well, okay.

I say how about Friday's at twelve.

She says well, okay, let me see, okay, that'll be fine.

This was a bad idea.

When she gets there, she's all hugs. She's wearing a new costume and a new hairdo and carrying a new purse—I assume it's a purse—and as we walk to our table she turns heads and I feel adolescent embarrassment. We sit down and she touches my arm and says how've you been, kid?

I want to tell her about Jake. I want to tell her I'm falling apart. I can't write anymore, I can't sing, I can't play, I can't concentrate. I can't turn on my dishwasher because the noise makes me feel like I'm getting sucked down the drain, but I'm afraid if I turn it on and leave, the house will burn down because when I turn it on I can hear a fire inside there that will only stay under control as long as I'm in the house, but then I'll get sucked down the drain. I know how crazy that sounds, but I can't hear right. We get these tapes in all the time at work, and I'm supposed to listen to them, but I can't tell good music from crap. It all sounds the same to me. And it's burning up outside but I can't turn on the air conditioner in my car, I don't even want to explain why, but it has to do with the noise, it has too much static in it and it makes me feel like crying, so by the time I get to work I'm sweaty and then I feel dirty the rest of the day. I always feel dirty, I can't get clean. And I hate taking a shower, I hate being naked, I hate looking at my body, I hate looking at Buddy's body, I can't stand being in the same bed with him. I can't sleep.

I say oh, I'm all right, how about you?

She says I'm up and down. She demonstrates with her hand.

All the sudden I'm very hungry. Deedee orders a California salad and water and I ask for a cheeseburger, French fries, and a diet Coke, then change that to a real Coke. I say I was wondering about your divorce.

She says yeah.

I say are you glad you did it.

She says uh-oh.

I say don't ask me any questions, I don't know the answers to them anyway. I just want to know if you're okay.

Well, yeah, now I am, she says, but it was hard for a long time, and I knew that it hurt you and I still feel really bad about that. She won't look at me.

Why'd you do it. I mean how do you know the difference

between a hard time that you just have to wait out but someday you'll get over it and the end of the marriage.

She still won't look at me, and I'm glad. I can't control my face.

Deedee says where do I start. She takes a long drink of water. She says it wasn't you, it was not your fault, but a lot of old problems did start surfacing when you came.

I say I know, and I'm sorry.

She says no, Sylvia, I'm telling you, it wasn't you. It was the way Mull just couldn't deal with you, he couldn't live with his own past.

She's touching me and I look at her hand, willing it off my arm. This is not what I wanted to know. I already know my father can't deal with me.

She says I mean like when your grandmother died.

I look at her.

She moves her hand. She says of course it wasn't that she died that bothered me, I mean.

I say of course not.

It was just that he didn't even tell me in person.

Now she's tearing up her napkin. I think Deedee, you're too old to be tearing up your napkin. And you're too old for fingernail polish that color. I'm okay now, and I don't make a face.

He left me a note, she says, a one-sentence note. And I read it and I thought shit, now my whole life's going to change. *Mitilene's dead.* That's what he wrote. No Dear Deedee, just *D*, the letter D, *Mitilene's dead. I'm in PC. Call you tonight. M.* Like he couldn't have waited one hour for me to get home. But I stood there in the kitchen reading that damn note on the back of an envelope—he couldn't even use a fresh piece of paper, he had to write it on the back of our trash. That pissed me off.

Our food has come and I'm eating my French fries, dipping them in a little puddle of ketchup. I haven't had French fries in a long time, and that strikes me as a mistake. I should be better to myself. I'm going to order dessert. A chocolate milkshake. I can't even remember the last time I had a chocolate shake.

She picks at her salad. I notice for the first time that she has very thin arms. I wonder if her arms used to be that thin, and I think about asking her, or would that be a rude question. Lately I've started looking at people, really trying to see what's around me, and you notice things you never did before. Like her hair is turning gray. This is the first time I've noticed that. It seems like Deedee of all people would dye out her gray. People get old too fast, this constant rush toward death. I eat two fries at once.

She says Mull and I had barely talked about it. I knew about you, I mean I knew you existed, and I knew your grandfather had cancer, but your grandmother was so much younger than your grandfather, we'd always figured she'd still be there to take care of you. And then suddenly there I was all alone and Mull was half-way there for all I knew and I kept thinking about what was going to happen to you and telling myself what a selfish bastard I was and arguing with Mull in my head, saying I didn't mind when he started sending you money—and I didn't, I really didn't—I didn't mind when we were barely married two weeks and he went to spend a weekend with you, I didn't mind when he offered to pay your tuition for a private school even though things were already tight, and one time before we were married I even went down there with him to try to talk your grandparents into letting you come live with us after the wedding, remember that?

Yeah.

Of course they wouldn't hear of it. Your grandfather was furious. He said Sylvia's ours, like you were a piece of property.

And your grandmother was heartbroken, couldn't stop crying, and she said they just couldn't live without you. Mull said she's my daughter, for God's sake, and they wouldn't even acknowledge that. They went at it like that for two days, but we couldn't get anywhere. I told him the only way you're going to get her out of here is to kidnap her, and I believed it. So finally we just gave up. Maybe we shouldn't have, but we did. And then five years later she was dead and there I was standing there holding the note going Mull, how much more do you want out of me.

This is not what I wanted to know. I've changed my mind about the milkshake. I wish I could leave. I wish I could make her shut up. I've opened a Pandora's box and I can't shut her up again. I used to have a record of that story. I can still hear it— *don't open the box, don't open the box, whatever you do, don't open the box.* I couldn't move during that part. Nothing could stop her. When the needle got to the end, I'd leave it there and turn up the volume. It sounded like a heart.

Deedee says I tried, though. I went downstairs and started walking around the basement, thinking about how Mull had wanted to redo it before the wedding. He knew a lot of good contractors from his work, and I'd agreed five years before because I was marrying him, I felt like I had to, and I didn't expect to make it in the music business anyway, but this time I thought if Mull still wants to finish the basement for her then where am I going to practice. And you were a seven-year-old child the first time, not a teenager. But by this time I'd played a few bars and talked with several people about playing on their albums, and I really believed I was going to get a break soon if I just kept hanging in there. I'd busted my butt for it, and I was afraid to let anything jeopardize it. Surely you can understand that, you're working just as hard for the same thing now.

She stops. She wants me to say something. I say sure.

And you, she says, pointing at me with the palm of her hand, I thought we couldn't uproot you right after your grandmother died and put you in a new home with new parents, a new school, a new state—you just can't do that, you were at a very delicate age. And I thought if I'm not ready to be a mother to a baby of my own, what in hell makes him think I'm ready to be a mother to a teenager. I was only twenty-five years old, I didn't think of myself as being in a totally different generation from teenagers, and I was arguing with him in my mind, saying you can say whatever you want about her being your kid and you'll take care of her, but I know that when it comes down to it, I'm going to be the one who takes her shopping, I'm going to cook her dinner, I'm going to—I don't know what, I have no idea what the mother of a thirteen-year-old has to do, but I know I'm going to have to do it. I'm not saying I was right to feel that way, I'm just saying it's the way I felt. I was young. We were both so young. We were all young. I'd say to myself I know she doesn't have a mother and I feel bad for her, but jeez, I don't even know her. You can't expect me to love somebody, open my home to somebody I barely know.

This was a mistake. This whole lunch was a mistake. My whole life is this lunch—one horrible mistake.

Deedee has the whitest skin I've ever seen. She won't go out in the sun because she's paranoid about skin cancer, and her lips are pencil thin, so she puts on this dark lipstick to compensate for how thin they are, and she looks like a vampire.

She keeps talking and I don't make a face. She says but then I said to myself this is not the time to be selfish, or to let Mull handle things alone. We can work all this out. We have to. So of course I decided to go to Pell City. I said I'll give them tonight, then I'll go down tomorrow.

Of course. What is going on in here, do they have somebody full-time just to crash silverware. It sounds like they have a vat in the middle of the restaurant and they keep hurling handfuls of knives and forks into it. Then every so often they bring out an entrée on one of those metal plates that sizzles, which ought to be against the law, you're supposed to cook the food in the kitchen, not on the way to the table. My ears hurt. This was one of my stupidest ideas ever.

Deedee says part of the problem was that she wasn't even a member of the family. She says when I married Mull his father made a toast welcoming me into the family—one of the only times he's ever spoken to me by name, and then he called me Dorothy instead of Deedee. So I didn't even feel like I was a member of that family, much less Ned and Mitilene's. I didn't even call them Ned and Mitilene, I didn't call them anything, and I called Mull's parents Gloria and Mr. Mullins. So it just wasn't my place to barge in and make them tell you the truth. But you know, it's hell living with lies you didn't make up and you never agreed to tell and then being trapped by them into becoming a passive liar.

I think about asking her if she wants me to feel sorry for her. I decide against it. I say I can imagine.

In a way, she says, passive liars are the worst kind, like truth isn't something they went up against and violated even though they knew what it was, but just something they disregarded. The whole thing made me sick.

I say yeah. I think why are you telling me this, why do people want to tell their life stories, broadcast all their terrible little secrets to anybody who'll listen, what is wrong with them. Why is Deedee telling me this, why did Jake tell me what he told me, why does anybody tell anybody anything. It just makes everything worse.

She says it's no wonder they all hated each other—Mull hated his parents, his parents hated your grandparents, your grandparents hated Mull and his parents, and poor you, Sylvia, you were caught in the middle and didn't even know what was going on. You didn't even know who your own father was, how could they live with that hanging over their heads? I told Mull when we got married, if you keep letting these lies fester inside you they're going to spoil and turn to hatred and you'll start to fear the truth, and you'll have good reason to, because if it goes on any longer then when Sylvia does find out, which she will, she'll be mad as hell at every single one of you and she won't have anybody to turn to and it will absolutely devastate her. And then time passed and I became just as bad as them and had as much reason to fear the truth as they did because I knew you could say to me why didn't you tell me, and I could say it wasn't my place, but that would mean nothing to you. You'd have every right to say to me that at some point in those five years I'd been married to Mull I should have done something. God. I just didn't know when or what, you know?

Yeah.

It was hell.

Yeah.

I tried, though. I really did. Like he was telling me a dream he had one morning, this was before we went down there to try to get you, and I'd been taking a class on dream interpretation, reading parts of our book to him, and I said Mull, do you realize how often you dream you're missing a part? He goes no. And I said you do, last night your teeth were falling out, last week you couldn't find your boots—since I've known you, you've told me dreams about looking down and seeing your fingernails missing or your toes missing or your hair falling out—and it's all the same dream, over and over. You need your daughter back. You feel like you lost a part of yourself when you gave her to them. He goes God, Deedee, I didn't give her to them. And I said okay, when they took her. But he didn't want to hear it. He closed up and he said I think it's castration anxiety. He got that from the book. So I said I don't need this, I'm just trying to help, and I went downstairs to practice.

She's talking too fast, and I can't follow her. Her words are scrambling themselves, piling up inside my ears. I finish my Coke and flatten my forehead.

She says and then when you did come, you were so hungry for a mother. I just felt drained. Every day you would ask me what to wear and how to fix your hair—that wasn't it, though. It's that you would hover over me all the time, offering to help in the kitchen, laughing at my jokes, complimenting me. That's not it either.

She's looking for the words with her hands in the air, elbows on the table.

You were just so damn cheerful, you just made me want to shake you and say stop smiling, stop being so goddamned good, it's not normal. I felt like I was losing control of my own house. I know how awful I sound. You were an orphan, for God's sake, and I'm resenting you for taking up space in my life. But that's how it felt at the time. So I started playing more and more to get away from you, both of you. Mull didn't want you in the bars where I played. That's another thing, that you were turning him inside out. He was becoming a Puritan. Like a month after you got there he said, he whispered in our bedroom behind a closed door, take her to get a bra. Like it was unthinkable that he would do it—this, the same man who brought seven pairs of edible panties on our honeymoon and ate every one, is embarrassed to take a twelve-year-old girl down to Caster-Knott for a bra. So I took you, but for your sake, not his. And I told him that. I said it's because I wouldn't want to buy my first bra with a man like you either. Scar her for life.

She picks up her fork and starts bouncing the tines on her plate. I want to say do you honestly think you kept me from being scarred? And was it really his idea to get me a bra, my father's? And do you really think anybody in the world wants to know how many pairs of panties their father has eaten? I want to say eat the bite already, Deedee, you're driving me crazy.

She says you know it wasn't anything about you personally, you know that, don't you.

Sure.

But now you're almost the age I was then, can you imagine coming home from work one day and finding out you're now the mother of a twelve-year-old child? Can you? She's pointing her fork at me.

No.

I was used to making love with the door open and for the life of me I could not see myself as the mother figure for a twelve-year-old, you know?

Yeah.

And then the whispering and the closed doors and twelve-year-old lies and Mull all of the sudden embarrassed for me to do laundry in my own house, afraid of what you'd think if you saw my teddies and my bustier—it all started closing in on me. Even now I can't tell you what a release it is to get all this out in the open. And then after your friend died—

I don't want to talk about him.

She looks at her plate. Finally she puts her fork in her mouth. I wait while she chews. Well, anyway, she says, her mouth still full of salad, one day I just decided I'd had enough, I'd had enough lies and secrets and deceptions to last me a lifetime, and I left.

She takes a drink of water, looks at me for a response.

I look at my watch, put a twenty on the table, and say thanks, Deedee, but I have to go.

I think about calling her a selfish bastard. I think about telling her my father never spent a weekend with me two weeks after they were married. I think about tearing her makeup off her face and throwing it in her salad and making her eat French fries until her precious skinny little arms turn into regular arms.

I kiss her on the cheek and leave her fumbling with her purse.

I tell myself it was her life, she could leave if she wanted to, she didn't owe me anything. She didn't owe me a damn thing.

I get in the car, and the heat pressing on my skin calms me down.

On my way back to work I redo lunch with Deedee.

We sit down in a booth, and she's wearing just one color and her hair is soft and it's obeying the laws of gravity and she's not wearing fingernail polish and she says she's so glad I called, she wants to know how I've been.

I say I'm having a hard time right now.

She says what can I do.

I say there's nothing.

She says do you want to talk about it. Then she's quiet.

I lick my lips. I say well, for one thing, I can't write. I haven't written a word in a month.

She knows that's bad. She remembers that I used to write poetry, but she thinks I just mean songs now.

I tell her I don't. I mean I haven't written a song, a poem, a letter, a thought. I haven't written one word. I haven't written a grocery list. I go to Kroger and wander around looking for food I think Buddy would want, feeling like I'm in a Korean grocery store. I pick up something thinking why would anybody want to eat this stuff and throw it in the cart and move on to the next display and do it again. And when I sit down to write, really write, I feel panicked like I'm inside a trash compactor, my brain is, and it's dark, and maybe if I could think, if I could come up with the right words, they would become flesh and they would stop the walls, they would push it back, and the light would shine in the darkness and the darkness wouldn't overcome it and I'd be safe, but who can think when they're jammed inside a trash compactor for a skull and the walls are closing and the only reason I don't get crushed to death is I'm shrinking, my brain is shrinking. Only I don't know how much smaller I can get. And I'm running out of time and you can't just sit down and make yourself come up with the words you need to save yourself out of thin air because it's all like it's from God, it's all being given to you, and if it is being given to you, all you have to do is concentrate and you'll have it, and if it's not, then it doesn't matter how hard you try, it won't be there, and the harder you try, the more clearly you hear the void, pounding, echoing its own emptiness. And I mean a physical pounding, so hard it hurts.

I look at Deedee for a response and she doesn't know what to say. I put her out of my mind.

I get on the freeway and drive fast. I pretend I'm going to Canada. I could do it, I wouldn't even need a map, just keep going north. It's not like you could miss it. I flip on the radio as loud as it will go and turn the base all the way up and the treble all the way down so I can feel the words in my hair. The sound waves hit my face like jolts of novocaine.

Three exits later I turn around.

When I get back to the office there's a letter on my desk from Jake marked personal. It's just one of those days. I go in the bathroom, wash my hands, and lock the door to read it.

My wife is gone to visit her parents for two weeks. She left yesterday with the baby, and I'm really no good at being alone. I found myself out late last night, drinking too much and not at all afraid to test myself. Nothing happened, but the potential was there. Maybe it'll be the other way around next time. I don't know. There's a side of me that I do not like and that I'm sure will cost me dearly someday if I don't watch it.

I think about you. I think about the graveyard. I think about the heat.

I'm coming to Nashville in October for the Country Music Awards. I hope you'll be there. I want to see you again.

He signs the letter with his love.

It's too much.

I put it in my purse, take it out, read it again and memorize it, then tear it up and throw half of it away. I wash my hands again and go back to my office. I take the rest of the pieces with me and throw them away there.

I call him and say are you alone.

Yeah.

Jake, don't send me letters like that, there's too much of a chance somebody would open it, people are going to ask me what it was as it is, and what am I going to say?

He says I'm sorry, I was drunk when I wrote that, I'm okay now. I want him to say I can't help it, I just miss you, I'm surprising myself at how much I miss you. He says it won't happen again.

Pictures run through my head before I can stop them. Buddy and Jake's wife have a head-on collision and die simultaneously, and Jake and I have only each other for comfort. Or all four of us are in a plane crash, and miraculously Jake and I survive without a scratch, but we're the only ones. We get married and I quit my job and adopt his daughter and we all go on tour and we hire a nanny to keep her backstage. Or Buddy and Jake's wife meet at the Country Music Awards and run off with each other to Mexico, Jake moves to Nashville, we get married and we write a love song for the wedding and it goes to platinum. Deedee and my father are in the plane crash too.

I say I just hope you're okay.

He says I'm okay.

I say well, David's going to kill me, I'm late for a meeting. I hang up and grab my purse, fishing for my car keys as I walk down the hall.

I decide to put Jake out of my mind, put the whole day out. I want to go home, make love with Buddy, cook a big dinner, all his favorite things, then watch a romantic comedy and snuggle together all night. I'll take my panties off in the car and lay them on the kitchen counter when I walk in. He loves that.

I pick up some steaks, *Chapter Two,* and *The Witches of Eastwick* on the way home. If Buddy's in a bad mood I'll watch *The Witches of Eastwick* by myself.

Only Buddy's car isn't in the driveway. I tell myself it's early, it's a pretty day, maybe he went to the driving range, maybe he went to get his car washed, maybe he's having his hair cut. I tell myself he didn't leave me, he wouldn't leave me. I deserve for him to leave me, but he won't do it, he just said this morning he wouldn't do it. What was it he said. I picture myself looking in his closet, figuring out what he packed, whether he took the big suitcase or his overnight bag or both, which shoes are gone. You can tell a lot about a man's plans by what shoes he takes.

I'm working up a sweat just parking my car in the driveway, wondering where Buddy would go if he left me, telling myself he wouldn't leave me. He needs me. If he leaves me, he'll be back before three days of eating cheap restaurant food. How long can a person live on Shoney's fried shrimp and vanilla pudding off the salad bar?

I'm walking in the house praying don't leave me and my eyes go straight to the message on the refrigerator and I'm afraid to read it, I know what it says. I pull it off and the magnet crashes and rolls under the refrigerator and I lay it face down on the counter so I can't see the words.

I tell myself if he did leave me, I'd be okay. I'd do better without him than he would without me. People have left me my whole life, and I've always done just fine. Buddy could leave me, Jake could leave me, and what would be the difference? My mother left me before I was born, my father left me, my grandmother, my grandfather, Bo Schifflett, Junior—I can't even think of the whole list of people who've left me, and it's never destroyed me yet and I'm stronger now than I've ever been.

Okay, Buddy, just do it. You don't even have to leave, I'll do it. I hope this note says you've gone so you'll save me the trouble. Come to think of it, don't do me any favors, I'll leave. Jake's wife is gone for two weeks, so maybe I'll just take a little vacation to California. I'll tell David I'm going to Disneyland. And I will. I'll go to Disneyland and Universal Studios and Rodeo Drive and Hollywood Boulevard and the Pacific Ocean and *The Tonight Show* and I'll charge it all to you, Buddy.

I turn over the note to read it. *I'm in Knoxville. Sorry, but it was an emergency. I'll call you tonight. See you tomorrow A.M. Love, Buddy.*

I crumple up the note and go downstairs to do laundry. A dry-walling emergency. I'm a fool.

The clothes are piled up high. I could do three or four loads. I look at how much of it will have to be ironed—hours' worth. I feel overwhelmed.

I think of the terrible probability of dying alone of old age in this house. I think I'll die carrying a load of laundry down the stairs, falling. I'll break my neck, and if I'm lucky I'll die instantly because otherwise I'll be paralyzed and I'll lie here by the drain on the cement floor in my own filth until I die of starvation, and by the time they find me I'll be partially disintegrated.

We have no food in the house. I make a mental grocery list. *Chocolate chips, eggs, bananas, ketchup, laundry detergent.* I sit down at my drums. *Yogurt, raisins, brownie mix.* I'll get two boxes of brownie mix. It's not like it ever goes bad. *Nuts.*

The basement is lit by a bare bulb, and it's too bright. It's too hot in here, and it hurts my eyes. I should put a lower-watt bulb in. *Light bulbs, chicken breasts, potatoes.* I pull the string to turn it off. Already it feels cooler. Buddy must have turned off the attic fan before he left. Saved thirty cents on our power bill.

I sit at my drums in the darkness, comforted by the thought that there are no phones here, and no windows. I am completely underground, completely alone.

I take off my denim jacket and drop it on the floor. I slip my feet out of my shoes, take off my earrings and my watch, and put them in a shoe. I listen to the hot silence of the empty house above me. I tell myself don't think, and I don't.

I pull my T-shirt over my head and throw it toward the dirty laundry. Slowly, my eyes are adjusting to the darkness. Everywhere I look I see black emptiness beginning to organize itself into shapes. I tell myself you can get used to anything.

I stand up, unzip my jeans, and slide them off, sitting down again. I touch my stomach, my arms. I hold myself. I reach forward with my left arm and move my right palm slowly from my wrist to my shoulder, then back down, touching the inside of my elbow both times. I do it again on the other arm. I take off my bra and touch my breasts shyly, first with my fingertips, like a self-examination, then like a caress. I cup them in my hands the way Jake did, then shake him out of my mind. I move my hands up my shoulders to the back of my neck and lift my hair. I close my eyes and arch my back, stretching out this slow pleasure.

I stand up and turn on the tape player as high as it will go without putting in a tape, and I hear static in the distance. I am surrounded by audible silence, visible darkness, moving toward me, closing in.

I wish I were dust.

I take off my panties and my wedding ring. I put in Jake's tape, pick up my drumsticks, and sit down at my drums again. His voice moves over my skin.

IT STRIKES ME AS ODD NOW, BUT IT WAS THE DAY PAW PAW
died of all days that I started plotting in earnest how I was going
to get Bo Schifflett, Junior. If it's the last thing I do—that's what I
said to myself.

Deedee was in hysterics and Uncle Mull was running around
crazy and Paw Paw was slumped over the kitchen table in his
bathrobe, and I just washed the dishes and went down in the
basement and climbed up on some old boxes like nothing had
happened. Then I got out my poetry notebook where before I'd
never written anything but poems and a flashlight and I sat there
in the dark and wrote Sylvia Schifflett, Mrs. Bo Schifflett, Junior,
and Bo and Sylvia Schifflett all over the page. I even wrote Sylvia
Mullins-Schifflett because that's what Deedee does, her name is
Deedee Henning-Mullins, but I decided Bo wouldn't go in for
hyphenating. He had a thing about feminists and Communists. I
could have turned on the light but it was just one of those times
where you'd rather sit there in the dark.

So I wrote all those Mrs. Schiffletts in my best, curliest hand-
writing, dotting the *i*'s with circles and hearts and little-bitty dai-
sies like Marylou Manderberry does, and I was making notes

about what color did I want my bridesmaids to wear, and who besides M'Lea would I get, and Mrs. Schifflett was going to be my mother-in-law so maybe I would have to learn Vietnamese, and all I had to do to make everything start falling into place was prove to Bo that I was a born-again Christian despite what I'd said on the phone the night before, which I figured shouldn't be too hard because I was, and everything would turn out fine.

I'd been carrying Bo's torch before Paw Paw got so bad sick, of course, but I think watching Paw Paw get sicker and sicker and skinnier and skinnier day after day and week after week to the point where you couldn't hardly even recognize him, and listening all that time to Uncle Mull and Deedee arguing about him, Deedee wanting to put him in the hospital, put him in a nursing home, anywhere but here in her house, and Uncle Mull saying Dee, they *said* there's nothing they can do for him, they *said* to bring him home and let him die in peace, and Deedee saying fine, let him die in peace, but this is not his home, and Uncle Mull saying Dee, like just her name was a warning, and Deedee saying do you want Sylvia to be the one to find him when it happens, do you want to do that to your own daughter, and me hiding in the basement where I could hear them better and thinking at least Paw Paw can't hear this because his hearing was pretty much shot by then and wondering what Memaw would have said to all this and wishing she were there—I think it was all that on top of itself that sent me off the deep end with Bo Schifflett, Junior, and I think Paw Paw dying was the straw that broke the camel's back.

At the time I thought Bo was my saving grace. Mrs. Tinkler said he was the salt of the earth, and he wasn't any taller than me but she said he was a spiritual giant, a man after God's own heart. It was so true that I didn't know I needed him at all, I just knew I wanted him badder than I'd ever wanted anything in my life. That's how in over my head I was.

Not having any way of knowing, of course, that at that very minute when I was sitting on my boxes in the basement under the kitchen where Paw Paw's body was, he was sitting on his bed with his Bible and his *Newsweek* and his Rapture notebook setting his own trap for me. And the other Rapture Watchers and the football team and his father and Nashville Christian Academy and Nashville and Tennessee and the United States of America and Canada and the whole entire rest of the world if he had time, except possibly Russia, which was the birthplace of the Antichrist so it was best in his opinion not to even bother with them.

Bo would never say why tempt fate because he believed in God, not fate, but that was his basic plan. Stay away from the Antichrist and get ready for Rapture Watch.

Paw Paw died Halloween night and they found him the next morning, but when I start trying to undo the whole thing in my head I have to go at least as far back as the last Wednesday in September at the second meeting of the Rapture Club. That's when I first planted doubts in Bo's head about my salvation which him finally asking me about it is what made me make the Roach-Prufe milkshake that killed Paw Paw.

There were still only four of us in the Rapture Club not counting Bo, which Bo said our having so much trouble getting anybody else to join was a sign of the times, but we had to persevere all the more because of it. So homecoming was a month away, and Bo said Nashville Christian Academy alumni from all over Tennessee were going to be there and he wanted to use the opportunity for the Lord, to get people fired up about the Rapture so they'd take the message throughout the state and beyond. He said has the Lord given anybody any ideas about how we could do that.

I didn't quite know what Bo meant, but at St. Clair County Middle School they always have a dance at homecoming and everybody gets all excited over it, blowing up balloons and stuff, so I said you mean like a dance?

And Bo said what kind of dance?

I didn't know there was more than one kind. I said just a regular dance, you play records and you dance. I was in trouble because I'd never actually been to one.

Bo said with rock music?

I said well, yeah, I guess so. I could tell he didn't like it, but I didn't know why.

Bo said Sylvia, rock music is the poison of the devil. It's a cancer of the soul. It gets inside you and it eats you alive like acid.

I said how. Because I really wanted to know.

And Bo said like he was explaining why we couldn't have a séance, we couldn't have a dance because rock music was sinful because between the beat and the words it led to concupiscence.

So I shut up. I didn't ask him what concupiscence was or whether country-western music was sinful too and I just hoped he'd never meet Deedee.

One of the other Rapture Watchers said what about a square dance.

And Bo said no dances, we're not going to have a dance.

So I said hey, why don't we have a Halloween party. Homecoming was going to be on Halloween night, and the idea hit me so fast right out of the clear blue sky I thought maybe it was from the Lord. So I started thinking up a costume party like the one M'Lea's mother gave M'Lea the year before, flipping through in my head what everybody from the St. Clair County Middle School seventh grade had worn so I could copy the best costume.

M'Lea's birthday was October 29, so she always had great birthday parties. M'Lea's mother said I believe in celebrating everyday life, that's all there is to celebrate, but she'd go crazy on holidays. So everybody in Riff Raff Acres got together and they decorated the whole mobile home park with ghosts and bats and witches and they all put their radios on the same station and put them in their windows and they got all the fish they'd caught that summer out of their freezers and they had a huge fish fry, the biggest one I'd ever seen. Everybody in Riff Raff Acres was always trying to feed M'Lea on account of she didn't have a daddy and they all knew about her mother and the Melba toast.

So I was thinking we could have a costume contest like M'Lea's and we could say if you come as a punk rocker—which half the people came to M'Lea's party as because it's the easiest thing—you're not going to win, and we could bob for apples and we'd set out big bowls of M&M's and peanuts and Cokes. And then it occurred to me that Marylou Manderberry lives out on a farm in Franklin, and maybe we could take a hayride out there after the game and have a bonfire and sing songs and roast hot dogs and maybe Deedee would even come out and lead the singing only I'd warn her beforehand about concupiscence and she'd stick to "Kum Ba Ya" and "Michael Row the Boat Ashore." I was thinking I could get her a songbook from Mrs. Tinkler before so she could learn them. I was also thinking hayrides can do something romantic to you and I was wondering what would all that do to Bo.

Meanwhile, Bo's looking at me horrified while I'm explaining all this and I know he doesn't get it, so I'm going into more and more detail trying to make him understand, explaining about bobbing for apples because I figure they don't do that in Tennessee and he's never heard of it and explaining how you do a hayride, saying you just fill up the back of a truck with hay and you ride around in it, only it's funner than it sounds because there's a lot of hay and people are sneezing and you're all packed in there and in Pell City they have them all the time at Halloween because it's just cold enough and you take the hayride out to a haunted house with people dressed up like monsters and dead people and vampires and scary music and maybe Marylou has a barn, she probably does, Marylou has everything, and we could turn it into a haunted house because I've always wanted to do that, to be dead with a cut-off hand and blood all over my face, dragging chains around—only Bo gets more and more horrified and his ears are always red on the rims but now they're solid red, tip to lobe, and I've been talking faster than I was thinking, this is the most I've said at one time since I got to Nashville, and finally I stop.

Bo doesn't say anything. He just looks at me like I've cussed or smoked a cigarette or worse, and finally he says I don't think our celebrating Satan's holiday would be appropriate.

Which shut me up fast. I wanted to say that's not how I meant it, Bo. But I didn't.

It turned out there was a dance in the gym after the game, though. They called it a Harvest Dance instead of a Halloween Dance, and there were hay bales under the basketball goals and red and yellow cardboard leaves on the walls. It looked more like Thanksgiving than Halloween to me, but I thought it was right pretty, for a gym. The Women of God decorated.

Nashville Christian Academy had won the game and it was

the first game that season they'd won, so everybody was running around crazy, pouring Cokes on each other, and we were all standing around in the gym waiting for the team to come in from the locker room but they were taking so long I thought maybe they're having a Bible study in there. But finally they came in, led by Terry Roberts and Coach Schifflett. Everybody was clapping and screaming and whistling and the cheerleaders weren't even in their costumes but they started a cheer, and pretty soon everybody was doing it with them. Crusaay-*ders!* Crusaay-*ders!* Cr'saay-*ders!* 'Saay-*ders!* Some people were in the bleachers, stomping their feet on the metal so loud it took over your heartbeat and you could feel it pounding through your head and your stomach like when you've run too fast, and everybody was clapping or punching the air with their fist, making the most commotion I'd ever heard in my life.

Except Bo. He just stood there, staring at his daddy and his daddy's arm around Terry Roberts, not moving a muscle. I thought maybe he was praying with his eyes open.

Then Coach Schifflett put out his hands palms down like he was saying go in peace, like Reverend Tutwiler used to do after the benediction, except Coach Schifflett was saying thank you, only you couldn't hear him, you had to read his lips, and finally people started calming down. Bo still didn't move, though. Then Coach Schifflett was standing in front of a microphone and he turned it on and it did that scream that microphones sometimes do which set everybody to cheering again, and then he put out his hands again and he said thank you again, but this time the microphone was on so you could hear him, and eventually everybody quieted down. By that time I already had a headache from the noise and I was pretty sure Bo did too, so I went over to him to see if he was okay.

Coach Schifflett started in on this speech about how proud he was of his boys, he couldn't be prouder of a group of guys for anything, and people kept interrupting him every other sentence to cheer. It was bugging me, so I could imagine it was driving Bo crazy. Coach Schifflett told the story of how the football team had endured the tribulation of summer practices, every morning in August at seven A.M., and they'd persevered through the heat and the rain and the sore muscles and they'd pulled together and they'd learned the meaning of the words discipline and commitment and teamwork. It got to the point where I thought to myself the Israelites themselves couldn't have suffered more getting to the Promised Land. Which was a sin because of bad attitude, but I thought it anyway, knowing even at the time I'd have to repent for it later. So he went on and on about their dedication and he kept quoting the Bible and explaining how it wasn't just a football victory—everybody cheered there—it was a spiritual victory, and God had finally made us all the victors. Everybody went crazy again.

By now he's already said he's proud of them a million times but then he turns toward the team—they're standing behind him like they're posing for a wedding picture, all lined up side by side, feet shoulder-width apart and hands clasped in front—and then Coach Schifflett takes the microphone out of the holder and it makes that scream which just about breaks my head open and everybody starts cheering again—'Saay-*ders!* 'Saay-*ders!*—and he quiets them down again with his hands and he turns to the team and he puts his arm around Terry Roberts and he says I want each and every one of you guys to know how proud I am of you and how much I love you. You're winners.

Then the whole gym goes out of control, chanting and stomping to the point where it was almost scary, like something could have broken, and Bo takes my hand and I follow him out the back door.

We walked all the way past the graveyard over to the football field without saying a word, which seemed like it took forever, and I could hear Coach Schifflett telling Terry Roberts he loved him as clear as if he was standing in front of my face, and without even asking I knew Coach Schifflett had never told Bo he loved him. Matter of fact, I was pretty sure he'd never told Mrs. Schifflett he loved her. Who he loved was Terry Roberts, and I didn't know anything I could say to make that any less terrible than it was.

Terry and Marylou were king and queen of homecoming, and Bo and I couldn't help knowing what Coach Schifflett was doing at that very minute, putting their crowns on their heads, shaking Terry's hand, calling him son, and kissing Marylou Manderberry on the cheek. We could hear the gym practically exploding with sound even with all the doors closed, and before I could stop it this picture ran through my head of the whole gym actually blowing up. It was a horribly pleasant thought.

Bo and I hadn't said anything. We came to the bleachers and Bo sat down and put his face in his hands and I was scared to death and I didn't even know what I was scared of, so I just sat down there beside him, wondering if it would help to pray since I couldn't think what to pray for and thinking it probably wouldn't since I still wasn't sorry about the Israelites, much less about the gym blowing up.

Finally the cheering died down in the distance, and it got real terrible quiet, and Bo said we've only got two months.

I said what?

He said two months until the end of the year, the Rapture's coming sometime in the next two months and I'm not doing enough to prepare for it, we're just not ready.

The Rapture Club had been slowly falling apart. In fact last meeting had been just me and him.

He said look at them in there, even my own father doesn't believe me.

I was searching through every thought I'd ever had, looking for something to tell him, but the only thing Bo hears is the Bible, and finally I said well, Bo, maybe it's like this. Maybe you're a lot like Jesus. I didn't think I was making any sense.

But Bo nodded and he said a prophet is not without honor except in his own country and in his own house.

I said yeah.

And he looked at me and he said Sylvia, you're the only person in the world who understands me, you're the only one who believes in me.

I thought boy. I was more confused than anybody.

We started walking back toward the gym. Bo had his hands in his pockets and I had mine in mine and it was a terrible kind of quiet. You could hear music coming from the gym as we got closer, only it felt like the music was a different world away and the only sound that really existed was me and Bo's feet on the gravel.

And then we were right outside the gym door and I could feel the music in my head, and before I knew it he'd kissed me right on the lips. I could feel the stomping in the gym through my feet and up my legs all the way to my female parts, and then he was gone.

It happened so fast I had to replay it in the mirror when I got home just to feel like I'd been there for it.

I stood there for a while, I don't know how long, trying to figure out what to do, waiting to see if Bo would come back, and I asked myself what would Christ do in this situation, what would

Amazing Grace do, but that didn't help. And then I thought I guess I'll just go on home.

Uncle Mull wasn't supposed to come get me until eleven o'clock, but I called him from the pay phone to come then, and I didn't even go back in the gym while I waited for him.

When I got home, I went straight to the bathroom and kissed myself in the mirror forty or fifty times, trying to remember every single detail and get that kiss fixed in my head so it'd last. After about thirty of them I remembered Bo's braces. He had railroad tracks and they'd hit against my lip and I was afraid maybe my lip had bled, maybe that's why he left so fast, but I couldn't see a scab. So I told myself he was just shy. I liked that about him.

Then I went in my room and lay on my bed and I couldn't stop saying to myself Bo Schifflett, Junior, loves me, Bo Schifflett, Junior, loves me. And I thought at that moment that as long as Bo loved me nobody could ever hurt me again. It was the happiest minute of my life.

I couldn't sleep, though. I couldn't think of sleeping. Uncle Mull had gone straight to bed and Deedee had a gig and would be out till all hours, so I got up and went back in the bathroom and looked in the mirror again. They had a tunnel of selves just like in Pell City, so I opened the medicine cabinet and put my face in the tunnel and let my mind wander down it thinking crazy thoughts like of all those me's, which one am I. Sometimes I think that's what happened to Mrs. Schifflett, she thought too long about something like that.

So then I closed the mirror and the tunnel went away and I washed my hands but I didn't wash my face so Bo's kiss would still be there, and I went in the kitchen. I thought about getting a snack only I didn't because I wanted to be thin for Bo. And the Rapture. I turned on the TV and turned it back off. I sat down at the kitchen table and flipped through Deedee's *Billboard*. I was just bored or something.

That's when I went into Paw Paw's bedroom. He was wide awake. He'd gotten to where he'd sleep three hours, then be awake for two, or sleep for one and be awake for three, but he'd never sleep through the night, so I went in there to see how he was doing.

He'd also gotten to where most of the time he'd smell pretty horrible, and he smelled so horrible that night that even with Bo's kiss and all those mirror replays fresh on my lips he gave me the creeps. Because it was like it wasn't Paw Paw at all, just some movie of him, like when you see old movies of yourself and you say did I really look like that? Only this was like a movie of Paw Paw ten years from now and you'd think is he really going to look like that? And then you'd say pull yourself together, Sylvia, he *does* look like that.

Plus he couldn't carry on a conversation anymore. For a while I'd tried to make him talk, asking him questions, trying to get him to tell me stories about the army or about me when I was a baby or Memaw or my mama. But that didn't work, so I'd gotten to where I'd go in there and I'd just talk, whatever came into my head. He couldn't hear too well, but I think he liked knowing I was sitting there talking.

So that night I told him we always play Westminster Presbyterian on homecoming, the only team in the state worse than us, and we'd won six to four. We made two field goals because we had a field goal kicker who grew up playing soccer in a boarding school in Canada for kids of missionaries before his daddy got eaten, and they'd sacked Terry Roberts in the end zone twice. Both times Terry'd rolled around on the ground for a while afterwards holding on to his private parts to the point where I thought maybe God was trying to tell him something about Marylou but which it turned out was just one of those things like the rain falling on the just and the unjust. When he finally stood up, everybody including Marylou cheered praise the Lord, and I watched Marylou's mother, who was sitting next to Terry's mother, lean over to Terry's mother and say bless his heart. I told Paw Paw pretty much everything that happened all night except Bo kissing me, which was private, but I did tell him about Bo's daddy and the speech.

Paw Paw knew all about Bo. I'd go in there every day after school and every night after I finished my homework, and I'd tell him all about how he wasn't going to have to die and how we'd all be together again soon, Memaw and my mama and the two of us, and we'd have a mansion and I'd have my own room there with a canopy bed and there'd be no more pain, no more sorrow, no more cancer or death or people fighting where you could hear them through the walls in the darkness. And you wouldn't have to wish somebody would love you and you wouldn't have to worry about that being wrong because Jesus would be there filling you up with love everywhere you turned around, like if God's love were sunshine you'd be sunburned inside and out, and you'd never be sad or mad or scared or lonely again. And just a little sunburned, like when Memaw would say the sun had kissed you. Not where it hurt.

So that night after I told Paw Paw about the dance I said you want a milkshake, Paw Paw. He couldn't answer, but I always asked him anyway, just to be polite, I guess. And then I went into the kitchen to make us some Slim-fast milkshakes. The kitchen was a mess and there were dirty dishes everywhere and the Roach-Prufe was sitting out—it comes in the same size can and it looks the same, just this white powder—and I cleared a space on the counter and I got two glasses out of the cabinet and I got the blender out of the dishwasher and I got the Slim-fast out of the pantry and I'd just started measuring out the Slim-fast when the phone rang.

I answered it on the first ring so it wouldn't wake up Uncle Mull, and it was Bo, and I said hey, Bo. Just hearing his voice made me feel fizzy.

But he didn't waste any time, he just went straight to the point, that's his way, and he said he was sorry.

I said you're sorry?

Yeah.

For what?

He took a big breath. For kissing you.

I said Bo, you don't have to be sorry.

I took advantage of you.

No you didn't.

You're my sister in Christ, and I treated you like you were just anybody.

I am.

I lusted after you, and it was wrong. I should have had more respect for you. Whoso looketh on a woman to lust after her hath committed adultery with her in his heart.

No it wasn't, Bo. I didn't tell Bo this, but the idea that he'd committed adultery with me in his heart was just about the most exciting news I'd ever had.

There was a long silence, and I could hear other voices on the line in the distance but I couldn't make out what they were saying.

Then Bo said Sylvia, I've got to ask you something important.

Okay.

Are you born again.

I knew what he meant, I'd been at Nashville Christian Academy long enough to know exactly what he meant, and I was mad. It's not good enough to be a Christian there, you have to have a conversion experience, preferably one that makes you cry when you talk about it. You have to have a before-and-after story with big differences, like I was on drugs but now I'm clean, I was a wife abuser but now I'm nice, I was blind but now I see, and I didn't have anything like that. I was only twelve years old, how could I have anything like that. My grandmama and granddaddy had taken me to church and taught me about Jesus since I was a baby, and I'd sung in the choir and gone to Sunday school and I'd always believed them and I'd always loved God, I mean really loved him the way I loved Paw Paw, like I would have done anything in the world to make him love me back, and I wasn't even mad about him taking my mama because Memaw'd told me God has his reasons but he loves you, and I believed it, I believed every word of it and I always had. And then I get to Nashville Christian Academy, and that's not enough. And now I find out if I love God, I can't have Bo, and it just seems like the last straw. So something snaps, something perverse goes off inside me, and I'm mad enough to cuss, I'm so mad I feel possessed and I don't know if it's a demon or Amazing Grace, but I say Bo, I'm a Christian, but no, I'm not born again.

In Bo's mind you can't be a Christian if you're not born again, so I've just committed blasphemy, and he's stunned. He doesn't even say huh.

So I say how could I get born for a second time when I wasn't ever even really born the first one?

He said what?

And I said you don't know everything, do you. You don't know I was cut out of my mama's dead body and thrown into an incubator limp as a rag doll and hooked up to life support and the same time the doctors were digging me out of her body the funeral people were digging her grave, so by the time I could breathe on my own, by the time I was really and truly alive, my mama was already flat buried six feet underground, so I don't even call that being born, I call it being snatched out of the safety of the arms of death and thrust into the horrors of being alive, and I'd have to be crazy to want to do that again.

I didn't know if that part about the incubator and the life support was true, I just made it up on the spot, but it sounded good when I said it. The whole thing sounded so good I thought I must have heard this in a sermon or a movie or somewhere before.

And for once in his life Bo doesn't know what to say. There's a silence where I think I can hear him swallow, and finally he says can you forgive me, Sylvia?

At the time I thought he meant for asking me if I was born again, and I said yes. But come to think of it, he might still have been stuck on the kiss. He'd do that—get stuck on things.

So then I hung up the phone and I didn't have any idea what to think and I felt just like when Memaw died, like you're not even upset because you can't really believe what's happened. So I finished making the milkshakes and brought Paw Paw's in to him and drank mine with him but I couldn't think or hear or see or taste anything because I felt like I was far, far away, and I was directing my body to drink that milkshake like by remote control. Then I kissed Paw Paw goodnight and went in the bathroom and washed my face and hands and threw up and brushed my teeth like I always did and went to bed. The only thing different was I got up in the middle of the night and threw up some more, but I didn't think anything of it except good.

And the next morning Paw Paw was dead and the milkshakes were gone and for the first time I noticed that Roach-Prufe right there on the counter right next to the Slim-fast and I knew what the shepherds felt like when they were sore afraid. I was so scared my arms hurt.

I kept trying to undo the night before, unraveling everything in my head from the speech to the kiss to the milkshakes to Bo apologizing to the throwing up to Paw Paw dying, and I would have given anything in the world if I could have just made it all not have happened. But of course I couldn't, and I didn't know what I should do and I didn't know what Christ would do or what Amazing Grace would do, but I knew what Memaw would do. Clean up your own mess. So I started cleaning. I put the Roach-Prufe under the sink and I put the Slim-fast back in the pantry and washed both our glasses out with soap and put them in the dishwasher and poured some detergent in there and turned it on even though it wasn't half full and I knew Uncle Mull would complain stop wasting electricity but I wanted to get my fingerprints off the glass and I wanted the Roach-Prufe not to be there, never to have been there, and all I could think was run the dishwasher.

I didn't tell a soul. I tried not even to think about it because God can read your thoughts, and everybody just figured it was the cancer. The doctors didn't even check him out, they were so sure it was cancer, and I didn't say a word. I just acted like the innocent victim, like the reason I was so upset was that my poor beloved granddaddy had died of prostate cancer which had spread to his intestines and then to his stomach and then his bones and I don't know where else and by the end had spread through his whole system. I just let everybody feel sorry for me, and I went down in the basement and wrote out my married name till I covered three sheets of paper with it and I listened to Deedee and Uncle Mull go on about the body and the coffin and the funeral and the insurance till I couldn't stand it anymore.

Then I put on Deedee's earphones just to shut them out only I could still hear them. So then I turned on her stereo and it was set to a rock station and I thought good. And I opened myself up and I turned the sound up as high as it would go and I tried to hollow myself out and let that music go inside me and fill me with poison and eat me alive like acid.

I didn't really want him to die. If I'd really and truly wanted him to die, he'd have been dead before then. Because since Memaw died and we'd moved in with Uncle Mull I'd stopped him three times from doing it himself. I'd hid his pistol in the toolshed and I'd flushed his sleeping pills down the toilet and up to a point I'd done everything a person could do. But then the thought that the world was about to end anyway and he'd go to heaven anyway, the thought that I should just let him do it came into my head, and I couldn't get it back out.

I'd say get thee behind me, Satan, but it'd just stick like gum on hair.

And it'd say this is what he wants, you got to do unto him as you would have him do unto you, and you can't know what you'd want until you've walked a mile in his shoes, but you know what he wants.

And I'd say no.

And it'd say what does it matter if Christ is coming back before the end of the year anyway, what's a few months.

I kept trying to fight it, I kept trying to do the right thing, only it was like a voice telling me don't make him keep hurting and hurting, sleeping every night in what's going to be your room after he dies, waking up every morning to another day full of pain, stinking up the house, do the merciful thing. It was like a talking serpent you know you're not supposed to listen to and you try with all your might not to, but think about it, if a serpent came up and started talking to you, wouldn't you listen? If for nothing else out of curiosity? You couldn't hardly help it. But I'd try with all my heart not to, and I'd say it's evil and I'd try to put it out of my head. But I couldn't help it, I'd just keep getting these pictures of myself getting the pistol out of the toolshed and putting it back in his drawer, or buying some more sleeping pills, the extra-strong kind, and putting them in the medicine cabinet—horrible, horrible thoughts I wouldn't have allowed myself to even think for one minute if I could have stopped them, only I couldn't.

And then the whole thing happened with the speech and the kiss and the phone call and the Roach-Prufe milkshake, and then he was dead.

Bo always said be careful what you pray for because you'll get it. Of course I'd never once in my life even thought of praying for Paw Paw to die, but sometimes I think maybe God read my mind anyway and he said whoso looketh on a woman to lust after her hath committed adultery with her in his heart, and that applies to murder too, so wishing Paw Paw was dead was the same as killing him. And I have to admit, terrible as it is, that the thought that I wished he was dead had flashed into my head before. I don't know why.

Only I'd also wished I could marry Bo and I'd pictured myself doing it, wearing this long white dress with a train that dragged all the way down the aisle and carrying a huge bouquet full of tiny pink roses and baby's breath and Marylou Manderberry being in the audience crying. I'd even prayed for it about a thousand times. And once Bo died I said to myself God might make you get some things you wish for, but that proves you don't get everything you pray for. I'd had my doubts before, but that was the first time I was sure.

Paw Paw was my second dead body, third if you count my mama. So Bo was fourth.

12

I CALL MY FATHER. IT'S BEEN SIX MONTHS SINCE WE TALKED.
I ask him what he's been up to.

Oh, nothing much, how about you.

Well, I got a promotion at work, I'm going to be in publicity now, and I'm trying to get some session work.

Really.

I can't tell what he thinks.

He asks who I'm going to be playing with.

I say he's a new artist, his name's Jake Harris.

Oh.

You haven't heard of him, but you will.

I wish I hadn't called. I *said* I'm *trying* to get some session work, it's not definite yet. He doesn't listen to me. Why can't I just hang up now.

He says well, you got to start somewhere.

I say he's going to be really big, they've budgeted over a hundred thousand dollars for publicity.

Hey.

I have no idea what Jake's publicity budget is, Sony probably hasn't even decided yet, I don't know why I'm making this up.

How much are they paying you.

I did get a raise, a small one, but I don't want to tell him. I wish I hadn't brought this up, I wish I hadn't called. I say I don't know yet, I just got the job.

Don't do it unless they pay you right for it.

I won't.

Hold out for the best because you're the best.

I'm not stupid.

They're just out to take advantage of young pretty girls like you, it's a dog-eat-dog world out there.

I say don't worry, I'm looking out for myself. I'm thinking who gave you a Harvard MBA, and what right do you have to tell me to protect myself.

He says that's my girl.

I'm not going to tell him how much I make. He had no right to ask, and I don't have to tell him. Jerk. If I did tell him he wouldn't care. Anything under six figures wouldn't be enough, although he's never made anywhere near that in his life. And if I ever did make enough to impress him, he still wouldn't see the point. The point is the music, the point is I'm doing what I want to do with my life. If the point was the money, I could have earned the same amount several times over doing just about anything else in the world.

Why does he make me so mad. I wanted to know what they'd pay me too. But it wasn't my first question. Maybe I'm the jerk. Maybe Buddy was right, I'm impossible to please, maybe he was just asking to show interest, concern. Yeah, right. My father.

I say I have to go, and hang up.

. . .

I was sick, I had a stomach virus, and I was in my bed and Uncle Mull came in and I pulled up the sheets around my neck. I didn't want him in my room.

He brought me a Coke and he put his hand on my forehead and he said are you going to be okay.

I didn't want him touching me. I said yeah.

He set the Coke down and I looked at him like get out of my room, but he didn't. He looked out the window and said without looking at me I'm not too good at taking care of sick people.

I said I can take care of myself.

Deedee was at work.

His eyes were working like flies, going from here to there to there, looking everywhere but at me, and then he was sitting on my bed and I stared at him like get off my bed now.

He said we haven't spent too much time together.

I didn't say anything and I didn't make a face.

He said you know, if you wanted you could call me Dad.

But I couldn't say it, I was sick.

I got up to run to the bathroom but I didn't make it.

Uncle Mull cleaned it up.

I kept telling him I was sorry and he kept saying he wasn't mad.

I pick up the phone again, look at the numbers I would dial if I called him back, then slam the receiver down like in movies. It doesn't help.

I take a walk around the office, partially to get my father out of my head and partially because it's late in the afternoon and I'm enough of a butt-kisser to think it's worth my while to let certain people know I'm still here. When I get to David's office, I pause outside and act like something's wrong with my shoe so he'll be sure to see me. I'm a jerk.

Jake and David are arguing about Jake's album on the speakerphone. Jake wants to use all his own material and David wants to do a mix. Jake wants very simple accompaniment, mostly acoustical guitar and vocals and some percussions, and David wants synthesizers. Jake doesn't want twang, and David says he didn't say twang, he said synthesizers. Jake just doesn't want to sound like he's wearing a cowboy hat. David wants to know who said a goddamned thing about cowboy hats. Jake wants to know if he's going to have any artistic control at all on this project. David asks what he wants. Jake would like to choose his own musicians, he's got a drummer in mind. Okay, David will take a look at his list of credits. She doesn't have a list of credits, she's new to the business. No, at a thousand bucks an hour David's going with an experienced professional. The person Jake has in mind is good, damn good. David doesn't care, if he hasn't done a lot of session work David isn't going to waste the money on him. Jake doesn't know how anybody gets experience with producers like David running the business. That's not David's problem. Jake signed with Sony because he thought David respected him as an artist, and now he doesn't get to choose his material, he doesn't get to choose his musicians. David wants to be blunt, he wants to know if he can be perfectly frank with Jake. Jake thinks that would be refreshing. David says I respect you as an artist, Jake, but grow up, this is business. David says artist like it's a cuss word. Jake says okay, from now on you do business with me through my manager.

I've seen this happen before. Jake's recording date will get moved back a month or two, his manager will talk him into compromising on the material, and David will throw in some minor concessions to make it look like he plays fair. Hopefully that's all.

I go back to my office and call Jake. I say I heard you going to bat for me, and I just wanted to say thanks.

He says you're welcome, but I didn't do it for you. I thought you would be the best person for the job, I think you have a good feel for my music, I think you're a talented woman, and I think somebody ought to give you a break.

Thanks.

And I think David ought to give me a break, I ought to have a little say on who plays on my own damn recording, not to mention what gets played. He's just the producer, it's my album, it's my career, it's my butt in a sling if we do a shitty job.

I'm sorry.

The man's a maniac. The man's an idiot. The man understands nothing of what I'm trying to do. He ought to be selling computers, he ought to be selling goddamn cars.

I promise Jake I'll try to use what little influence I have with David. I say sometimes he's not so rigid when he's had some time to think over the other person's point of view. It's a lie. We hang up.

I close my eyes.

I'm sitting on the dock at Riff Raff Acres with M'Lea. We're both wearing shorts, and we're hugging our legs. It's dark and hot and muggy with a cool breeze, and we're watching the lake being lit up with heat lightning like firecrackers. I think we should go inside, we could get hit by lightning, we could die. I'm not allowed on the dock when it's lightning.

But M'Lea loves heat lightning. She says it's not regular lightning, it won't hurt you.

I tell myself we're safe. M'Lea's mother would make us come inside if we weren't safe. I hug my legs tighter, and I can feel the lightning in my stomach.

A week later I get a note from Jake. *Thanks for speaking to David on my behalf. I guess you heard my recording date's been moved back two months and I don't know if I'll be able to use you on the drums. Sorry. See you in Oct. J.*

I tear up the note, wad up the pieces, and throw them away. He couldn't even write out the month. He couldn't even write out his own name.

I've been thinking he was coming to the Country Music Awards to see me. Why else would he come, his album isn't even recorded yet so obviously he's not up for an award, and every time he's mentioned it before he's said he was looking forward to seeing me in October, he couldn't wait to see me in October, it would be good to see me next month. And now two weeks before he says see you in Oct.

I tell myself he may have been in a hurry. He's got a million things on his mind, he's under a lot of stress, and he was just in a hurry.

He calls that afternoon, and when I hear his voice say my name I forgive his cryptic note. I say the Country Music Awards are coming up pretty soon.

He says yeah, I'm looking forward to it.

I think I hear affection in his voice. I say I am too.

He says I just heard from an old buddy who used to be in my first band, did I ever tell you about the Headbangers?

Yeah, when we were in Birmingham.

Right. I didn't know he'd kept playing, but he's in the business and he's going to be there and I'm going to have a drink with him.

I say how nice for you.

He says and my manager is going to be there, believe it or not I've never met my manager in person. Can you hold on a second?

There's somebody else in the room where he's calling me from, and it doesn't bother him, there's nothing he has to say to me that anybody else couldn't hear.

This means something totally different to him than it does to me. I've been working myself up to sleep with him, thinking he couldn't wait for it, he's replaced the bathtub man. When I can't sleep I put myself in his arms with his breath on my hair, our bodies folded together, and I feel his heart beating between my shoulder blades, his toes on my feet, and he whispers stories to me until I fall asleep. While he barely thinks about me.

I feel another depression moving in, and I hang up.

I take another walk around the office.

I need some fresh air, and I take a walk around the block. It's raining.

It's thundering and I'm standing in my room in the dark and my grandparents are in the kitchen where it's light and my nightgown is on backwards, pressing at my neck, and he's saying nothing happened. She says I saw and he says you're making this whole thing up out of thin air, it was nothing. She says my God, what kind of man and he says I was tucking her in bed, I was putting on her pajamas and tucking her in bed. Loud whispers.

I can't see them, but I can see the light from the kitchen creeping low down the hall under my door, and I can hear.

I stand in my room shivering. My fingers are cold. I open a window and put my face in the rain where it's quiet.

I walk back to the office through the rain holding my hand over my face.

I have to be wrong about Jake. Obviously I'm not thinking clearly. I'm not crazy, I think I'm not, but I'm not sure I'm completely in touch with reality either. Why else would I have these things, I don't know what to call them, these hallucinations. I don't know, but I have to pull myself together. I have to get a clear picture of what exactly is going on now, in real life, in the present. What's passed is passed. Think of forgetting the past.

I close my door and call him back. If I'm not wrong I may as well know it now.

I say hi, it's me.

He says hi.

I say I was confused about something you said earlier.

He says yeah, we got cut off, I was going to call you back.

Yeah.

So what are you confused about, Sylvia.

Are you alone.

Slight hesitation. Yeah.

Well, I don't know how to say it. Now I wish I hadn't called him back. What was I thinking. It's so obvious and I've been an idiot and I'm just making things worse, but I can't stop. It's like picking at a scab until it bleeds and then squeezing the blood out. I want to hear him say you mean nothing to me, Sylvia. You were a cheap thrill, you weren't even much of a thrill, and it meant nothing. I think I deserve that much. I say I just want to know if I'm in the same category as your old band member.

He laughs although nothing's funny. What are you talking about.

I mean when you think about me am I just your publicist, like you want to see me and your manager who you've never even met in the same way.

No, I didn't mean that.

Then what did you mean.

I'm looking forward to seeing you, what else do you want to hear, I don't know what you're driving at.

I think you do.

Trust me, I don't.

Okay, I guess I'm asking if our, if your feelings toward me are totally professional or if you have some affection for me.

I can't believe I'm degrading myself like this, asking a man who obviously cares nothing about me to tell me he cares about me anyway. I should forget him, I should quit my job and get a better job with a different label and really work at getting some session work and making some demos. I should just go on with my life and my marriage and not look back at this painful memory until years later when it will be one of those crazy things I did when I was young, an adolescent fling, and I can forgive myself and forgive him and enjoy the memory of how tender he was in the beginning.

But there's a part of me that can't do that until I hear him say it—no, I don't have any affection for you, I couldn't care less about you, I was just using you and now I'm done.

He says whoa, we have to be careful here.

I think what do you think I'm asking, I'm not flipping out over you, I'm not telling you I can't live without you, I'm just saying we practically made love, and now three months later all

I'm asking is whether you have any affection for me, not whether you're in love with me, not whether you want to marry me. Whether you have any affection for me at all. I don't think that's asking too much. I say I know, I'm being careful.

Long silence while he's waiting for me to say forget it, but I don't.

He says this isn't really the kind of thing we should do over the phone.

What does he think? We can't do it in the mail, neither of us wants a written record of this, and I don't think one discussion of our feelings in three months is too extravagant. I don't answer him.

He says well, I can't really say until I know how you feel.

Something hot rushes over me like a panic. I don't want to tell him how I feel. I don't know how I feel. If he had been wanting to see me the way I've been wanting to see him I would never have asked because I would have assumed like I've been doing for the past three and a half months that he felt what I did, but if he doesn't, I have to stop feeling this way, and the sooner the better, so I'm not going to tell him.

He says I asked for you to be my publicist because I believe you're a smart, talented, ambitious, hard-working woman. I respect you, and I wanted your talents working for me. I wouldn't have tried to get you promoted if you'd been great in bed but a bimbo.

I can't answer him. I know I'm not a bimbo, he doesn't have to tell me that. What I didn't know is that I got the promotion because he helped me. I'm not a bimbo, I'm an idiot. The thought had crossed my mind, but I told myself no, you earned this, you got the job because you were the best person for it, and now I don't know whether to be grateful or mad. It's not like I couldn't have gotten it without him, so what's so wrong with him putting in a good word for me. It was a nice thing to do. It's how things get done in this crappy business.

I also know I'm being defensive, and I don't feel like defending myself to him. The best thing is just to get the conversation over with as quickly and smoothly as possible and still leave room for a working relationship.

I say well, good, I appreciate your confidence in me.

He says wait a minute, I'm not saying I did this completely for my career advancement, I also thought it would be nice to have you in a situation where I'd get to talk to you regularly, see you occasionally.

Okay, thanks.

I mean we have to be careful.

I know that.

But yes, I still have some feelings for you.

I don't know why he's telling me this. Some feelings—what is that supposed to mean, I have some feelings about my dry cleaners. I say I have to go, and I hang up and go to the gym.

After dinner, Buddy and I make love with the lights on. I think he senses my urgency, or he mistakes my desperation for desire, which in a sense it is. But because of it or for reasons of his own he wants it as hard and fast and long and slow as I do, and when he says my name it sounds foreign, odd in its familiarity, and I come. And for the first time since Birmingham, I don't imagine Jake when Buddy comes inside me.

Afterwards we lie side by side on our backs, holding hands, and Buddy falls asleep.

I get up and turn out the lights. I try counting sheep, but I can't get them to keep moving after they jump the fence, and soon I have twenty sheep in a pile on one side of the fence and no more sheep will come near it.

I get up again, put on panties and a nightgown, wash my hands, and brush my teeth in the dark.

I HAVE FINISHED THE TENS, AND I GO ON TO THE ELEVENS.
Eleven times one is eleven. Eleven times two is twenty-two.

He keeps rubbing.

*Elevens are easy, you can watch the numbers line up in your
head. Twenty-two, thirty-three, forty-four.*

*I am naked and I'm covered with medicine and I'm tingling
and cold and he keeps rubbing and rubbing and rubbing and I
keep multiplying and he tells me I'm pretty.*

*Eleven times ten is a hundred and ten. I stop. I can't do
twelves.*

He says that's okay, we'll go over the twelves later.

I say I need to know my twelves, I have to know them now.

*He pushes my shoulder down. Right now you just concen-
trate on feeling better, then we'll do the twelves.*

Yessir.

Is your tummy feeling better.

Yessir.

*My stomach is not sick, but he keeps rubbing and rubbing, I
can't stop him from rubbing.*

How does your throat feel.

Fine.

Let me see.

I swallow, then open my mouth, and he shines a flashlight in me. He puts his finger on my tongue. He says say aah.

I force out something full of vowels. I feel like throwing up.

He moves his finger in my mouth. He takes it out and puts it in again, pressing my tongue up and down. He touches my teeth, and I'm searching my mind for the twelves, and he's inside my cheeks and I wish I could throw up and I might. Twelve times one is one.

I start going away. I can't move my body.

He lays the flashlight beside me on the bed and gets a cool washcloth. He wipes my face with it and it feels soothing and good and clean and I have come back. He folds it carefully and lays it on my forehead.

That feels good, doesn't it, he says.

Yes.

He moves it over my eyes. He is rubbing my stomach again.

He says let's put a fresh nightgown on you, that will help you feel better.

I don't move.

I feel my covers come off my feet and he touches my feet. He picks up both my feet in one hand and squeezes them like Play-Doh. He says we have to warm up these feet.

My underpants are on my knees, and he bends my knees. He is holding my feet, and my underpants come off and he says we'll get you some clean underwear, that will help you feel better.

Twelve times two, what is twelve times two, twelve plus twelve, add your twos.

He says I just want to make sure my little girl's all right, and he opens my legs. Be a good girl now. That's a good girl. That's a pretty girl.

I am a good girl, I am being a good girl, I do whatever he says, I always do what he says. I will learn my twelves and get well and take a makeup test and make a hundred and the teacher will give me a smiley face and I'll bring it home and he'll say that's my girl. Twelve times two is twenty-four.

Be a good girl and lie still and Paw Paw will get you a chocolate milkshake when we're through. Would you like a chocolate milkshake.

Yes.

He bends my legs and he puts one foot on each side of him and I am under the washcloth and I can't see him with my eyes but I see him. I see him pick up the flashlight and point it between my legs. I feel the light from the flashlight like it's hot and my feet are cold and my hands are cold and I can't move and I feel his hands on my legs where it's bright and he spreads open my dark place and the light touches me, hot, and his fingers touch me where it's bright and then inside where it's dark and he says you're a pretty girl. He has opened me up and the light goes inside me and it fills me with something hollow and it's hot in my stomach where it's bright and then his fingers, somehow his fingers go into me, like I'm broken, full of holes. I don't stop where I thought I stopped, and I feel his hands moving inside me, deep in my self, how did he get in there what is happening.

I can't look and I can't move and the washcloth starts to slip off my eyes and he puts it back but he's still inside me and I don't know how to get him out, and I don't know where he begins and where I end and I have too much inside me, first Jesus in my heart and now Paw Paw in my stomach and sometimes I think I hear someone else in my head and it's too much, and he keeps telling me I'm pretty, I'm a good girl and I'm pretty, now be still.

I am still. I have things moving inside me I can't stop but I am perfectly still. I am still as death.

That's a good girl, that's Paw Paw's good little girl.

I lie very still and I don't make a face. It doesn't hurt as bad when I'm still. I am sick and I'm sweating and it hurts but it's for my own good and it goes on forever but soon it will be over, it will be over soon.

Okay, I'll get you a milkshake in a minute, but we won't tell Memaw about it, right?

Nosir.

Memaw doesn't like you to have milkshakes in the middle of the day.

Nosir.

Especially not when you're sick.

No.

It's over. The washcloth comes off my eyes, and he's putting a fresh nightgown on me, my yellow one, and I lie there like I'm nothing and I let him do it.

It'll be our little secret.

Yessir.

Just between me and my pretty Sylvia.

I lie very still.

I think of my mother, who was dead with a living thing inside her. I killed my mother and then I lived inside her where she couldn't move and couldn't live and couldn't even die, and now I have become her.

THIS CAN'T BE RIGHT. THIS IS ALL WRONG. I CANNOT BE RE-
membering right, what is wrong with me. I'm either going crazy—
I'm not crazy, I'm just tired, I've been working too hard, I've seen
too many talk shows. Dammit, this is ridiculous. I'm just nervous
because I'm going to see Jake and I don't know how to think
about him.

Why would a person think this about somebody they loved.
It's sick. It makes me sick, I make myself sick.

I can't even remember the milkshake. If it really happened I
would be able to remember the milkshake after, you should remember a thing like that. But I think milkshake and I draw a total
and absolute blank.

What is happening to me.

I pick up the tweezers and pluck some stray eyebrow hairs.
I have hair on my stomach, dark brown hairs in a row like
an overtweezed eyebrow. It's the most disgusting thing I've
ever seen. I pull them out. I wish I could get my whole body
waxed.

I turn on the TV. Another talk show, another celebrity talking about being molested as a child. What is wrong with people

like that, don't they have any sense of shame, decency. And it's not fair. The people they accuse always deny it and nobody ever believes them, but what if they really didn't do it? What if the celebrities are really mad about something else and they made this up, or they want to get on the cover of *People,* or they're just insane? That's not right. The people being accused get no defense. It's un-American. You're supposed to get a fair trial, you're supposed to be presumed innocent, this country was founded on the presumption of innocence and now it's all shot to hell. It makes me sick.

Why would you go on national television to talk about a thing like that, why can't they just leave it the hell alone instead of turning themselves into cheap time-fillers for talk shows that measure their success by how many maxipads they can sell. They're worse than prostitutes.

I turn it off.

I look at the blank screen, and I feel like it's staring at me, watching my every move. I think fuck you and feel slightly better. Fuck you. I say it out loud.

I think about telling Buddy, Buddy saying what is wrong with you, and me saying fuck you.

I think about going on TV to talk about my grandfather and the talk show host asking if my husband is being supportive and me saying he doesn't believe me, and I realize why people do it. Revenge. Any audience would take my side.

I wouldn't talk about this on TV to save my life, but if I did I would lose some weight first. TV adds ten pounds.

I put on more mascara and some perfume. I open the closet door and look at myself in the full-length mirror. I have on too much makeup, I look like a slut. At least I don't have any hair on my stomach. It's a cheap mirror, and it's distorting my stomach.

Someday I'm going to buy a full-length mirror from somewhere other than Wal-Mart and Buddy's not going to say a damn thing and I'm going to look in it and I'm going to see what I really look like, it's going to be a three-way mirror, and by that time I'll be thin. When I sell my first song, that's what I'm going to buy with the money. No matter how much it is, I'm going to spend the whole amount on a mirror.

I want to be thin. I want to be pretty. That's why I put on too much mascara, I was just trying to look pretty.

I look at my arms. I pull the fat back under my armpits to see how I'll look when I'm thin. I feel like crying.

I have to stop this. I'm just nervous. I'm excited and I'm nervous. How many cups of coffee have I had today. My hands are shaking.

I go in the bathroom and throw up without trying. I look in the mirror. It was a stupid idea. I'm not going to buy a new mirror. I'll put it in a savings account, only in my name. Or I'll buy some stock, if there's enough. I wonder how you buy stock. Maybe I'll buy a tile floor for the kitchen. I hate linoleum. You can't get it clean, it has built-in grooves that hang on to the dirt and you have to put stuff on it to make it shine, so it seals in the dirt and over the years you build up layer after layer of sediment and you could excavate it and uncover your whole pathetic little history but what would you find, no fossils, no treasures, no buried civilizations, just dirt. Just goddamned dirt.

I look at my watch and brush my teeth quickly. I dig some Scope out from under the sink and swallow it. I take the price tag off my outfit and stuff it to the bottom of the trash so Buddy won't see it. I step into the dress and zip it up.

. . .

Buddy meets me in front of the Opryland Hotel, and the first thing he says is dammit, Sylvia, I shelled out $78.50 for this monkey suit and you've got people here wearing goddamn blue jeans.

They're not blue jeans and those people are stars, Buddy. I could say something here about him being fifteen minutes late. I could say something about how much trouble he made me go through to get him a ticket without even thanking me when I told him it wasn't his kind of thing, but no, he just had to see Garth, and I don't think telling him to dress appropriately when my boss is here and my coworkers are here and everybody who is anybody in my whole industry is here, I don't think that's asking too much. But I don't. I'm not going to fight with him tonight. We're in public, and it's not worth the effort even if we weren't.

He says I don't recognize them.

Well, they are.

What difference does it make, if Waylon Jennings can wear blue jeans why can't I?

I'm sorry, Buddy. I'm sorry I made you wear a tux, I'm sorry I made you get a haircut, I'm sorry you're here, okay? But there's nothing we can do about any of that right now so can you just please forget about the tux and have a nice time?

He's visibly sulking, struggling with his bow tie like it's about to kill him, and I try to maneuver us to our seats in the Opryhouse before I have to introduce him to anybody.

After the awards Buddy says he has to go home and get to bed, he drove two hours to get here tonight and he has to leave for Atlanta early tomorrow.

Buddy, I have to stay for the parties, it's my job.

Fine, stay.

I see Jake on the other side of the lobby, and I feel him moving toward me as Buddy walks out the revolving door. I feel lighter as soon as Buddy is out of the room.

Buddy's waiting for his car while Jake and I kiss hello professionally. Jake tells me how beautiful I look as Buddy gets into his car. I believe him.

He says you're here alone?

I had told him Buddy might come. I say yeah.

He smiles, and I'm smiling back.

I say are you.

He is. I knew that.

It's crowded, and we get shuffled into the ballroom, and then we're standing beside a buffet table and I pick at the food because I'm nervous. It's a loud party, there's loud music and everybody's screaming at each other. Sometimes people scream and then hug each other, which reminds me of high school and gives me a sick feeling. Jake introduces me to Barbara Mandrell, who is prettier and thinner and older and shorter than I expected. I don't know how he knows her, but I get a glimpse of his life and how much bigger his is than mine. I think about telling Buddy I met Barbara Mandrell, but I don't know if I will. He wanted to meet Garth Brooks.

Waiters keep pouring champagne. Miller comes up and kisses me on the face and I kiss him back like I've been watching everybody else do only I don't scream. He stumbles a little and I try to hold him up and I slosh champagne on him, but his tux is damp where I grab him as if he's been sloshed several times already tonight and doesn't much care. I look at Jake like I need help, and he introduces Miller to some other woman, who Miller immediately starts kissing. Jake takes my arm and begins to steer me out of the room. I follow his lead without asking where we're going because the band has gotten louder and I couldn't hear his answer anyway. Sony is giving a private party at a club downtown, and I figure Jake may be wanting to head on over there.

When we get to the lobby he says didn't I once promise you chart-reading lessons?

This is the first time either of us has referred to anything that happened in Birmingham, and I'm flustered. I say oh, that's all right. We're walking toward the elevators.

He says you ought to learn.

I say really, Jake, it's okay. I'm shaking my head. We get in the elevator and I'm nervous and I start talking. I tell him I do want to learn to read charts but it's not something he should worry about, I have people here who can teach me, tons of people, it's just that I've been so busy lately, what with work, you wouldn't believe how swamped we've been, and this week of all weeks, Andrea, the only competent secretary in the publicity department, has had jury duty—and then the elevator doors close and we're kissing again and his tongue makes me think of a hummingbird.

The elevator dings and we straighten ourselves and the doors open to an empty hallway.

I've missed you, Sylvia, he says.

I can't answer him.

We go to his room and I'm nervous and I don't know how I smell, I ate something oniony at the party, and he kisses me softly on the cheek. He takes off his jacket and hangs it on a chair, gets some papers out of his suitcase and drops them on the bed, and I lean against the wallpaper and look at them and I feel the champagne like it's in my hair.

He goes to the mini-refrigerator and gets out another bottle of champagne, asks me if I'd like some. His back is to me, he's not looking at me.

I say okay and take two cups off the dresser and start unwrapping them because I want to be busy. They're tied in tissue paper with ribbon, like presents.

He opens the champagne and I hold the glasses while he pours, and I like it that he doesn't say cheers or make some stupid toast. He looks at me while he drinks and I look at him looking at me and we don't say anything.

I sit on the bed and pick up the pages. It's the song about fading love he was working on before, only he's finished it now. He has the words on one page, and the other page is all numbers, mostly fours and ones and a few fives, arranged in groups of four. I look at the chart, then at Jake.

He says it's not hard, do you read music?

No. I'm blushing.

That's okay, it's basically that one is the key it's in, so if you're in A, then one is A, two is B, three is C.

One is A.

When you see a one, play an A chord.

Okay.

And if you're playing and somebody says change to C, then you're in the key of C, and now C is one and D is two. You just need to learn your scales so you'll know when to play sharps and flats, although you already know which chords go together, so you can figure it out.

It's like learning to read. All the sudden all those squiggles make sense.

You're a fast learner.

And this means what? I'm pointing to a plus sign.

It's an augmented chord. Hold on. He gets his guitar and

shows me. He says if you're doing drums you're not really going to need to follow the chord changes, but you'll want to know what the other musicians are doing so you can communicate with them.

I'm reading his song and I can hear the numbers and I say this is wonderful.

He says you want to try it on the guitar?

I start playing and I remember the tempo from Birmingham and he sings and something happens. I hum a soft backup and he uses his guitar case for drums and our bodies go out and there's just the music filling up the room, and my playing and his singing and my singing and his playing all come together into one and the harmony is physical, you can feel the rhythm bouncing off your skin like in ultraviolet photographs, everything bigger than itself, merging with everything else, and your boundaries dissolve and it opens you up and it seeps past your skin through your muscles into your bones and you start to feel weak, and you give yourself over to it and it takes over your body and it pulses through you like echoes.

When it's over, we look at each other and we can't talk and I'm too aware of my breathing.

He puts the charts and the guitar in its case and slides it onto the floor and the music is starting to disintegrate and my body is coming back and it's over and a little awkward and I should say something but I can't think of anything.

He says you're a natural.

I smile and shake my head.

He says you're a very talented woman, and I believe him because he means it and because it's coming easy to me and not just because he's a good teacher.

He says you anchor me and I can communicate with you,

Sylvia, and you understand my music. I really want you on my album.

I tell myself it's happening. A whole new world is opening up. And I feel afraid.

Then we're fully clothed, lying on his bed, holding each other, and I could fall apart and I want him to hold me together.

He's kissing me, and I get flashes of my front yard where I've been meaning to plant flowers for the past few months. I meant to plant bulbs last fall, daffodils and tulips, and I was going to do it right, spread bone over them or whatever it is you're supposed to do with bones. He's kissing my shoulders, my collarbone, and I can feel him in my ribs, I'm too aware of my skeleton, and I wonder if bonemeal is actual bones and what kind of bones— probably chicken, or cows maybe, or maybe it's not bones at all, maybe it's chalk. I feel my bones turning into meal and I feel him ossify in my hand and I wonder if I really want to plant bones in my yard, like I live in a graveyard. I wonder if it would attract dogs.

He's kissing my arms, he touches his tongue to the insides of my elbows, and my fingers move in his hair and I feel the shape of his skull and I'm coming open.

I think of Buddy, flicking his ashes into the yard as he heads into the house, grinding his butt into the dirt with his heel. I think of the front yard opening up, cataclysmic, a big crack down the middle like a tear showing black, utter nothingness underneath. Then it grows and I can see the center of the earth, the red, hot burning without oxygen that is the core, and then Buddy falling in, pulling at the grass, tearing out onion weeds as he goes, calling my name like an oath before he's swallowed completely and the yard closes in over him and zips itself up.

I sit up suddenly and call out something full of vowels, the kind of thing people call out in passion, and Jake unzips my dress.

Two days later my period comes. It's early, and the flow is heavy and painful and it feels like my body is trying to empty itself, turn itself inside out. I try not to wonder if it's more than this. If it's a miscarriage. If it's symbolic. If my body is doing penance. The ache is comforting to me in the sense that it's the only thing that seems appropriate in my life right now. This goes on for a week and a half, and I start to feel anemic.

At night I dream of leathery prehistoric creatures with long curved necks and bodies that are somehow hidden but I know they're big enough for me to fit inside. I could be eaten, and I want to be. I want to be torn apart as I go in and then pull myself back together inside, nourished by the blood of a vanished species, stained red. I want to curl myself up there and go to sleep, then wake up to find myself being slowly, painlessly digested, transformed. I want to know what it's like to be extinct.

I want to be swallowed whole by a whale and I want to live in its belly and breathe through its blowhole. I want to be spit up on the shore of some exotic island, bleached white from digestive acids, and shining, a miracle.

I want to be presumed dead.

I want to live in a cave with a great big boulder rolled over the door, a warm cave so small you have to creep everywhere and there's straw on the ground for sleeping and a spring for bathing and you don't need to eat, you don't want to eat, you have everything you want, which is nothing, and you never lose anything because you have nothing to lose.

I want to live in a dead cave and sleep on dead leaves, hibernating, healing, drawing on secret reservoirs inside myself for sustenance, just barely surviving while everything around me rots into nothingness and I suck the life out of the air.

I want to be rock solid and deep and cavernous and dark.

I want to be locked in, safe.

I want to hide in the center of the earth and to find me you have to open layer after layer after layer, inside what's inside what's inside, like papier-maché eggs.

I want to dig a bomb shelter for myself and live underground, unseen, alone.

And I don't want anyone to touch me and I don't want anyone inside of me anywhere and I don't want to be inside of anyone and I want to know the whole world could blow up and I could be buried alive and I'd survive.

I don't want to have sex with anyone, I don't want sex to exist, and I don't want to be pregnant, I don't want somebody else's bones inside me, I don't want his heart inside me, beating inside me, pulsing, his hands moving, opening, grasping, sucking, and I don't want cancer or God or Buddy or Jake or my grandfather or any man or anyone or anything ever to come inside me again. I want to be inviolate, inviolable, indestructible, closed.

I want to go into a coma and wake up in the next century, a new woman in a new world, and I want to have to learn all over again how to walk and how to talk and who are the people I love.

At night I can't sleep and I just want to be held, but I don't want Buddy to touch me. I don't want anybody who's real.

I woke up screaming once as I slid down the throat of a reptile. Buddy stirred in his sleep, rolled over, adjusted the covers. I tried hard to go back to sleep, back to reptilian dreams.

I always think about suicide when I'm depressed. When you feel that dead inside, suicide is a comforting idea because it seems true in the way that the rest of the world is a lie. It's the only thing you can think of that would even you out. There's something almost sexual about the attraction, like a one-night stand. It seems like it would create that kind of release of tension and passion and anger and everything else inside you and if you could find some way to keep from feeling the physical pain of it and still be fully aware, then the moment your soul finally freed itself from your body, opened you up and tore itself out, would be like the ultimate climax.

And then it would be over, and you'd be transformed with a new mind and a new body into a new world, a whole new reality, and you'd never have to think about it again.

But until now, it's always been in the abstract. I have known there were certain limits beyond which I would not go. I would not sleep with another woman's husband. I would not kill myself.

I think about Jake's sister.

I think about what Buddy would do, whether he'd feel just a little bit relieved. He could start over. He is nothing if not resilient. He'd show up at my funeral just barely drunk and somebody, some morbid matchmaker, would already know at the funeral who he'd be dating next. There's something terrifyingly romantic about widowers. Buddy, a tragic figure. One of his middle-aged friends' wives would invite him over to dinner, where she also just happened to invite her cousin or her younger sister, a nurse from Murfreesboro. The younger sister would have been told about me, of course. And nobody would blame Buddy. It turns out, they would say, she was abused as a child and she never was very stable. Then she had an affair and went crazy. No, then she went crazy and had an affair and killed herself and Buddy, poor Buddy, there wasn't a thing he could do. Tore him apart, literally tore him apart. He was absolutely devoted to her.

And Jake would go on with his singing career and go back to his model wife and model daughter and model life and never so much as write a song about it.

I asked him if he'd ever write a song about it.

He said no, but you will.

I said you wouldn't mind if I did?

He said not if you make it a good one.

I wanted to know how he was so sure he'd never write about it, how could you be a writer and know you're not going to write about it, the only way is if it meant nothing in the first place. So I didn't ask. I didn't want to hear it.

Sony would get a new publicist, but I'd mess up the files before I left.

My father would feel sorry for himself. I must have gotten this from him.

On top of everything I was terrible. He said so himself, he said are you this inhibited with your husband.

I had thought about buying condoms, paying cash, tearing up the receipt, putting them in my purse, sitting through the awards next to Buddy with a package of condoms in my purse, but I couldn't do it. So I thought maybe Jake would take care of it or we'd go to the Sony party first and then we could get some on the way back to the hotel and I didn't know for sure we'd need them at all, it wasn't that planned, this was all just in case, and then I had this crazy idea that I knew wasn't true but I thought maybe the hotel would provide them with the shampoo and the sewing kit because which is it more likely you'll need unexpectedly. But they didn't and he didn't, and we were on his bed and my clothes were off and his shirt was off and the lights were on and I said I want you to make love to me and it felt funny to say it even though I'd thought it a thousand times and I'd wanted to say it because I'd never said it to a man before and he looked surprised and I thought didn't you know, but he didn't mind, it was a pleasant surprise. But then I thought it would have been okay with him if we didn't and I knew he didn't have condoms and I wasn't so sure anymore but what could I do, this is in the middle of kissing and his socks are coming off and his cummerbund and then we're completely undressed and I don't know if it's a matter of proportion like Buddy has a forty-six-inch waist and Jake's is closer to thirty-three or thirty-four, I guess, but not everything is smaller and I try not to show it but Buddy's the only other man I've seen and people say size doesn't matter but it's a pleasant surprise anyway and it makes me curious. So you try to put the lack of condoms in there and I can still feel champagne bubbles popping in my ears, in my hair, on my neck, and his hands go through my skin to my nerve endings and my bones are like chalk, disintegrating into dust every time they move, and I say we need a condom, I pull the sentence out of another room, and he doesn't stop kissing me and he mutters we don't have one, I'll be careful, and we're still kissing and he likes long kisses that Buddy doesn't have the patience for and I say shouldn't we get one and he says there's not as much pleasure for the man, which has never bothered Buddy, and I think yes there is if it keeps me from being scared to death but what am I going to do, and he says he'll be careful and he is careful. He's very slow and very gentle and he doesn't do anything that hurts and he keeps looking at my face to see what I like and he would never hurt me and it's too late and I open myself up and he comes in and just being there he fills up the hollow part with something like pink.

And then I can't. I'm splitting in two, then in a million pieces. I'm too many, and part of me is under him, melting into him, reverberating against his chest, and then I see an AIDS commercial, I see another part of myself looking straight into the camera, saying I'm HIV positive, it can happen to you, and I see Buddy sitting in his chair watching TV, folding the newspaper and slapping it onto the floor.

I'm standing in the kitchen, wearing shorts, stirring something on the stove. No matter how much they give them, he says, they want more, when that money could be going to cancer research, heart disease research. I say Buddy, do you know how many people have AIDS. He says yeah, but look how they got it, you have to be an idiot to get it. I say you think there are that many thousands of idiots in this country. At least, he says.

I couldn't tell him, I'd just have to leave, disappear into a Third World country. You didn't even know how many people he'd slept with, how could you be so stupid, what happened to your brain. Then he'd open a beer. Christ.

I hear Mrs. Tinkler at Nashville Christian Academy. If you have sex outside of marriage, girls, you will get syphilis and tuberculosis and you will go crazy and die. Now how many of you want that.

I see my grandfather in his pajamas opening my bedroom door, pulling me out of sleep, giant and glowing from the hall light behind him.

Coach Schifflett muttering durn fool, holding a football, winking at a cheerleader, his muscles looking flexed and dangerous even when he was relaxed.

Bo Schifflett, Junior, with his Bible and his *Newsweek* and his Rapture Club notebook and his red ears. I see Bo Schifflett, Junior, kissing me outside the gym, his hands still in his pockets, and I hear his voice crackly over the phone at the same time. He's sorry.

My father asleep in front of the TV after another long day, and I tiptoe around the kitchen, my feet heavy like books dropping.

And I see Buddy. Buddy mowing the grass, driving the car, making coffee, Buddy sleeping beside me in bed, trusting. I hear him snoring.

I see my father and Deedee and Deedee's lingerie on the clothesline in the basement and my grandfather slumped over the kitchen table and I feel him in my stomach and I see myself as a child asking Jesus into my heart, please forgive all my sins, erase my old life and let me be born again and come live here in my heart. I'm repeating the words after my teacher, pointing to my heart, and I feel him there when it beats. She says today is your spiritual birthday, Sylvia, and she hugs me tight.

I see Buddy sitting across the table from me at dinner, cutting his steak, talking about dry walling and bottom lines and politics and whether to buy the Jacuzzi now or next year, Buddy in the shower, his arms and his stomach soft and soapy, Buddy stepping into the shower with me, kissing me, but I can't do it standing up, it hurts.

I see all their faces rushing past me like I'm drowning. I feel their faces rough on my skin, and I hear the purring sound they make when they brush my cheek.

I see my face, thousands of my faces blinking in unison, splitting, diminishing down the dark tunnel of selves, and I can't go on, I have to stop.

I push him away and I can't look at him and I say I have to stop.

I'm afraid he'll be mad now and I look at him and I see his eyes and I'm waiting, I'm even curious to know what he's like when he's mad. But he isn't. So I want him to hold me and I say will you just hold me and he doesn't ask why, he just does it, he holds me tight and gentle and long and he says you're just starved for affection and I've never thought of myself like that but it seems sort of true in a terrible way I don't want to admit and he doesn't ask me to say anything and he's so gentle he wouldn't have hurt me, he would never do anything to hurt me. Only he couldn't have helped it, he can't help it.

He says are you okay.

I laugh, sort of, and I say I'm okay.

He says are you sure.

I'm shivering.

He says are you cold, you want me to turn up the heat.

No, I'm okay.

Are your feet cold, you want me to warm up your feet. He reaches for a foot and I straighten.

No, I'm okay.

Then he moves his hand and I say no, just hold me and he holds me. I like the way he holds me. He says are you this inhibited with your husband.

No. I move. I say but he's my husband.

He says okay, relax. Look, I'm not going to hurt you, we're not going to do anything you don't want to do.

I'm sorry, I just—

It's okay, you don't have to be sorry.

I think he's afraid of me.

I can't explain. I'm all messed up inside and my mouth is dry and I keep thinking he knows things I don't know, he's expecting me to do something that's never occurred to me. I've never even watched an X-rated movie and he's been with how many other women, and I'm worried about the condoms, I'm not on the pill, he probably thinks I'm on the pill, and I can't stop thinking about

Buddy so I'm trapped in a cycle—when I'm with Buddy I can't stop thinking about Jake. I can't put my whole self in one place anymore.

I just want to fall asleep in his arms and wake up another person, wake up married to him, wake up with Buddy and the whole thing was a fantasy. I want what we're doing to be okay.

I have to say something, so I say I don't feel good enough.

He says you're good enough.

You're just being nice.

No I'm not.

Yes you are, you've been with other women, you could be with another woman right now, I saw how women were looking at you downstairs, and other women don't do this, but I'm not like other women.

Well, that's true, I've never met a woman like you. He's laughing.

I look at the wall.

He says Sylvia, and he turns my face. He says it's okay, everybody has their hangups.

Like what. We're lying side by side now, facing each other, our hands touching. I don't know why I asked that.

Like, well, there was this waitress I met in a club where I was playing one time, her name was Sherry, and she wouldn't let me take off her bra.

I don't say anything.

And this UCLA undergraduate, Ann, she had a great body, but she wouldn't do it with the lights on, it had to be pitch black, she wouldn't let me look at her.

I don't make a face.

She was the one who kept calling me afterwards.

I say the fan.

Yeah, and there was this Mormon, former Mormon, I guess, she was from Utah, what was her name, she wouldn't move when she came.

What was her name.

What *was* her name, I can't remember, but she wouldn't move and she wouldn't make a sound, either. I had to do all the work.

I say you're going to forget my name. It's not a question.

No I'm not, he says.

I lie very still. I make my face be still. I think maybe he needs to do this. I tell myself lies, like he cares so much about me it hurts, so he needs a defense mechanism to distance himself from me so he tries to put me in the same category as meaning-less affairs that were nothing but sex whose names he can't re-member.

But I don't care, I don't want to hear it. I think about asking him to shut up. I think about sitting up and screaming what kind of shit would forget the name of a woman he'd fucked. But I don't. I don't want our last few minutes to be full of accusations and recriminations, negotiations of apologies.

It doesn't matter anyway. I'll never do this again, so what does it matter.

I try to memorize his face. There are parts of tonight I will want to remember.

He starts kissing my hair, very softly, very tenderly picking up my hair and kissing the ends. I like the way he kisses my hair, like he's never heard of split ends. I will remember the way he kissed my hair.

He says enough about former lovers.

I say Jake, I can't do this, I have to go.

He knows. He rubs my back like a cat's and he says okay,

Sylvia, and I feel stung by my name, accused by it, and he lies there in bed watching me dress, watching me fumble around the sheets for my panties, watching me pull on my pantyhose and hook my bra and zip my dress like some kind of bizarre backward striptease, watching me and my mirror image brushing our hair, putting on lipstick.

I put my brush in my purse and come to him. I want it to end sweetly. I kiss him softly on the lips and I say I'm sorry, but I have to go.

He doesn't say anything, and he kisses me for the last time and I close my eyes. I can still close my eyes and feel his breath on my face.

Then I take the long way home, half hoping to get hit by a truck.

I think about nothing. I concentrate on it.

I think of Bo Schifflett, Junior. Bo tapping his Bible saying Jesus was perfect and he was human, God and man become one, the Word made flesh. I said if he was perfect what was human about him. Bo's ears turned red and I said never mind.

I think of taking Communion, the taste of sweet grape juice and those little floury squares on your tongue and the preacher saying do this in remembrance of me and the whole church drinking shot glasses of grape juice at once, our hands moving in a loud mumble to our mouths.

I think that's what was human about him. Nobody wants to be forgotten.

There was nothing in this world I could have done to make Jake remember me, except possibly what I did.

I think of my mother, driving herself and her lover and her unborn baby into a train.

Buddy's asleep when I get in, and I take a long, hot shower and scrub myself raw with a loofah sponge. I crawl into bed beside him and lie there wide awake until dawn, a new depression creeping over me like the sun sulking in through the curtains.

By the time Buddy's alarm rings I'm deep in a hard, terrible sleep, the kind that gives you a headache when you come out of it.

When he gets out of the shower he asks me if I want some coffee, he says I look like I need some.

I can't think what to answer. I tell myself just act normal, what's a normal answer, but I feel like he's speaking through a long, dark tunnel, he's calling from the top of a well I've fallen into, and I keep falling, my eyes won't focus, and I pretend to go back to sleep.

Once, after the eleven o'clock service, my grandmother and I went into the church kitchen. I don't remember why. And on the counter I saw thirty or forty empty bottles of Welch's grape juice with purple cartoons of grapes on the labels like musical notes. The grapes may have had faces with goofy teeth, I can't remember. But I felt an impulse to cover them up like if you saw a dead body.

It was just grape juice.

I'd always thought it was something else.

I put my finger in my mouth to get the Communion wafer out of my teeth.

I was terrible the first time with Buddy, too, but that was on purpose. Part of his attraction to me was his belief that I was more or less untouched by human hands. This after his first wife had been unfaithful to him.

And I was a virgin, I think. Whatever that is. I just wasn't completely clueless. He started touching me and showing me where to touch him and he wanted to be the only one there who knew, who had any idea what to do. I'd expected the same thing, I had thought I'd feel lost and I'd need him, but halfway through I had this horrifying sense that it wasn't the first time, the first time had been erased.

He'd bought me a long white lacy nightgown and I went in the bathroom to put it on and I washed myself with a washcloth and I left my panties on the counter and I put perfume on my legs and he didn't take it off. I had thought he would take it off, I wanted to stand there, barefoot, and feel the straps come off my shoulders and slide down my back and I wanted it to land in a white halo at my feet and I'd take his hand and step out of it. But he left it on. Pulled it up around my stomach and left my breasts covered.

After, I kept wanting to try again. I thought the second time wouldn't hurt as bad, but I didn't think of telling him that was why. He rolled over and said Sylvia, you just don't understand, men can't do it again that fast.

I think he wanted me to bleed. If it were now I'd say it hurt like hell, isn't that enough, do I have to actually shed blood. But at the time I didn't say anything. I didn't want to be melodramatic about it and I didn't want to argue on our honeymoon and I never wanted to argue about sex, so I didn't say anything about any of it. What was the point.

The next day I wanted to talk, but I couldn't find the words. I wanted to say Buddy, I gave you the only thing in the world that was all mine to give, and it's not enough because I didn't bleed doing it. Dammit, you kill me, Buddy, you just kill me.

This while I'm rubbing suntan lotion on his back, kissing his neck, acting like a honeymooner, desperately trying to think like one.

Afterwards, after Jake, the world gets bigger and smaller.

You could have an affair with anybody. People do it all the time. You could meet somebody at lunch and be having sex with them that night. There's no limit. Life is short.

I'm standing in line at the bank when I could have gone through the drive-through but I have some time to kill, and all the sudden it isn't abstract anymore. I could have an affair with some man who's right here in this bank this minute. I could meet his eyes and do my mouth a certain way and then meet his eyes again, smile. I could look at his hands and finger the zipper on my purse and I don't know what to do after that, but he'll know and if he doesn't I'll forget it and find somebody else and if he does I can follow anybody's lead.

I'm not going to do it. I just like thinking about it. It makes me feel like part of the world.

So I try to pick somebody out, like if I were going to, only every man here is too old or too young or too fat or too skinny or dumpy.

I think about a woman, but I don't know about that. I wouldn't know where to start.

I try to figure out what they do for a living. He may as well be rich. But I'm no judge of shoes, and beepers don't tell you anything anymore. You can get a small one and put it in your jacket pocket and that's the most expensive kind, anybody with a big one on his belt you wonder about, what he's trying to prove. Some of them are big enough to be phones, but if they are phones, forget it. I have a thing about people who carry around phones. I don't even like car phones.

Once, Buddy said I'm thinking about getting a car phone.

I said what for.

It was just a game. I wasn't going to have an affair, but if I had been considering it I would have decided not to once I looked at my choices. When you really look at them, most people aren't that attractive.

You just want to touch somebody. You want that kind of connection. Kindness, humankindness.

But you know beforehand it's not going to work. Nobody could really be what you needed.

You can name people, maybe just one person, who tried to kill you and you lived through it but it made that kind of impression on you like if you'd died. It was that permanent. Maybe they tried to strangle you or suffocate you or starve you or cut you open. Not always literally.

You wish you could do that to somebody so they'd never forget you. Not kill them. The other thing, what they did to you. Go inside them and leave a part of yourself there that would eat them alive like acid.

But you don't. You don't know how. They were all men.

1 5

EVER SINCE HOMECOMING I'D BEEN TRYING TO PROVE TO BO I was one of the faithful, so by Thanksgiving I'd quit studying just like him. I thought that might help. I wanted to go to the Tuesday night Bible study with him too, but it had broken up. It turned out the leader was exhausted and his wife, who never had gone to the Bible study and who was being used by the devil, put him in a mental hospital. Which is typical of what's going to happen in the Tribulation, people getting thrown in mental hospitals just for preaching the word of God. Bo said the Russians had been doing it for years, but he never would have believed it would happen here in the United States of America if he hadn't seen it with his own two eyes.

The other Rapture Watchers had dropped out of the Rapture Club, and I have to admit the thought had occurred that I might should too, but I felt so bad for Bo and he was all alone and I thought he needed me and then he told me so. He said are you going to desert me too, and I said no, Bo, I'm not, and he said good, because I need you. Which made me feel like Cinderella and Snow White and Sleeping Beauty all rolled into one.

So we just kept trying to get ready and watch and get everybody else ready only nobody would, and Bo'd memorized Matthew and Mark and Luke and moved on to Genesis while I was still working on John, which slows down fast after the first couple of verses, and Bo'd find himself in every story. Like first he was Adam because he was made in the image of God and he communed with God and then he was Abel because he was a keeper of sheep and he'd suffered the wrath of his brothers in Christ and even his own father because of their jealousy when God found Bo's offerings more pleasing than theirs. And then he was Noah, being asked by God to be a visionary, to prepare for a coming the world didn't foresee and he was willing to be laughed at and spat upon if that was the cost of obeying God. And then Nashville Christian Academy was a tower of Babel because people there were trying to get to heaven by means other than the grace of God. And then he was Lot, and God's wrath was going to come down on Nashville and destroy it and he was being told ahead of time to save people but nobody would listen and God was going to be merciful to him and he'd come out all right but everybody else was damned.

It was scary. It was scary in the way just about everything in the Old Testament is, God killing people right and left when they don't do things his way, turning them into pillars of salt and changing their rivers to blood, setting locusts on them and killing their children just to see if they'll still love him after. You think too hard about that being God and somebody believing they're a prophet of God, and you start to feel scared.

But you grow up listening to these stories every Sunday and reading books about them with color pictures and sometimes even pop-up illustrations, like Noah's Ark, all those little animals trotting into the ark and even the snakes look cute, like sideways s's with an extra squiggle on the end and they're smiling and the girl snake has eyelashes—somehow the destruction of the world becomes a pleasant thing to contemplate. They all get that way. The water turning into blood looks like pools of velvet, and the blood of Jesus is something you sing songs about, swaying to the music and saying halleluia, and I had comic books that showed Jesus on the cross with blood dripping down his legs and people swimming around in the lake of fire, only there was something about their arms that made you think they were wearing roller skates under the fire.

But the thing was, they all end up happy if you're a Christian. Good triumphs over evil and everything works out fine. So you just teach yourself not to think about the people who died or whose firstborn sons died or who got taken into slavery because that's not the point. You have to have faith and not live in fear because if God is for you, who can be against you. Only godless people live in fear and they ought to be afraid, maybe the fear of God is what will save them. So you just learn not to think about it, and it's the hardest kind of learning to unlearn because nobody ever taught you.

So when Bo said he was Abraham, it was a little scary, but I already had a whole roomful of things in my brain I wasn't allowing myself to worry about, so I just threw Abraham in there and shut the door. What I was afraid of was Bo and the Rapture and him getting more and more carried away with it with every passing day to the point where I thought he might I don't know what. I didn't let myself finish that sentence.

And then before I knew it, it was New Year's Eve, and if God was coming by the end of the year like he'd told Bo he was, he was coming before midnight that night.

I felt real funny in my gut that whole day, like I knew something bad was fixing to happen, only I didn't know if it'd be the

Rapture or not but I tried to believe it was the Rapture in case it was so I would have had faith.

Bo called me about eight o'clock that night. Deedee and Uncle Mull had just left for a party and the phone rang and I said hey, Bo.

He said do you want to go with me to watch the dead in Christ rise first?

I did not. I thought it sounded like an R-rated horror movie I wasn't allowed to watch even when they edited them for TV. But with Bo, even when the question is what do you want or what do you think, there's always a right answer and a wrong one, and I knew what the right answer was so I said it. Yes.

Okay, meet me at the graveyard at school in half an hour.

Bo, I can't, there's nobody here to take me.

Okay, I'll come get you but be ready fast, we don't have any time to waste. There was something hollow like panic in his voice, so I didn't remind him that he couldn't drive either.

It turned out he could, anyway, and he came and picked me up in his daddy's Jeep and I didn't ask questions. His clothes were torn and his hair was messed up and his eyes looked funny, almost like he'd been crying, but I didn't ask anything or say anything all the way to the graveyard. Bo would get this certain kind of intense that just made you be quiet, and he had it that night.

So we got there and we parked and Bo opened the back door and he had logs and rope and a Bible and two burlap bags and some newspaper and I was scared. I felt like I was an actor in a movie and my character was about to commit murder. The weather felt like that too. Here it was December thirty-first but it wasn't all that cold and it was almost muggy if there's such a thing as muggy in the winter, it was just hard to breathe, and the clouds were swirling around in the sky like they were getting ready to bake something and there was thunder everywhere, and thunder has just always done something to me, so I said to myself it's just thunder, it's just thunder. It's not going to hurt you.

I said it sure looks like it's fixing to storm, which Bo said was because the Bible said Jesus will be trailing clouds of glory, but I said I always thought it would be during the day and the clouds of glory would be big old white fluffy things and there'd maybe be a rainbow up there or something.

Bo said the Word says be filled with the fear of the Lord, for he is a just and vengeful God, and those clouds are supposed to put the fear of the Lord in you.

Which they did. It was lightning and thundering something crazy and Bo had such a crazed look on him that I started thinking maybe this whole Rapture was a bad idea.

There wasn't any turning back then, though, and Bo started scooping all that stuff out of the back seat and he was giving off that don't-ask thing of his worse than ever, so I didn't say anything else, and I held out my arms and Bo gave me the burlap bags and the newspaper and one of the logs and he took the rest of the logs and I followed him.

He was walking toward a grave, and it didn't take much knowing Bo to know which one. There was a cross about seven feet high in the middle of the graveyard, and I knew that's where we were headed. I was nervous, but just looking at that cross thinking that's where we're going helped.

And then we got there and we put our stuff on the ground and I was thinking now he'd explain but he didn't. He just handed me a burlap bag and said put this on.

I said wear it?

He said yeah.

I said over my clothes?

He thought a minute, a second really, and he said okay.

So I looked at it and it had two armholes cut in it and his did too and he was putting his over his head and I said okay, but why?

He said haven't you ever heard of sackcloth and ashes, don't you know what they're for?

I said oh, okay, I just didn't know what sackcloth was, exactly, and I pulled mine on fast. I was trying to think who was it that put on sackcloth and ashes and I thought it might have been David after Bathsheba and I thought is this still about the kiss, am I going to be living with that kiss forever, only I wasn't sure if it wasn't more than one person who did sackcloth and ashes, but I was also relieved because he seemed to be off of Abraham and I couldn't remember what David did after the sackcloth and ashes but I was thinking he just went back to being king and everything turned out fine. That's what I was also hoping.

Then Bo started balling up the newspaper and he was building a fire, which I didn't think you should make a fire in a graveyard and I was afraid we'd get arrested or something so I was trying to talk to him so I said what'd you do today and I said to myself it's just to make ashes for sackcloth and ashes, how else do you make ashes if you're not going to have a fire, and I thought if the police come we can explain and it's a free country, freedom of religion and all that, so we won't be arrested. But in the back of my mind I kept thinking about the Bible study leader who'd been thrown in a mental hospital, so I was still scared.

Bo said I spent the day in prayer and fasting, but he looked at me like what else would I be doing, you idiot.

I'd slept late and woken up to the sound of Deedee and Uncle Mull fighting in the kitchen, so I'd stayed in bed till Deedee left and slammed the kitchen door behind her and I put on some blue jeans and a sweatshirt and went out in the den where Uncle Mull was watching TV. We didn't say anything. Then I went in the kitchen and the only thing we had to eat was black-eyed peas but Deedee never put bacon fat in there like Memaw used to so hers weren't as good, but you could put ketchup on them and they'd be all right, so that's what I did and I ate the whole pot. Then I watched a football game with Uncle Mull and he fell asleep in his chair and I drank a sip of his beer, just to see what it tasted like, which was terrible.

By the time Deedee got home, I'd remembered about the Rapture coming and I had kept trying to tell myself no but I was getting scared anyway because I'd been praying every morning and every night since Paw Paw died, please save Deedee and Uncle Mull, please let them get born again, only it hadn't happened. I was afraid about them living without me, going through the seven years of Tribulation which start right after the Rapture. Bo'd said when you think about it, between no Christians being there to leaven the bread and nuclear fallout making them all lose their minds and get cancer and their skin fall off their flesh, it's a wonder they'll last that long. I kept telling myself God was a just God and if it happened to them they deserved it, but I couldn't help it, just thinking it made me scared. So that afternoon Deedee was in the basement doing laundry and I went down there and finally I told Deedee please, please just be a Christian, just try it for one night.

Deedee started laughing. She could laugh at anything, and she said honey, your daddy and I are Christians.

I said you are?

She dumped Uncle Mull's underwear into the washing machine and she said come here, and she hugged me and she said married people fight sometimes, we just see things differently, but that doesn't mean we're not Christians.

I said I know, that's not it. I squirmed out of her arms.

She said it's your school, right?

Yeah. I felt embarrassed, but Bo had said are you embarrassed by Jesus, are you going to let a few minutes of discomfort keep the people you love from spending eternity with Christ.

Deedee said Sylvia, not all Christians are like the ones at your school.

I knew that. Memaw and Paw Paw for just one example weren't anything like Bo.

She said but that's okay, God's a very big God and there's room for all kinds.

I wasn't too sure about that.

She said look at all the different kinds of trees he made, all the flowers, different kinds of fish and animals and rocks. Look how many stars there are in the universe, there may be completely other worlds, other galaxies. God has the capacity to embrace difference, that's why he's God, and when we accept difference in other people, when we love those differences and enjoy them, we're being like God.

I knew what Bo would say to that. That's Scripture watered down, turned lukewarm, and made palatable to the masses and it makes God sick, he wants to spew that kind of thinking from his mouth. He'd spit when he said spew. Bo would, I mean.

So when Bo didn't ask me what I did that day I didn't offer to tell him.

So then Bo had his fire going and then he opened his Bible and it was dark, there were clouds everywhere and it was fixing to rain hard and the fire was going but you couldn't read, not the Bible where the words are smaller than anywhere else, but he opened his Bible anyway and he was standing there beside the cross like he was giving a sermon and then he started talking loud, like he was talking to more than just me, and he said as Abraham was called to leave his homeland to prove he loved God more than his father, as he was called to sacrifice Isaac to prove he loved God more than his only begotten son, so I have been called to prove I love God more than myself.

Abraham had always made me nervous, and I said what are you going to do, Bo?

Bo said God tested Abraham's faith, not to lead him into temptation but to reveal his grace. Grace can't be revealed without faith and the testing of your faith produces endurance.

What are you going to do?

He looked at his Bible like he was reading only it was too dark and by now it had started to rain on the pages and he said and it came to pass after these things that God did tempt Abraham and said unto him, Abraham. And Abraham said behold, here I am.

Then Bo stopped and looked into the rain and said even louder, behold, here *I* am, Lord.

Then he looked at the Bible again and said and God said take now thy son, thine only son Isaac whom thou lovest, and get thee into the land of Moriah and offer him there for a burnt offering upon one of the mountains which I will tell thee of.

Now I was really scared. For one thing, I was scared I was Isaac. I said tell me what you're going to do, Bo.

He kept reading.

I said tell me, now.

He said and Abraham said unto his young men, abide ye here with the ass and I and the lad will go yonder and worship and come again to you.

Now I was hoping I could be one of the young men, and he looked at me and I didn't say anything.

Bo said Abraham said we will come again to you. Abraham knew what he was about to do and yet he said that he *and Isaac* would return. Was he lying?

I didn't know.

No! He wasn't *lying.* He *believed* in the promise of God. He *knew* that God had promised to make of Isaac a great nation, and how could he do that if he stayed dead?

Bo was laughing now and the rain was coming harder, smashing his hair onto his head and starting to make his burlap bag sag on his shoulders.

I said I don't know.

By faith. That's how he knew, by faith. By faith Abraham when he was tried offered up Isaac and he that had received the promises offered up his only begotten son of whom it was said that in Isaac shall thy seed be called, accounting that *God* was *able* to *raise* him *up,* even from the dead. Bo snapped his Bible shut and pointed to it and said so Isaac went willingly. He was a grown man, probably stronger than his father. He could have escaped, just like you could escape, Sylvia, but you don't because *you* have faith *too.*

I thought he was going to kill me. I had this strange sense of not being real, of nothing being real, not even death, and I thought to myself okay, now he's going to kill me, and it seemed like times I'd felt before like when Memaw died, like my soul went out of my body and somebody else went in. Not Amazing Grace, but somebody like her inside me protecting me only this one didn't have a sense of touch, so whatever happened would have been okay because she didn't care, and I didn't care either because it wasn't me. So I thought if Bo kills me it's not going to hurt because it's not going to be me that dies, it'll be her. I could already feel her hovering around my ears, fixing to take over.

Bo just kept reading the Bible from memory. He said and they came to the place which God had told him of and Abraham built an altar there and laid the wood in order and bound Isaac his son and laid him upon the altar upon the wood and Abraham stretched forth his hand and took the knife to slay his son.

Then Bo stopped and picked up the rope and said tie me up.

I didn't know who was who anymore. I said no.

He shoved the rope at me and I let it drop and he said do it, God says for you to do it.

No.

You have to, God says. You have to tie me up and cut my throat and offer me up to God as a burnt offering.

I shook my head no.

He was pressing the rope at my chest and he said God says. Are you going to disobey God?

He didn't say it to me.

That's because he doesn't talk to girls, name one girl he ever told anything to.

Well, he should have made an exception if he wanted me to do it because I'm not doing it, I just don't go around killing people. I was shaking in my jaw.

He said I won't die, God will protect me just like he did Isaac.

I said no, no way, just wait a minute. I was scared. I was scared to death.

Bo looked at his watch so I looked at mine and I thought Mary, but I didn't say it. The rain was putting the fire out and there was smoke everywhere and I was coughing and it was five minutes after ten.

He said we've got less than two hours, the Lord is coming before midnight, so just tell me, are you going to do it or not.

Not.

Okay, I'll do it myself. God's looking down from heaven for one faithful man and that's what he's going to find, one.

Then he pulled a pocket knife out of his blue jeans and I said wait, Bo, just wait, wait a minute, what are you doing, why are you doing this. I was dragging him away from the cross but he wasn't moving.

He said God didn't give Abraham a reason, he didn't give Job a reason, and he didn't give me one. He just said do it. I'm a prophet, Sylvia, it's my calling. I am a lamb of God ready for the slaughter. And the angel of the Lord called unto him out of heaven and said Abraham, Abraham, and he said here am I.

And then Bo held the knife up to the lightning and he said God will provide himself the lamb for the burnt offering.

Bo'd just told me he was going to do it but somehow I hadn't believed him or I'd thought God would stop him like he stopped Abraham, I don't know what I thought, but I think Bo had thought the same thing, because it all happened in slow motion with that same sense that you can't stop it as an instant replay on TV, and then he'd done it, he'd cut his own throat wide open, and I'd just stood there holding the rope, just holding it, but it had felt like that rope was tying my hands down because I couldn't move. Then he got this look of terror on his face like he'd seen God, and his eyes went big like he couldn't believe only it was like he wasn't seeing anything, and I jumped up and I couldn't believe it and I was shaking head to foot and I thought it was happening, I thought it was the end of the world, I thought the thunder was breaking the sky open, and it was too late but I said stop, Bo, and he just looked at me like I wasn't there, and the blood wasn't just coming out and dripping down like Jesus on the cross, it was shooting out, spraying all over the place like a fountain, like a hose, and I said oh God oh Bo oh no and he lay back on the grave and the blood was everywhere, out of control, and he said my God, my God, why hast thou forsaken me, his voice already going away, and I said Bo, screaming it like I was screaming down a tunnel, *Bo,* like when somebody's lost and the search party is calling for them in the dark, *Bo,* shaking him and shaking him not even feeling real and my hands could hardly believe a person could get that wet from their own blood.

I didn't know anybody had that much blood in them but it just kept coming and coming so fast I was thinking of the parable where the oil lamps just always have more in them, thinking he couldn't possibly have started out with this much blood, it wouldn't all fit. And I put my arms around him and I put my head on his chest and the blood was getting all over me and I thought about that song that says washed in the blood of the lamb and I thought whoever wrote that song had no idea how gross this is and he said wipe my blood on the cross and I didn't know what to do and he was going to sleep, he was dying, and I knew he needed help but I couldn't just leave him and I was screaming for help afraid to leave him, screaming so hard my throat hurt and I could hear cars but nobody came but I thought maybe somebody's on their way so I just kept screaming but the whole time I was screaming I was doing what he said, wiping blood everywhere, tearing our clothes up, rubbing ashes on our faces, and I was screaming Bo, wake up, please don't die, Bo, and I was begging him so hard I just knew if he was in the tunnel of light between earth and heaven where you can still change your mind, I knew if he heard me he'd come back, so I was screaming Bo, come back, help, somebody help, Bo, come back, trying to aim my voice down the tunnel and out to the street at the same time.

1 6

I HAVE TO SEE MY FATHER.

I call his office and he's out on a job but I say it's an emergency, it's a family emergency. I say I'm his daughter. I listen to my voice. There's something cracking and desperate in the way I say it.

The receptionist says honey, he's on a site, you can't reach him by phone. She thinks I'm a child.

I say where is he, each word separate.

She gives me the address and directions. It's in Montgomery County, practically in Kentucky.

I hang up the phone. I close my eyes with my fingers. I tell myself you've waited your whole life for this, another forty-five minutes isn't going to kill you. I'm feeling funny, like my face is pink and my head is too big and I need food. I cover my face with my hands and try to remember if this is the normal size of my face. My hands feel small, and my wedding ring is loose. I eat a brownie straight from the pan and I keep eating until I feel the sugar hit my bloodstream and my arms come into focus, then I keep going until we're out of brownies. I decide not to brush my teeth so I can keep the taste of brownies in my mouth. It's comforting, and you take what you can get.

On the drive up there I practice. I tell him you're the only link I have to my past, and I have to know some things. I tell him I have these memories, but I don't know what's true. I'm missing big pieces of my life, and I don't know if that's normal. I don't know how to think about all this, but I don't know how not to and there's nobody to ask. I ask him if he has any pictures. I tell him my grandparents didn't take many. I tell him do you know what it's like to grow up without a father or a mother, I need you to know what that's like, all your friends have parents, everybody you know, and you feel like a freak. I say did you know that I prayed for you every night, every damn night I'd get in bed, and sometimes I'd pray you'd come get me and I could go live with you, sometimes I'd pray that you really were my father—I'd guessed but I didn't know—and other times I just prayed you were alive, I just asked God not to kill you, whether you were my father or not. I tell him I don't pray that anymore.

I start over. You're the only link I have to my past, and I need to know some things.

When I get there, he's sweaty and he smells bad and there's a Port-a-John but no bathroom and I've never been in a Port-a-John but I don't think they have sinks, so everybody here has germs all over their hands. I look at his hands, and they're filthy. There's dirt everywhere, on his hands, on his clothes, but also everywhere else, like the landscape is naked, no grass, no groundcover, not even any weeds. It's embarrassing.

I look back at him. His hair hangs in strings out of his baseball cap and he takes the hat off and his hair is stuck to his head like gravy over a skull, only where the hat ended, his hair sticks out like the edge around a scoop of mashed potatoes in a cafeteria. He walks over to me slowly. A drop of sweat runs through the grime down his cheek onto his neck and into his shirt. I don't like to think about him having bodily functions. I think about Deedee and the edible panties. I look at the ground.

I say so this is what you do with your life. Like I've never seen a landscaper at work.

He scratches his neck behind his ear. Yep.

I say other people tear down forests and you come back and plant boxwoods in their place.

He looks around. He doesn't think this was ever a forest.

How do you know, how the hell do you know what used to be here.

Well, for one thing, we haven't come across the root systems.

You don't know. God, root systems, my father thinks he can read the past by root systems.

He looks at me, opens his hands. I don't know if I've ever called him my father to his face. I'm crying. I pick up some dirt. I want him to be wrong. I hold it out to him and I say you can't find any root systems here?

He shakes his head no. He's scared of me and I like that.

I let the dirt fall through my fingers. I wipe my hands on each other, then on my jeans. I feel ridiculous. I say well, neither can I, what do you know. I turn and look at my car. I want to leave now.

He says Sylvia? He's quiet.

I wait until I can speak. We both wait. The sun pulses on my hair, and machines in the distance plow the dirt rhythmically. I feel the ground trembling under my feet while it tears itself apart, and I think about the molten lava ready to explode at the center of the earth.

I'm not going to be able to say much to him, it's too hard, so I pick one thing. I say Paw Paw molested me.

I look him in the eye. He believes me, and I've hurt him.

Finally. I'm suddenly very calm. I think about the peace that passes understanding and I wonder if this is it.

I say without emotion Memaw knew.

His eyes are holes and I have poured acid into them and it's eating him alive.

I could say more, but I'm done, and I turn to leave.

He touches my arm, then recoils. He says wait, and his voice is raw. His face and his arms are red and wet with perspiration. His whole body makes me think of steak still in the package.

I can't stay, though, there's nothing more to say. I just wanted him to know, I don't even know why, but now he does and I want to go home. I'm walking toward my car and he's walking half behind me, half beside me, and I don't know what I'm going to do when I get there. I locked it, which was stupid but also habit, and the keys are in my purse and I don't want to take my wallet and my checkbook out and make a big production out of finding them but I always have to with this purse, it's too big, I hate this purse, I just bought it because it was on sale, and I'm going to have to get a new one. I just want to go.

He puts his hand on my car door as if to stop it and I look at him. I tell myself there's nothing he can say.

He says Sylvia, you have no idea what I've been through.

I say what you've been through, without inflection.

He says that's not what I mean, let me start over.

I look at him. It's that simple to him, you just say let me start over.

He says what can I say or do at this point.

I don't say anything because the answer is nothing.

He says I can't deny being the world's worst father in the world.

I think about a plaque: WORLD'S WORST FATHER IN THE WORLD.

He's at an international awards banquet, each father dressed in a costume representing his country like the first part of the Miss Universe pageant. Some woman in a tight black dress kisses him on the cheek, and he walks up to the podium to make a speech. He pulls out a folded-up piece of paper and says just in case. The other bad fathers smile. I'm not there.

He keeps talking. I'm a total screw-up. I've screwed my life up, I screwed Deedee's life up, I screwed your mother's life up, and worst of all, I screwed your life up, that's the worst part of it all, I would give anything— He's shaking his head.

I lean against my car, facing him. I can feel the hot metal on my spine, and it reminds me that I'm real. This is all real.

He can't stop shaking his head and he can't say anything. He starts over. He says I fucked up, I'm not saying I didn't fuck up, but I want you to know what happened.

He waits.

I'm being cruel, and I like it.

He says please try to understand. He lets out a breath. He never says please.

I say okay.

He looks at me like he's surprised I've said okay, but what else could I say.

He looks at the sky, at the site, the machines droning. He puts his hat back on, which is a relief. He looks younger, more human, when you don't have to think about his skull.

He says I was seventeen years old, I was a kid myself. I know that doesn't make up for anything. But put yourself in my shoes. I was in a coma when you were born, f' God's—they didn't know if I'd live, they didn't know if I'd be a vegetable. It took a long time, I had to start my whole life over, learn how to walk, stuff like that. I'd been an athlete, I'd run the four-forty.

He shakes his head, erases the words in the air with his hands. What I mean is, he says, the thing is, by the time I got to a point where I was capable of raising you, it just seemed sort of too late. You already had your own home and your own life and they'd already told you all these damn lies about me—goddammit, I'm not saying I did the right thing, but I swear to you, Sylvia, I didn't know what else to do. I was only seventeen when you were born, and then it took me a few years. I don't know where I'm going with all this, but for what it's worth I want you to know I loved your mother. And I loved you. I'm not big on saying that kind of thing, but it's true.

I can't say anything and I can feel the silence between us like sunlight on my skin. I think about skin cancer. I don't know what it looks like, how I'll recognize it if I get it, but I think of my skin hardening into a crust, then flaking off like paint chips, exposing wet pink open wounds underneath.

He says I still miss her. Sometimes I think that had something to do with Deedee leaving, like having you was too much like having Gracie back. I don't know what I'm saying, I'm not very good at this, I'm not one of these guys who can talk about their feelings.

I say it's okay. I've never seen him so uncomfortable. He's sweating more now than he was when I got here. I think he needs to sit down but I'm afraid if I suggest it we'll never get back here.

He says I mean I would give anything to make none of this have happened. God, I don't know, I mean, what did he do to you, is that okay to ask.

He touched me. I can't say it.

He's looking at me to figure out what I mean, but I can't say it. He lowers his chin and his forehead but keeps his eyes on me. He says you mean?

Yeah.

His face withers and he sits on the ground, his back against my car, elbows on his knees, face in his hands. He's whispering. I didn't know, I didn't know.

I have an impulse to comfort him, but I'm not going to do it.

I think about my father waking up from his coma. We lived parallel lives for a while, both of us learning to walk, falling down, pulling ourselves back up, learning to talk. I wonder what his first words were. I wonder what he said when they told him about my mother, about me. Did he ask them my name. Did he want to name me something else. Did he wish I'd died with my mother.

I think he wants me to forgive him, but I can't do it and I'm not going to lie. I just want to get out of here, I can't remember why it seemed so important to talk to him in the first place. I think how would Amazing Grace get out of here, but she wouldn't have come in the first place. I'm on my own.

I look at my watch. I say I better let you get back to work.

Wait, Sylvia, he says. He stands up.

I'm feeling for my keys. I say please.

He steps back.

I unlock my door slowly, concentrating on it. I can't look at him. I get in the car and feel cold against the hot seat.

He says I love you.

I nod my head and pull the door closed. I leave without looking back.

I tell myself you don't have to think about this anymore. You don't have to do anything you don't want to do. Just think about something pleasant. Brownies. Clouds. Hearts. Flowers.

I had a red construction-paper heart on my wall. It had a door you could open like an Advent calendar and behind it was Jesus, with stick legs and stick arms and a head that glowed with yellow dashes like sun rays. I got it for learning behold, I stand at the door and knock, if any man hear my voice and open the door I will come in to him and sup with him and he with me.

I knew what it meant to have Jesus in my heart, and I knew what sup meant—have supper. When old people had heartburn it meant Jesus didn't like what they gave him for supper, and if you had a heart attack it was because he threw a tantrum. He does that. If you go to Sunday school long enough, eventually they'll get to the tantrum stories, so I tried to eat things he'd like. I tried not to make anybody mad.

Sometimes I'd lie in bed at night and I could feel him in my heart, walking around on those little prickly stick feet, bored.

I turn up the air conditioner as high as it will go.

I'm not going to tell Buddy I saw my father. It's over now, and there's no point in dwelling on the past. That's one thing about Buddy, he never dwells on the past, never thinks about it. You'd never guess he'd been married before, that whole mess is like it never happened. Sometimes I wonder how much of it he even remembers. It must be a man thing.

I try to learn from him.

I look around the kitchen. Look at the floor. I have to pull myself together, I have to do something, I have to clean up this mess. I put on old clothes, the kind that seem like they never were new, and I put my hair in a ponytail and I'm going to strip the linoleum and get that bottom layer of dirt up once and for all. I hate that floor. I've taken a flat-headed screwdriver before and scraped along the walls where the edges turn to a gray crust.

I open the cabinet under the sink and start reading bottles. You're supposed to remove old buildup with ammonia and all-purpose cleaner, but I don't know what all-purpose cleaner is. I know what every cleaner I have is for, none of it is for everything. Why do they have to make everything so difficult, I just want a clean floor, is that too much to ask.

Once, I broke a bottle of red wine on the floor. It just rolled out of the grocery bag onto the floor and ate up the finish. But it was a mess and you had this feeling like if you didn't mop it up fast you were going to have a pink floor. I think about white wine, whether it was just something about red. I wonder if beer would work. I think about opening a six-pack onto the floor.

I end up using dishwashing detergent, which I needed to get rid of anyway, and a screwdriver. When I'm finished I mop with Brite and start the whole process over.

I clean the bathroom, then go in the bedroom and clean under the bed along the wall and behind the nightstand and places that haven't been cleaned in months, and when I finally get it all clean, cleaner than I can remember it's ever been, I sit down on the bed. I feel my grandmother, warm on my neck, like she's looking down from heaven, saying you did real good, Sylvie. It's a comfort.

I hear my grandmother's voice, angry—cut that out, you two.

Stop it. I've had enough for one day. Just stop it. Keep moving, keep talking, keep doing whatever you have to do to keep from sitting there reliving things you shouldn't ever have had to live through the first time.

I say out loud, she knew.

I close my eyes while I feel the heat drain out of my face, then I run to the bathroom and throw up. I think about maggots and dead bodies disintegrating and the way your skin tightens when semen is drying on it so I can keep throwing up, and I do. I vomit brownies and coffee and orange juice and everything I've eaten for two days until I get to the yellow bile at the bottom of my stomach where my soul is, and then I vomit that and flush.

I lie down on the floor on my side with my eyes closed, and Amazing Grace watches me from the ceiling. I'm sweating and she tries to cool me off but I don't look at her. Through my teeth I say get out, but she doesn't. I hold my knees. I think where the hell have you been, but I don't ask her. I just lie there. I have to lie there. I can't move.

I hold my shins. I'm sweating and I'm cold and I'm spinning around the room and then I'm up on the ceiling with Amazing Grace, then thud, back on the floor, and I can't stop spinning. I try to hold on to the tile but my hands are too small.

I say you knew. He touched me and you knew it and you didn't do a damn thing.

Somewhere in my mind, I'm talking to Memaw. Somewhere, I'm talking to God.

I close my eyes. I rock shut and don't open my mouth, saying how could you know and let it keep happening, how could you leave the house. I scream out loud at all of them. What was wrong with you.

I feel Amazing Grace trying to take over, but I won't let her. I want to do this myself. I hold myself in my arms. I rock myself like a baby.

Amazing Grace wants to sing to me so I let her. She sings slowly and softly and she doesn't trill the notes like she's showing off and I let the music move over me and seep into my skin. *'Twas grace that taught my heart to fear.* I feel it pounding through my bloodstream, bathing my heart and my stomach and my uterus. *And grace my fears relieved.* All my selves rising out of me separately, singing harmony with Amazing Grace on the ceiling, then pouring themselves back into me as one. *How precious did that grace appear.* And I'm alone in the room.

I go back to the beginning and start over, singing harmony with myself in my head.

When I get to the end, I open my hands and close my eyes and say to my grandmother I forgive you. It is not a lie. It is an act of faith.

I can still hear the music, and I leave my hands open and I let Amazing Grace pull things out of my fingers.

There is a part of forgiveness that is letting go, giving, and there is a part that is receiving. This time, for the first time, I receive, and it is something like grace.

I take a shower and wash my hair, then go to the grocery store without makeup while my hair's still wet. I buy beer, two steaks, a lot of fruit, a mix for homemade bread, brownie mix, a Snickers bar. I'm going to cut up the Snickers bar into the brownie mix. And I'm going to arrange some fruit in a wooden bowl on the kitchen table. I buy one of every color. I take my time, getting just the right shapes. I get two bananas so it won't matter if Buddy eats one. I buy a new dishtowel, a new package of sponges. I get ice cream and soft chocolate chip cookies and raisins and condoms and fingernail polish and Heinz 57 and a bottle of red wine that's fifty cents off, which is how I always choose wine. I write a check.

I just want to be happy.

I just want to forget and be happy.

I think of a poem I read somewhere. Think of the past, think of forgetting the past. Practice forgetting.

I put the food away and put the steaks in a red wine marinade. I like the smell of red wine. I like the way it feels to have a clean house and a full refrigerator.

When Buddy gets home I get him a beer and lock all the doors and windows.

He says what are you doing.

I say I just want to be safe.

He says okay, I just wondered.

How was your trip.

It was good, he thinks things are finally starting to pick up, housing starts are up, and pressed wood siding is the way to go when you're coming out of a recession—it's cheap, it's low maintenance, it comes with a twenty-year guarantee. He's got a whole subdivision account—sixty-six houses, he's providing all the timber products and all the dry walling and he's using a new distributor so he doesn't expect to have any more dry-walling problems.

I'm peeling potatoes.

He comes in the kitchen and hugs me for no reason. He's lost some weight, and more of him touches me when he holds me now. I put my hands on his stomach and smile.

He starts setting the table. He's going to build a deck next summer, maybe even before that, a huge deck with seats around the edges that you can get to from the kitchen or the den, and off to the side a Jacuzzi, big enough for six people, he picked up a brochure in Atlanta. And while we're at it we'll clear out the back yard and put in some landscaping, would I like that.

Yeah, that'd be nice.

Maybe a fence.

Not a chainlink one.

No, a privacy fence, a pretty wood one.

I smile and lean into him. He keeps talking. He's been thinking about getting a dog, if we had a fence he could get a big dog and put a doghouse out there, and it'll be a safe place for children to play.

I try not to stiffen.

Whenever, he says, no pressure. His voice is soothing to me, it's old and familiar. I take out his belt, his dop kit, his shoes, and his razor, put them on the kitchen counter, then close the suitcase to carry it down to the wash. I set it by the basement door.

I take the steaks out of the refrigerator and ask Buddy if he wants to cook them or if he wants me to.

He wants to.

I say I don't mind.

No, he wants to.

I finish setting the table. I put out candles and cloth napkins and turn on Miles Davis. I remember something new—my grand-mother holding me, singing, my little pink record player, the choir at church. There was always music.

After dinner I'm full and I feel good and pretty and I'm washing dishes and Buddy comes up behind me and washes a dish with me, holding my hands, and I lean my head back on his shoulder and he's singing in my ear and he's not really a bad singer, not as good as Jake, but it's okay.

I pick up another dish and he puts it down and then we're not really dancing, just swaying to the music, and then too many things flood into my head, too many people, mistakes, and I push them out but they crowd back in and our hands are wet and soapy and we're dancing in the kitchen and his hands move down my back then into my clothes, making me wet, and he is my husband, he is not my grandfather, he is not Jake, it's not wrong, it's not the same thing but it feels the same and my skin starts remembering things and I can't do it, I can't stand it, I'm too crowded, stop.

God, Sylvia, what'd I do now.

I'm crying uncontrollably and I can't stop and everything from this afternoon is coming undone and his face blinks in and out of focus and I'm scared and I can't explain. I say Buddy, you don't know, I don't know, you don't know things about me, but you wouldn't love me if you did. I sit down at the table and hide my face.

Yes I would.

No you wouldn't. I hear Jake. Whatever happens you don't let go of this. I think nobody can ever really completely know me again. Jake knows a side of me nobody else knows but he barely knows me at all and Bo knew me better than anybody at one point and he wouldn't even recognize me now and my grandfather knew a part of me I don't even know myself and it goes on and on like that, everybody only knowing fragments, including yourself. All those selves in the tunnel of selves, they don't even know each other, they just stare. And then people who barely know you can tell you things about yourself you never would have guessed and then they forget your name.

He waits. He's listening.

I can't talk. I don't know where to start. I've never told Buddy about Bo. I've never told him about the Rapture Club and the Rapture and how Bo died. I've never told him how my grandfather died. I haven't told him much about my grandparents. I haven't told him about Jake and I won't, I can't, and I get that quick little panic you get when something spills and you run for a dishrag thinking what's going to get ruined. Sometimes I feel torn apart and sometimes I feel like maybe I'm coming back together and sometimes I feel like coming back together would be impossible because there are too many of me scattered around, so many I can't keep track of them all because part of me died with my

grandfather and part of me died with Bo and part with my grandmother and part with my mother and I can't even imagine what it
would feel like to be whole again, I can't even say it.

I say Buddy, just hold me, and he holds me tight. We go into
the den and he sits on the sofa and I curl up into a ball and put
my head on his lap and he holds me and he strokes my hair and I
breathe all the gravity in the house and I can feel things floating
around me but I close my eyes so I can't see them and the gravity
sits in my sinuses and my lungs and I feel it slowly pumping itself
into my bloodstream, gravity disseminating throughout my body,
until I fall into a weighted sleep.

Buddy brings me coffee when I wake up and he sits on the bed.
He says do you want to talk.

No. I sit up.

Okay.

I look at him and drink the coffee.

He wants to know what he can do.

I just want you to be here for me.

I'm here.

And love me.

I love you.

I set down the coffee and lean into him and he holds me.

I think what I need is to get away from Jake, what I need is
to write some new songs, some whole ones, and make some
demos and send them to Miller and start making my future instead of living in my past. I say Buddy, I think I want to take some
time off from work.

He says sure, quit your job, maybe what you need is a baby,
maybe that's the loneliness.

I put my head in his lap, and he strokes my hair.

I say maybe I'll just take a week off.

Buddy says yeah, take two weeks off.

It's not the greatest job in the world, I know, but it's a good job. A lot of the time it's fun. And there are things about it that are better than not having a job at all. Jake's album has been moved back again, so nobody in publicity needs to do anything for him for a while.

I call David at home. I say David, I've got some vacation days saved up, and I really need some time off.

He says are you okay. There must be something in my voice. This isn't like him.

I say yeah, I just have some things I've got to work out, family things.

He says sure, you know, things are kind of quiet this week anyway.

Yeah.

Well, take all the time you need.

Thanks, I just need a few days. I, uh, I'm all right.

Yeah.

Okay, thanks.

I can't remember my dreams, but I know Jake is in them. They are falling-away dreams like fog, and I wake up feeling like you feel after you've dreamed about someone you love who is dead.

I find myself praying pathetic, immoral little prayers that he doesn't forget me, and that he doesn't remember me and I don't remember him and the whole thing never happened.

I argue with him in my sleep. You do not have to love me.

I'll be standing in the shower and I'll feel the water moving hot like hands over my back, down my legs, and I hear myself saying his name into the water and it comes out warbled. Then I close my eyes and drop my head back and listen to the water until it's over.

I start a new song. It's about Amazing Grace, and she helps me write it.

Once, I had a Magic Writing Pad where you could write things, anything you wanted, with a little plastic stick onto a clear plastic piece of paper and the words would show up on the layer below it and then you could lift up the sheet and it all disappeared, forgotten.

After a while, though, it stopped working. I pressed too hard when I wrote and the bottom layer got scarred with everything I'd ever put there and every line I'd draw would come out fragmented.

I wanted a new one but we couldn't find one.

I was arguing with Bo Schifflett, Junior, in my head. Bo said we have sinful natures, we're fallen from birth.

I said if Jesus was perfect, he didn't have a sinful nature so he wasn't human.

Bo said yes he was, he took on our human frailties.

Like what.

Like he could die.

I said it doesn't count when you don't stay dead, if you don't stay dead it's just a bad vacation, you have to die and stay dead.

He'd get me so mad.

I have an eraser in my fist and I keep rubbing the paper, I can't stop rubbing, and I tear a hole in it and I have eraser crumbs in my lap, all over my guitar, everywhere, and I keep rubbing. It's that kind of eraser that's the color of mucus and it falls apart.

I get a new sheet of paper and start over.

I think about spitting in the sink after brushing my teeth and seeing blood and knowing it's mine, driving up to a car accident and thinking that could have been me, turning off the TV and watching the little point of light in the middle of the screen disappear, thinking that could have been me.

You come up with new ways of seeing the world, new definitions of love, of God, yourself. Otherwise, you don't want anything to do with any of it.

You make a decision. He's not going to take one more thing from me. I'm not going to lose one thing more. I can't.

After a week at home I go back to work. I've rewritten my song about a hundred times, and I think it's good enough to demo now, and I think I'm ready to deal with it if there's a message from Jake. I wear a black dress and put on old foundation, darker than what I wear now, so people will think I've either had a death in the family or gotten a tan. Nobody asks.

There's no word from Jake, and I tell myself what a relief.

By Thursday, though, I want to hear his voice, just hear it. I still need some kind of ending or something, not just a fade-out. I call him late in the afternoon and I hear his voice on his machine and I leave a message for him. I say call me back, overly casual.

He could be anywhere, he could have gone away for the weekend. Friday morning I'm jittery. In the afternoon I'm depressed. What is his problem, is he tired of me. Okay, fine, I'm tired of him too, and I'm tired of being alive. Not suicidal, just bored.

It's a slow weekend.

I call him Monday morning and he's still not there and I listen to his voice on his machine and I try to imagine it's saying something else and I don't leave a message. He probably took a long weekend away with his wife, left their daughter with a neighbor or something. Buddy and I should do that. He had to do it to get me out of his system and go on with his life. I should do that, ask Buddy to take me to Memphis and we'll stay in the Peabody. We'll see Graceland, we should have seen Graceland by now, we're the only people in Tennessee who haven't, and we'll have a nice dinner and drink piña coladas. The Peabody probably has some kind of weekend special. We could tell them it's our honeymoon.

I wait all week.

Then it's Friday afternoon and most people have slipped out early and I have some unexpected privacy—Buddy and I talked about going to Memphis this weekend, but Buddy can't get away right now—so I call Jake and he answers the phone. I say hi, it's Sylvia.

He says he got my message and he's been meaning to call me back, he was just about to call me, but he's had the flu and he's been trying to take care of himself.

I say that's good, you ought to take better care of yourself. I think maybe it's true, maybe he did have the flu. But it's not like I asked him to move my furniture. How much effort would it have taken to return a phone call. I've returned phone calls when I felt bad, important ones. I've gone to work when I was sick, I've taken aspirin and worked nine-hour days and had to take what I wore that day to the cleaners because I kept sweating in it. You can find a way to do whatever's important to you. And whoever heard of a flu lasting from Thursday through the weekend all the way to the next Friday. What kind of idiot does he take me for.

I decide I'll get my own version of the flu and I'll stop calling. I've stopped calling, only he doesn't know because it's just been two minutes, and I wonder how many days it will take before it dawns on him that I've stopped calling. Weeks, maybe. I should send him something—a newspaper article or a clipping from *Billboard* with a curt note scribbled across the top and signed with just my initials. So he'll know.

I think about telling him I wrote a song last week, a whole one, but I don't.

I think about calling Miller, telling him I've written a song he might be interested in. Leaving Sony right before Jake's album comes out and everyone in publicity is already swamped with work and his album falls through the cracks unnoticed. It happens. All the time.

I decide to wait until after Jake's recorded. I'm still holding out some crazy hope that I'll get to play, even though I know I won't. But in my fantasy I do, and then I call Miller and I send him Jake's tape and I say I did the percussions and he gets me more session work and I start meeting people and I get more work and pretty soon I have people wanting to pay me to go on tour with them and buying me clothes and sending me to their hair people and their makeup people, and then Jake's album comes out and he says what about my publicity and David says what can I do, I'm doing everything I can do, it's just not taking off. Jake calls me and says it's Jake, Jake Harris. And I say oh, Jake, it's good to hear from you, what are you doing these days, has your album come out yet. He wants me to get Miller to take his calls, and I say Miller's life is absolutely crazy right now, he's pulling his hair out, you know him, but if I can do anything, you know I will. He says should I call you tomorrow. I say I don't know when I'll see him next, things are insane right now, just let me call you if I can do something. Okay. Then I say I know I have your number somewhere, but give it to me again.

I had a ribbon, and every time I learned a Bible verse they'd pin a shape on the ribbon and the verse was written on the shape. Like a flower for the grass withers, the flower fades, but the word of our God lasts forever, a light bulb for thy word is a lamp unto my feet and a light unto my path, a globe for for God so loved the world. Something, I think it was a book, for in the beginning was the Word, and the Word was with God and the Word was God.

I believed it. I thought words were holy and eternal. I thought words were connected to God and I thought they were true in the way that God is truth and God is love. I didn't understand about lies.

I thought God loved me and I thought that was enough and I thought I would never die.

I call Miller and ask him if he wants to hear some of my songs. I hand-deliver them to his office.

We prayed the Lord's Prayer every Sunday and I meant it. I tried to forgive so my father in heaven would forgive me. I tried to be like Jesus in the garden of Gethsemane, saying not my will, but thine. Sometimes I would pray and my hands would go into fists. And then I'd open them, palms up, and say not my will but thine.

I thought if I did, God would protect me from evil and anything he didn't protect me from must not be evil.

I thought my father was in heaven.

You want a room, some space in the world that's all your own.

You would keep the door locked and you'd be the only one in the world who would have the key and nobody could come in unless you said and you would never say.

You just want a place where you feel safe.

I think my life has folded itself up so my past and my present are in the same place, touching.

I'm standing in the graveyard on a cold January morning getting ready to bury my best friend. I'm standing at his grave and I want to be inside it, I want to know what he feels like.

I'm wearing pantyhose and a dress and my legs are cold, my feet are cold, he was so cold. I was holding him and I could feel him go cold in my arms and I put my face on his face and it was cold.

Jake calls. He says are you okay.

I've had the flu, I say.

He says okay, Sylvia, I hear you.

I think I've hurt him. I think about his hands holding the phone, I think about the curves of his fingers dialing my number, touching my breasts, tangling themselves in my hair.

I say wait a minute, and I put down the phone hard. I close the door loud enough for him to hear, then come back and say I just had to close my door. I'm telling him I'll talk.

He says well, I just wanted to see if you were okay.

I say I'm okay.

Good.

I think about asking him if his wife and daughter are okay. I think about telling him Buddy's okay. I open a drawer, shuffle papers. I say I heard David put your recording date on hold again.

Yeah, it's a long wait.

I say it's been a long time. He hears me.

He says look, for what it's worth, I called you three times the week after CMA.

I didn't get your messages.

I didn't leave messages, but I called. I know you took the week off.

I want to ask him if he has any idea why, and if so, what kind of shit wouldn't have called me the next week, the next month. But I don't. I still don't know the rules for these things, what you're allowed to say, what you're supposed to say, how you end it, whatever it was, when you still expect to see the person professionally and you know you're not capable of just pretending it never happened. I want him to tell me what to say. I think he ought to tell me, he's the one who's done this before.

He says when I realized you'd taken the whole week off, God, I just didn't know what to think.

I think about saying so you got the flu, but I don't. I say it's okay.

He says I mean, I didn't mean to make you, ask you, I don't know. I didn't mean to hurt you.

I think maybe he hasn't done this before, not this part of it, and he doesn't know what to do any more than I do.

I say I know.

He says so you're okay now?

Yeah.

He says have you written anything lately?

Yeah, actually, I sold a couple of songs to Miller, the one you helped me with in Birmingham and a new one called "That Could Have Been Me."

That's just the beginning, I knew you had it in you.

Yeah, you did.

I think about him calling Miller, telling him I had talent. I think about him kissing me by the lake, and I can still feel his hands moving on my skin, my skin trembling at his touch. I close my eyes, and I listen to his voice.

He says so what's next?

I don't know what he's asking, if he wants to see me again. I close my drawer. I say I'm thinking about leaving Sony. What I mean is I'm leaving him, if he's there to be left. I have to.

He says what are you going to do?

I don't know. I say I'm going to try to get some session work and sell some more songs. I might go work for Miller.

You don't need to work for Miller, he says, you've got a lot of talent, don't sell yourself short.

Thanks.

You've got a lot going for you.

I think about my own hands. I think about touching his ears, how they felt scratchy on my tongue. I think I should say something, but I can't think of anything.

He says well, Sylvia, I better let you go.

Thanks for calling, I say. I want to tell him more than that. Thanks for the gesture, thanks for not forgetting me, for being there, three clichés in a row. I say it was good to hear your voice. Four.

I put down the phone and I let go.

They made me wash the blood off. Deedee came in the bathroom with me and it had dried on my skin, it was pulling at me, at the hair on my arms, and it had changed colors so it wasn't blood. And then in the shower it changed back to blood going down the drain, deep thick red blood sometimes flowing, sometimes in ribbons or clumps, and I could have thrown up, I almost did, and Deedee said don't look at it, just don't look down, and she was scrubbing me hard with a washcloth and I couldn't stop crying and she said just look up, look at the light fixture, and I couldn't move and I couldn't look and I couldn't stop crying and I thought I was crying tears of blood and Deedee said no, you just have it on your face, put your face in the water, and I didn't want to but she made me and she gave me a washrag and she said wash your face off, Sylvia, and I did.

That's how it was. I did what people told me to do.

I'm making love with Jake in my grandparents' graveyard and it's hot and we're sweating and he touches me and I'm alive in the way people are when they're dying and then I'm holding Bo Schifflett, Junior, I'm holding his body in my arms, and I think he's dying and I'm screaming for help and he's calling on God and he really believes it, he believes he's not going to die, and then he's cold and I know this cold from my grandmother, my grandfather, and I suddenly think I know it from my mother. It is that cold which is the absence of life.

.   .   .

I'm making breakfast for my dead grandmother, washing the breakfast dishes of my dead grandfather.

I take Communion and I like the sweetness of the grape juice which is the blood but I hate those little flour squares which are the body and I try not to think about what it means.

Bo said life on this earth is nothing. It's a flicker of a candle held up to eternity. All it is is preparation for the next life.

I said preparation for death.

No, for life. Eternal life.

I hear Jake—life is short.

They dig the hole before you get there. And then they fix it so the coffin lies right over the hole, hovering, but they don't put it in until people start leaving, and you're standing by the cars and you're cold and you want to go but they're talking over you like they don't even notice what's happening and you don't want to look but you can't help it, and you watch the coffin going into the hole and you think he's going in the hole but something about it doesn't seem real.

I feel like I'm a dead weight and Buddy's trying to pull me out of this terrible valley and I don't know if he's strong enough but I reach out to him as from a long way away. I say I wanted to stop, but I couldn't, I just didn't know how. I collapse into his arms and he lifts me up.

I tell him I don't think I'll ever heal, it's like a cancer, you just don't heal, the only way to survive is to rip part of yourself out, and even then, as a fragment, you might not make it. My fingers are trembling.

He holds my hands. He says it's not like cancer, it's like a flu, you'll get over it.

It's not a flu, Buddy.

I didn't mean flu, I can't do words like you can, I'm just trying to tell you it's something you'll heal from.

No I won't.

You will, give yourself some time.

I don't know if I can.

He says you will. You're a strong woman, and I'll be here for you, and you will.

I say Buddy, I know you want a baby, but I just don't know if I can, I'm afraid to.

Okay, we won't have one, it's okay.

I'm afraid because for one thing I can't separate my mother's death from her pregnancy and I don't want to die, I'm afraid to die.

Buddy says you're not going to die. He puts his arms around me and I lean into him.

I say I'm finally realizing the kinds of holds the past has on me. I press his arms tight around me. I feel a cracking in my chest like the first break in the ice before a long, slow thaw, and I let him pull me together. I say I can't remember the last time I was happy.

I hear my grandmother—the only two reasons you're alive today is you're a fighter and the power of prayer.

I think about sharing a hymnbook with my grandmother, pretending I could read the words. I hear Reverend Tutwiler— when you sing hymns you're praising God. I hear him preaching, the cadence of his voice like an incantation.

I remember knowing words and music were divine because they connect you with grace.

You can find things worth salvaging.

Buddy says you'll be all right. We'll be happy again.

I try hard to believe him. I think maybe I'll pray. I try hard to believe.

1 7

EARLY SPRING, THE WORLD STARTS BREAKING ITSELF OPEN, stretching life out of the last bits of winter, and if you listen hard enough you can hear it creaking, sucking, and if you let it, it will go inside you and break you apart.

It's Sunday morning, and Buddy wakes up with spring fever and we don't take showers and we put on old clothes and go to Wal-Mart and fill up the trunk of the car with flowers. The fence is up and the deck is finished and we're waiting for the Jacuzzi, there's a big hole in the deck for it, and we plant flowers everywhere so the yard begins to bubble with color like a party. I tell Buddy how M'Lea's mother used to believe in celebrating everyday life. We go back to Wal-Mart and get some more.

I like the cool dirt in my fingernails, the way it smells. I like pulling the roots out of their tiny plastic cups and thinking about them expanding in the ground, breathing, drinking. I like to think they were suffocating in there and I've rescued them. I like thinking of myself as a life-giver.

I think I can hear them slurping, struggling to untangle their hair, giggling. They make silly sounds like in cartoons, only very quiet because it's underground and they're not supposed to.

I haven't prayed in a long time. I don't know if I believe in God anymore. I think about my grandmother planting flowers up the front walk. I think about how Memaw said God sees our lives —past, present, and future, beginning, middle, and end all at the same time. God exists outside of time where nothing begins, nothing ends, nothing happens, and nothing is forgotten, everything just exists together like harmony. I hear the choir from Pell City Presbyterian Church singing the benediction in four-part harmony and I remember thinking it was beautiful. As it was in the beginning, is now and ever shall be, world without end, amen, amen.

I feel the sun touch my back. I feel my soul unfolding.

I say thank you, God, in my head without opening my mouth. I feel shy around God.

I start getting a new song.

Late in the afternoon I pack a picnic and I've saved some of the flowers and Buddy doesn't think it's a good idea but I say I need to do it and I need you with me, so we go to the graveyard.

It has a gate all the way around it, a beautiful wrought-iron gate. This is the first time I've noticed it, but I think it's important, marking off boundaries like that. It's comforting.

The days are getting longer now. It always happens and it always surprises me.

We find an empty space and spread out an old blanket. We eat bread and cheese and fruit and Snickers brownies and Buddy has a turkey sandwich and we split a bottle of wine. I still have dirt under my fingernails.

I plant some flowers at Bo Schifflett, Junior's headstone. They're pink, but I don't remember what they're called.

I close my eyes and my fists and say I forgive you, Bo. Then I open my hands. I try to pray without words. I forgive him again. Then I forgive my grandmother and my mother and Uncle Mull and Deedee and Jake and Buddy and, finally, myself. Then I forgive God. I don't forgive my grandfather. I don't want to and I don't have to, it's unforgivable, and I don't know if I ever will.

When I'm finished, my hands are muddy with sweat.

We go home, take a shower together, make love, and fall asleep.

I hear Buddy get up, lock the front door, and turn off the lights. When he comes back to bed, I pretend I'm still asleep and he arranges the covers and gets in beside me and I put his arms around me and lean my head into him. He fits me better than he used to.

Life is sweet. That's what Memaw used to say, and I'd wonder how, after everything, she could mean it.

I used to forgive her every day. I'd close my eyes and open my hands and forgive her for dying, for being human, for everything. I do it again. I know it's not my last time.

I write a song about that, about life being sweet. It's a love song that doesn't say what I was trying to say. It makes being loved and floating around heaven sound like the same thing.

But I finish it anyway and make a demo of it and sell it to RCA for a woman Miller just signed to do her first album, Mitty McDaniels.

Buddy and I go to the Bluebird Café when Mitty's there and when she sings it, it sounds sadder than I meant, and prettier, and Buddy and I hold hands under the table, listening.

He says remember our first date.

Yeah. I look at him and our eyes connect.

After the song I say let's go home.

Buddy says we'll stay as long as you want.

But I want to go home. I touch his knee, and we leave.

It's eleven o'clock and Buddy's fast asleep, just barely snoring, a sound I find comforting. I'm lying beside him, still, not to disturb him.

Sometimes he stops snoring and the silence wakes me up and I touch him to make sure he's still warm. Sometimes I can't get back to sleep and I can't count sheep and I play *Gilligan's Island* reruns in my head and pretend they've all driven each other insane. Sometimes I get Amazing Grace to sing to me.

I look towards him in the dark. There are no stars out tonight, but I know what I'm seeing. I listen to his breathing, the slow, peaceful rhythm of it. I think about my flowers unfolding their roots in the soil, opening. I stretch my back, my toes, and my muscles ache with a wonderful exhaustion. I put my hand low on my stomach and I feel things there.

I start getting a new song. I close my eyes and listen. I put myself to sleep singing harmony with myself in my head, not making a sound.